I

my book! ♡

UNRAVELED

C.F. Gonzi

Thanks for the support!

For Elyse and Parker; thanks for playing the games that inspired the story.

CHAPTER 1

Delilah

In conclusion, the subject is insane.

Signing my report in the loopiest letters I could muster, I shuffled my papers together and pulled the mini-stapler from my backpack. My hair fell over my shoulder, tickling my arm as it fell between the stapler's jaws. By now it had to be long enough to tuck into my belt loops, and as I pushed it back behind my ear I enjoyed the blanketed feeling it gave me. I noticed out of the corner of my eye that the guy in the faded AC/DC shirt was staring at me again.

I smiled. I was used to people staring at me, maybe not because I was pretty, but because I was a 6'2" half Native American woman with hair down to my waist. I stood up from my desk, careful not to bump into anyone else's chairs on my way up to the front of the classroom. Even though I was used to getting weird looks, I hated getting up in front of people; my height already made me stand out, but the fact that everyone else was still sitting made it an all-eyes-on-me kind of thing. Also, being the first to finish the final—with at least 30 minutes remaining—did not help my case. Professor Erickson peered up from behind his bulging glasses as I approached.

"Done so soon, Hadley?" he skeptically set down his thick book.

"A student is only as good as their professor, sir," I smiled as I handed him my final, and as I turned back to my desk, I added with a sweet sort of sarcasm, "I hope it isn't too much of a disappointment."

"Have any of them been?" he mumbled to himself. I raised my eyebrows as I went to my usual backrow seat. I sank into my chair with a relaxed smile curling my lips. It'd been a long week. But now that my last final was complete, the tension and stress from this semester eased in my shoulders and chest.

It took a few moments to gather my things, but soon I was walking out of Erickson's lecture hall for the last time. I breathed in the warm May air as I began to walk across campus and pulled out my phone to restore the volume from being silenced for exams all day. I felt pretty popular as I opened the one text message I had received.

I bit my lip when I saw it was from Jace, the bureau's lead profiler, as well as the guy I'd been harboring a crush on since he first got moved to my floor in January.

Jordine wants you in her office. 4:30, no excuses.

I sighed. No "Hey how's it going?" or "Hope

the exams are going well." It was all business all the time with him. Or, at least, most of the time; when he first asked me out, I had reluctantly told him I couldn't even think of a social life till I finished school. We are finally going out to dinner tonight as our first official date.

I glanced at the time on my phone. 3:15. I replied with a quick "Count on it" before sliding my phone back into my pocket. I had plenty of time to walk the two blocks to my apartment, but I made a beeline for the bus stop anyway, not wanting to risk being late.

Why did Jordine want me in her office? She usually didn't request meetings with me personally; it was always with my team. Maybe she'd heard I'd be getting my master's in a week and wanted to congratulate me.

I laughed to myself, the group of high school students taking a tour glancing at me nervously. Yeah, right. Jordine was not the kind to throw a party, even if I did just work my butt off for the last six years to graduate with the degree that will finally help me obtain a childhood dream.

* * *

I slammed the door behind me as I ran to my bedroom, calling for Dot as I went. It's a good thing the bus was actually on schedule today, or I would have had no time to change from street clothes to work attire.

As I was pulling on a blazer with my already fading badge attached, Dot came streaking into the room. Her fur was graying at the tips of her tail and ears, but the rest of her was as black as night. The cat jumped up onto my bed and lay right on top of my purse.

"Oh, Dot," I said as I pushed her over, stroked her tummy, then pulled my purse from under her. "What in the world does she want with me?" She meowed as I hobbled to the kitchen, trying to pull on my flats while rushing to put food in her bowl.

Dot followed me excitedly as I hurried back to the front door. "I'll be back tonight," I promised as I swung open the door and blocked her from walking out with me. "You stay put!"

I closed and locked the door before running back down the stairs to the front of my building, checking my watch as I went. It was already 4:00, and if I didn't make an appearance in front of Jordine Maxfield's desk in exactly thirty minutes, I knew I'd be toast. I only lived about 10 minutes away from the building, but with New York traffic, I had to be quick. Waving down a taxi and promising a good tip if we got there in time, I trusted my career to this cabbie's driving skills.

Thankfully, we arrived in one piece. I practically threw the cash at the guy as soon as we pulled up to the curb, sprinting inside and to the elevators. I punched the button to the sixteenth floor as I realized my hair was still down. I twisted and pulled as the elevator continued ticking off numbers as it passed each floor. Finally, I placed a neatly tied bun on top of my head and pulled a bobby pin from my purse to secure it. My hair was thick enough that if I pulled tight, the knot would hold on its own, but I was not going to let my long, tangled mess get me in trouble with the Executive Assistant Director of the FBI.

Trying to compose myself as the elevator reached my floor, I glanced at my watch again. I had exactly one and a half minutes to get to Jordine's office. Praying that all this hype wasn't just because she needed to ask me to fill out more paperwork on a cyber-attack, I stepped off the elevator and sped across the floor, veering in and out of cubicles toward the windowed office on the other end.

"You're cutting it close." Jace fell into step beside me as I passed the halfway mark to Jordine's door.

"You could've given me more of a heads up —I was in a final," I accused, glancing over into his big brown eyes. He was one of the few people in the office I didn't have to look down at to talk to.

"She didn't let me know till about a minute before I texted you. Be grateful I didn't wait longer." He winked, his smile revealing that chipped front tooth I had gotten so used to as he veered off my path. I watched him for a moment in front of Jordine's office as he headed to the copying machine, his white button-up stretched tight across the muscles of his back.

Taking a deep breath, I knocked on the door.

The man standing beside it, Jameson, smiled understandingly, his dark bald head shining under the luminescent lights of the office. "Good day so far, Rapunzel?"

I nodded, my voice caught in my throat as I wrung my hands behind my back. He turned his head, looking into the office. We could all see what was going on in there, but they still had to have a post to call the shots of any happenings outside her door. I watched as the shrewd woman inside nodded to Jameson and pushed a button on her desk, disabling the lock as the door swung open to let me in.

"You're late." Her deep voice seemed misplaced in her small stature. Her black hair was fashioned in a spiky pixie cut, giving more structure to her already chiseled face.

I glanced at the clock. 4:32. "I'm sorry, ma'am. I was finishing a final when I heard you wanted to see me."

"Don't call me ma'am, Hadley." She still had not looked up from the paper she was reading. "Which final was it?"

"It was a diagnosing report for a sociology course." I remained standing, waiting to be asked to be seated. Finally, she looked up.

"It amazes me that you are still in school and already have the position you hold here. Please, sit." She motioned to the three chairs in front of her ridiculously cluttered desk. "Has anyone ever told you that you're extraordinarily tall?"

I nodded. People rarely failed to remind me.

"It's slightly intimidating having you just stand in front of me like that," Jordine continued as she studied me with her light eyes. "You're probably driving yourself crazy, wondering why I asked to meet with you."

I nodded again, unsure of what to say. At this point, I was honestly just hoping I didn't file a report wrong and was now in legal trouble. It was hard to maintain eye contact with this powerful woman, and I struggled to keep my head up as my feet begged for my attention.

"As I understand it, you have been a probationary agent with us for two years. Is that correct?"

"Yes."

"And I heard from Avery that you are just about to receive your master's degree in... what, again?"

"Psychology with an emphasis in criminal sociology," I rehearsed, straining not to put a ma'am at the end of each sentence.

She must have noticed. "You can call me Jordine, Hadley. However, given the order of things, if you prefer my last name I will answer to that as well. Just not ma'am, please."

I nodded again. It would be so weird to call my commanding officer by her first name. I grew up in a home full of ma'ams and sirs, making it a hard habit to break.

Her face split into a smile. "Just relax, Delilah. I called you here to offer you another position with us. Something above data entry."

I fell into the back of my chair, sure my stomach had dropped through the floor. I took a deep breath and glanced down briefly to make sure it was still inside me.

"Your two-year period as probationary agent is up, you have passed entry level exams for a special field agent with flying scores, and apparently you are about to receive a master's degree in this very field. Would you be willing to accept this position?"

Big girls don't cry, I thought to myself as I sat up a bit straighter in my chair. "Yes ma—Jordine. I would be absolutely honored to take a position in the field." This is what I'd been working for. I could move on to so many new cases and get out and see the subjects that I'd been studying for the past six years.

Jordine stood and extended her hand. "We will hold a small ceremony. You should know by now how they usually go; you can invite family if you wish."

I stood and took her hand in mine. It was quite a bit smaller than mine but still firm and, surprisingly, a bit calloused. "I don't know if they'll make it, but I will definitely be letting them know. Thank you so much for this opportunity ma… Jordine. I look forward to working with you more."

She sat, resuming her shuffling through what had to be thousands of papers littering her desk. "Now I may not be the most organized…" she mumbled after a few minutes of searching, pulling out a calendar marked in reds and blues. "But there is a method to my madness. We will hold your ceremony on the twenty-fourth of next month, if that works for you."

I didn't even have to look at a calendar; my life was basically all work now that school was over. "That should be fine, Jordine. Thanks again."

Just as she was nodding her dismissal to me, the floor outside her office seemed to erupt into chaos. People were thundering in and out of cubicles while others were pulling their badges and guns to their waists before heading for the elevators.

"What do we have here?" Jordine mumbled, beckoning to me to follow her out her door.

Jace and Jameson stood right outside the office with their heads together in deep conversation, occasionally coming up to bark an order to an agent before exchanging papers and continuing their mumbling.

Jordine marched up to them. "Avery, Jameson, what happened?"

Jameson looked up, excitement in his eyes. "Avery just made a major breakthrough on the Mc —"

"That case we've been working on for four months," Jace gave a warning look to Jameson before glancing at me apologetically. "We may need to meet in private for this one, Director."

I tried not to feel hurt as they reconvened

in Jordine's office, leaving me alone in the hustle of busy agents. Straightening my shoulders and reminding myself the protocols of the FBI's clearance requirements, I made my way slowly through the mess of cubicles and people. A conversation floating over one wall made me stop dead in my tracks however, because these agents weren't being as careful as Jace.

". . . that they don't have the right tactics to apprehend him."

"Obviously, he's evaded us for four months. You would think the FBI could catch a drug lord working right under our noses."

"I personally think he's working elsewhere, and just trying to lead us on a fake trail. Again."

"I've got to get downstairs, but one thing's for sure; if Avery and Jameson are the ones to bring McGregor in, our branch will. . ."

I skirted around the cubicle as the speaker walked out of it. McGregor? *The* McGregor? That's the case Jace and Jameson have been so busy with? I may not have clearance to know it all, but I know two things for sure; first: McGregor was bad news. He was plaguing New York with new drugs every month. Second: I had to get on this case. If I could be the one to help bring down a major drug lord, straight out of probationary? I'd have it made in this bureau, new agent or not.

By the time I got to my desk, which was around a corner from the main part of the floor and down the break room hallway, I was too excited to sit. Looking over, I saw a big card on my keyboard, along with several colorful balloons around my chair that promptly drove the case out of my mind; balloons rarely made an appearance in this vicinity.

Edith, my cubicle partner, was watching me expectantly. I smiled. "How'd you know?" I asked, reaching for the card.

She stood and drew me into a hug, her strawberry blonde curls tickling my neck.

"We graduated training and started here at the same time, remember?" Edith had one missing tooth in her smile; it was one of the qualities I liked most about her. "I got my news this morning."

My excitement overflowed as I squealed, "We're going to be special agents!" We both turned to take our seats. "Sorry I didn't have time to decorate your desk."

She barked out a laugh. "I know you are either at school or here. Speaking of, how'd the finals go?"

"They went well; it's definitely nice to finally be done." I logged into my computer and picked up the file left on my desk.

"You could have just settled on a bachelor's like everyone else in the office," said Edith, ever attentive to details.

"Jace has his master's, and he's one of the highest-ranking profilers in the city. If I could get anywhere close to what he can do, it will be totally worth it."

"Or just close to him in general." She looked over at me slyly. "I heard you two got dinner tonight."

"*Ahem.* I need to file this report, Ms. Banks. Please do not distract me." I rolled my chair over one of the balloons, accidentally popping it as we both laughed.

* * *

As I turned the key in my door, I heard the pitter-patter of Dot's steps growing louder. She may look like a cat, but I genuinely think she was raised by dogs before I rescued her. As I pulled the door closed behind me she rounded the corner. Sometimes I felt like Dot could sense my emotions, and this was one of those times. What looked like a smile played on her little mouth as she bounded toward me, knowing I had good news. I scooped her into my arms, dropping my keys on the side table of the hall before switching on the lights and making my way to the front room.

My apartment was nice—better than some of my friends' anyway. It wasn't huge, but perfect for me. It had a small laundry room beside the fire escape, which was pretty convenient. The living room was big enough for my standing grand piano and to have game nights with friends, whereas the bedroom was just large enough to hold a full-size bed and dresser. With Dot in my arms, I plopped down onto the couch that sucked you up as soon as you put your weight into it. She purred as she twirled her tail around my fingers.

I looked at the clock. I had a bit of time to make some quick calls before Jace arrived. I slipped my phone out and hit Dad's name, knowing that he wouldn't take as long as Mom. As the phone started ringing I made my way to the bathroom to pull my hair out of the flyaway bun.

"Hello?" answered a woman's voice.

"Mom?" I asked. Why was Mom answering Dad's cell? They lived in different states and, as far as I knew, hadn't talked to each other in over a year.

"Liles? Why in the world does your father not have your number saved to his phone?" She sounded excited but tired. She yelled in the background, obviously trying to block the volume from the receiver but failing. "Emmit? Emmit! Liles is on the phone! Come here!" She came back on at full volume, "Sweetie, I'll just put you on speaker, okay?"

"Okay, Mom, thanks." I was still confused, but at least this way I could take care of both parents in one phone call, which hadn't happened since their divorce. "What are you doing with Dad?"

"Oh, we were just swapping some old boxes of things that have been sitting at our places for too long, hun." Mom had the sweetest country drawl, but her vagueness was slightly annoying.

"Oh that's...nice," I said, trying not to sound suspicious.

Her voice was far away again as I heard her ask my dad how to put the phone on speaker. I rolled my eyes as I heard him cuss and say he only knew how to make a normal call.

"Maybe try hitting the speaker button that comes on the screen when you pull it away from your face, Mom," I suggested as they started bickering over technology. Suddenly, Mom's voice sounded at the same faded volume as Dad's. "Did it work?" I asked, already knowing the answer.

"Oh yes, we can both hear you now, sweetie."

"Hey beautiful, how are things in the big city?" Dad's deep, Cherokee voice was so calming. It was nice to hear it again.

"Good Dad, thanks! How are you two?" I prayed they wouldn't try to talk over each other.

"Well, I'm fine, sweetie, thanks for asking!" my mom answered as my dad had started to mumble something in the background.

"We're all good here, Liles. Why such a late call in the middle of the week?" That was my dad, always getting to the point.

"Oh, hun, let us visit for a minute, unless something bad has happened, sweetie? I sure hope not, but I'm tickled you called. We are always here for you!" And that was my mom, always one for the conversation.

I decided to follow my dad's trait in this situation, seeing as Jace was coming in fifteen minutes and I still hadn't changed or fixed my make-up.

"Well Mom, I actually do need to be fast," I said, starting to make my way around my bedroom to find something cute to wear. "I just wanted to let you know that I got offered a promotion today!"

"Ah!" My mom exclaimed as I heard my dad

clap in the background. They may not be the best couple, but they have always been supportive parents. "Where you headed to now, gorgeous?" My dad asked, and by the tone of his voice I knew he was smiling.

"I'm now a special field agent; I get to go out and do the investigating instead of the filing," I said, a smile bouncing around my lips as the reality of it hit.

"That's my girl!" Dad said as Mom continued to make noises like she was choking back tears. My dad was a strong Cherokee man and believed in many of his people's traditions, but he never let those traditions get in the way of his pride in me, and that has always helped my confidence.

"Yeah, so they'll be holding a little ceremony on June 24th if you guys wanted to come, but I know coming up to New York can be hard, so I just thought I would let you know." Reality hit again, however this time it was the reality of how expensive plane tickets were and how neither of my parents had much money.

"Oh honey, I would love to come, but I've a conference I've got to make that week." My mom sounded genuinely disappointed, and I tried not to imagine her quivering lip.

"That's okay, Mom, I totally understand. It's not even a big deal, at least you made it to my training graduation; that one was a lot more important." I tried to tone it down for her, and it seemed to work because she agreed and told me she loved me before handing the phone to my dad. He took me off speaker.

"I'll be there, Liles," he said softly into the phone. I'm sure he did it that way because he didn't want to make my mom feel worse. It was her idea —the divorce, and I could tell he still cared for her. "Just let me know the time, and I will try and make it the night before."

"You can stay with me," I offered as I chanced another glance at the clock. "But Dad, I do have to get running. Is it okay if I call you another time to work out the details? Maybe tomorrow?"

"That's fine, sweetheart. Just let me know, and I will be there. Have a good night. We love you."

"Love you too, Dad."

CHAPTER 2

Jace

I'd like to think of myself as a punctual person. I was rarely late, and the two times I have been in my life it was no more than two minutes. So, it just fits perfectly that the universe would have me fall for one of the least punctual people I have ever met.

I sat in my car, knowing Delilah wouldn't be ready on time, but I had a reputation to uphold. Having everything timed perfectly, I knew I would be knocking on her door at 7:00 exactly.

As I climbed the stairs of the apartment complex, I smoothed my thick hair. It was impossible to tame, but messy is the style now, right? I checked my watch as I climbed. I'm usually not that fidgety, but this was our first actual date and I had no idea how to handle someone like Delilah outside of work. Knowing she was only 24, her confidence overwhelmed and slightly intimidated me. It started to dawn on me how little I actually knew about her, since we had only met a year and a half ago when she transferred to our office. I'd only ever seen her at work, and while I felt I'd gotten to know her well in office, I realized I only knew the work side of her. I guess that's what dating is for, though.

I made my way down the hall, looking at each door number as I went. There were only a few and they were placed far apart, so I could tell these were nicer apartments than what I could have afforded at her age. Just another thing to intrigue me; how in the world did she afford such a nice place while working a filing job *and* finishing school? Maybe she had rich parents. *Oh Jace, we are not going to bring up money on the first date.* My mother's nagging sounded loud and clear, always appearing when I felt nervous.

Finally, I reached 13C, the farthest door to the right. I checked my watch. Yep, 7:00 on the dot. Man, I'm good. I knocked on the door.

"Just a second," a voice called from the other side.

I smirked; totally called that.

The door swung open after a minute or two and there stood Delilah, her long, chocolatey hair spilling over her shoulders. It had a slight wave to it that must be the result of the bun I saw her sporting earlier that day. She wore a plain, fitted blue dress and sparkly sandals. Delilah was the tallest girl I had ever met, and definitely the most gorgeous. Her height didn't take away from her fit and curvy body, and her olive skin was smooth and hairless on her arms and legs. She had the most stunning blue eyes I had ever seen, and her high cheekbones gave her face a beautiful diamond shape. I hadn't felt tongue-tied because of a woman since high school, but Delilah. . . let's just say she gave me a run for my money.

"Hey Jace!" she said, flashing her brilliant white smile and grabbing her purse off of the hall table. I hate to sound shallow, but I have never been more grateful for my height—I was still three inches taller than her.

"Hey Delilah," Realizing my mouth was hanging open, I shut it quickly as she pulled her door closed behind her, locking it with a pink key. "Sorry if I'm early."

"Jace, I've told you a million times, call me Liles," She waved off my apology. "And you're right on time; you know I'm always the one running late. I just had to call my parents and. . ."

She stopped in the middle of the hall and looked at me. I faced her, trying to keep my face expressionless. She cocked her head.

"Do you know why Jordine called me to her office today?"

I broke, smiling as I turned back toward the empty hallway. "Why do you think I'm taking you out tonight? I thought the news deserved more celebration than what Jordine could give."

Her blush was subtle against her tan skin, but I could still make it out as she laughed. "You jerk!" She hit my shoulder, the force of it a bit harder than I would have expected. I guess she didn't realize that when girls flirt, they were supposed to hold back a little. "Your text made it sound like I was in trouble! I was literally stressing the entire way to the office."

“Hey,” I said, rubbing my shoulder as we continued down the stairs. “You know Jordine. She has to be the one to give the news.”

I continued to ask how the visit with Jordine went on our way to the car. Delilah shared the whole story of how she feared she had filed a report wrong and was surprised to the point of tears when she was offered the promotion. She spoke with so much animation that it wasn’t hard to be interested in everything she said.

In the car, I let her control the radio. I told her that as long as there was no country playing, I would be fine.

“You know I grew up in Oklahoma, right?” She laughed as she switched through the radio channels.

No, I didn’t, thanks.

“Wait, so you’re telling me because you grew up in Oklahoma, you love country music?”

“Wipe that smirk off your face, Avery,” she said, looking out the window as she finally decided on what channel she wanted. It was an old rock station. “I’m just saying I grew up with it. I’ve learned to recognize its better qualities. I thought people didn’t own cars in New York?”

I laughed. “I usually take the subway, but that’s a little too grungy for a date night. That’s why I keep this baby in reserve.” I patted my dashboard. “And I don’t mind the traffic. Gives more time for conversation. Do you own a car?”

“I’ve got this gorgeous red jeep I brought up with me when I moved, but it’s collecting dust pretty fast. I don't chance driving here often."

"Seriously, it can be scary sometimes for sure," I chuckled knowingly.

She nodded, and we continued the small talk for some time as I drove through the lit-up city. I wondered if it was still pretty to her, all the lights and flashing screens, now that she's been here for a couple of years. I watched her out of the corner of my eye whenever there was a lull in the conversation; she'd just glance out the window and then look back at me, smiling. Distracted driving at its best.

"Sometimes I forget what this city looks like at night," she said airily as we pulled up to the valet parking. "Oh, you didn't tell me we were going here!"

I laughed again as I handed the man my keys and walked around to open her door. Delilah looked up at the flashing sign for the *Blue Hill*, her mouth slightly open as she stepped out of the car, taking my hand.

"I should have worn a nicer dress..."

I smiled, offering her my arm. "I figured becoming a special agent required some sort of fancy dinner," I took a sidelong glance at her and saw a smile playing on her lips. "And don't worry, at least you're *in* a dress; I didn't even wear a tie."

We walked up the steps to the front of the restaurant, and thanks to the reservations I made earlier in the day, we were seated immediately. The waiter led us back to a tidy booth in a corner of the restaurant, which was nice because it kind of secluded us from the crowded main dining area. People stared as we passed, and I felt a twinge of jealousy of this table full of guys who kept glancing at Delilah, till I realized we probably looked like a pair of giants walking by. As we reached the booth, she defied the stereotype of clumsy tall people when she slipped her arm from mine and slid easily into the seat facing the rest of the restaurant. I made sure she was seated comfortably before taking my spot across from her.

"You're not vegetarian, are you?" I asked as the waiter passed out our menus and went to get us drinks.

"Once again, grew up in Oklahoma." Delilah smiled at me from over her menu. "I'd go hunting with my dad, and whatever we killed we ate. Sorry if that's weird to say on a date."

She disappeared behind her menu as I laughed. I had never met someone like Delilah, who kind of just said whatever she wanted. Things never got awkward with her though. I think it made her easier to talk to; you didn't have to guess what she was thinking.

Delilah apologized again as she ordered a double-stack beer burger with sweet potato fries, saying she knows it's a fancy restaurant, but that she'd heard they make the best burgers. I agreed and ordered a bacon cheeseburger with fries as well. I had asked if she wanted an appetizer, but she made a good point of how those usually fill her up before the actual meal. I appreciated her honesty; I could tell she wasn't ordering like that to save my money, like some girls might have. She just wanted to enjoy the meal—and so did I.

During dinner I found out that her parents divorced just a year or so ago, and while the blow had hurt her, she knew it was for the best, because her mom was such a free-spirited woman and would end up leaving her dad anyway. I discovered she never had an actual boyfriend because she always saw boys as the brothers she never had. Delilah was an open book—a down-to-earth conversationalist. Comparatively, my childhood was a lot happier than hers, but she talked about hers as if she wouldn't have had it any other way. I'm pretty sure she was flirting with me, you know, complimenting my plaid shirt or making fun of my messy hair. At one point she even reached across the table and felt my five o'clock shadow that I've been cursed with since high school. Her hands were soft and her fingers thin, making her touch light and quick. I enjoyed every minute, but the more I thought of a relationship with Delilah, the more I grew cautious. Dating other agents was dangerous business.

My last relationship was with a fellow agent. Long story short, the stress of the field got to her, and between that and her worrying about me constantly, she kind of went crazy. I broke it off, thinking it would be better for both of us, and within a week she had quit. I didn't want a mess like that on my hands again, but the more time I spent with Delilah, the more I was tempted to chance it.

The waiter ended our dinner by asking if we wanted any desserts, and Delilah whispered behind her hand that she had ice cream at her place. Walking out into the night, her arm through mine once more, Delilah looked around. The restaurant was placed at the top of a hill overlooking the bulk of the city, putting all the lights and buildings into plain view.

"You know, with so much school and work these past couple of years, I haven't had time to have this much fun," she said as I led her to the car.

I smiled as I opened the door for her once more. I hurried around to the other side and took the keys from the valet driver. "I'm glad," I said as we pulled out of the parking lot. "Does that mean we can go out more often now?"

"Of course!" Her blush was much more apparent this time, and my confidence skyrocketed.

"So," I started as we pulled into the jam-packed streets. "Would you like to go dancing, or to a movie?"

"You didn't plan further than dinner?"

"I thought we'd wing it." I shrugged sheepishly. "Makes it more fun."

"Hmm..." She looked over at me. "Mind going back to my place? I'm too full to dance."

Anticipation filled my stomach as we made our way back to her apartment. I didn't know what to expect; the few reasons I knew of getting invited to a woman's home filling my head with skepticism. I didn't think Delilah was that kind of girl, though, so I tried not to think about it.

As we walked in to her apartment, a fat cat came bounding toward the door with its tongue hanging out like a dog. *Well,* I thought, *you don't see that every day.*

"This is Dot," Delilah introduced as she led me down the hall to the living room, where a beautiful mahogany piano stood on the far side of the wall. "I found her in the trash can when I was 16 and we've been best friends ever since." She nudged the cat with her foot.

"She's cute," I stroked the sleek black hair of the feline. She purred and licked my hand, again like a dog. "She's pretty old then, isn't she?"

Delilah plopped down on a fat couch and patted the seat next to her, motioning for me to do the same. I walked over and sat down, feeling swallowed up at once by the cushy sofa.

"Old, but healthy as a horse." She smiled at the cat and then looked up at me. "Did you want some of that ice cream?"

"I am actually still pretty full from that bucket of fries they gave me," I said, patting my stomach for emphasis. "But if you want some, don't let me stop you."

"Oh, I'm full, too," she said, then leaned in and whispered, "And good, because my stash is actually only for emotional breakdowns that lead to chick-flick binges."

I laughed. "You like chick flicks?"

At that moment, my phone buzzed in my

pocket. Although on vibrate, it still made a racket as it was sitting right next to my keys. I looked down for a moment, confused.

"Do you need to get that?" Delilah asked, thankfully not looking offended at all.

"Well, I don't usually get texts from anyone after nine," I said, pulling out the phone apologetically. "Tell you what, if it isn't some top-secret mission, I'll fill you in."

She laughed. "Eh, I'm okay staying out of your personal life, I really don't mind. I mean, if I hadn't checked my phone earlier today I wouldn't have made it to Jordine's office on time." She crossed her long legs and looked toward the window, though I could tell she was watching me expectantly in her peripherals.

I quickly read through the text from Jameson. "They've got a break in our case!" I fist-pumped excitedly, and then looked back up at her as I realized she had no idea what I was talking about.

"Sorry," I explained as I put my phone back in my pocket. "It isn't top-secret, but I also don't know how much I can say. Apparently, we've made *another* break in this case we've been working on since January, and I've got to go in to the office early tomorrow morning." I couldn't keep the excitement out of my voice; this was huge.

Delilah smiled, admiration lighting up her eyes. It made my spirits soar even higher. "I cannot wait to be in that position." She leaned over and put her arms around me. I raised my eyebrows as I returned the surprise hug.

"Congratulations, that's awesome!"

I appreciated her sincerity. I have dealt with people in her position that avoided the topic of work altogether because they were jealous of how far ahead I was. It was nice to have some recognition. *Don't let it get to your head, Jace Avery,* my mom's voice nagged.

"Is there a chance I could be in the briefing, you think?" she asked hopefully, shyly tugging a stray strand of hair behind her ear after pulling away. "You know, now that I'm a special agent?"

"I'll ask Jordine, but it's definitely a possibility," I said, not wanting to make any promises but hoping this beautiful woman could come see my success in this ridiculous case. Then again, now that I was starting to understand just how much she cared about her position, the thought of an actual relationship with Delilah seemed even further away.

Delilah smiled gratefully, and the conversation turned from work to her finals and how they'd gone. She talked about them modestly, but I could tell she felt confident in how she had done, and I enjoyed hearing her bag on some of her professors. I remembered how I felt when I was that close to graduating; I'd grown to dislike every professor I had.

Delilah excused herself after that, but only for a moment, coming back with a deck of playing cards in her hands and all the confidence in the world that she would beat me; and though I hate to admit it, she was so right. I have never seen anyone match things up in a game of speed so quickly, but I guess that's why she was so good at her filing job at the office. After a couple of rounds, however, her eyelids had begun to droop slightly, her movements becoming increasingly less agile.

"I'll let you get some sleep," I said, standing to stretch.

She stood up hastily, pulling her dress down from where it had hiked up during the excitement of the game. "So soon?"

I couldn't tell if she meant it or if she was a little relieved that I was the one to bring up leaving.

I put my hands on her shoulders. "I know how the day's gone for you, I've been there," I pulled on my shoes that had been kicked off when the cards were broken out. I let her lead me to the door. "Next time we can stay up as late as you want."

Delilah pulled me into a tight hug. She lingered there for a moment, and I couldn't help but let my mind wander to her perfectly pink lips.

"Thanks, Jace," she said. "Dinner was wonderful, and I really loved getting to know you more." She pulled back a little sooner than I wanted.

"Any time," I said, walking out and looking back at her. "Really."

Basically floating down the hall, I made my way back down to the parking lot. Delilah was certainly not like any New York woman I had ever met.

* * *

"You played cards?" Lars asked incredulously as we sparred in the gym under the office. I dodged his left hook, grabbing his arm and swinging my elbow into his ribs. "On a date with the most modelesque woman in the office, and you stayed up to eleven *playing cards*?"

It was 6:00 in the morning. We had already been at the gym for half an hour, and I was due to the office by 7:00. That gave me just enough time to finish here, shower, and grab some breakfast. My life was very scheduled, but it would work better if Lars wasn't trying to draw out what I did with Delilah the night before. As he doubled over from my blow, I grabbed the back of his head and ran him into the wall, pinning him there as I used my knees against his sparring helmet.

"Yes, we played cards," I said, breaking off. Lars was short but agile, and he quickly recovered, aiming for my legs and bringing me crashing down to the padded floor. "It was a nice relaxing game after a heavy dinner. On a first date."

"Sure," he teased as I flipped him on to his back and pulled him into an arm bar. "Maybe I should ask her out. See if she 'plays cards' with me, too."

Lars was all talk, but the thought of him taking Delilah out caused my grip to tighten and his arm to creak dangerously.

"Okay, okay!" he yelled, tapping the ground. I released him, and he stood, rubbing his shoulder. "I won't ask her out okay? Dating other agents is risky anyway."

I nodded, out of breath from the exertion it took not to break his arm. Lars is a good friend, and while I would trust him with my life, I would never trust him with Delilah. The thought made me angry, which was weird; I had never been the jealous type. But I had to admit he was right; the aspect of chancing another in-office relationship made me indecisive. What if it did work out, and we fell madly in love? Being an FBI agent wasn't really the safest gig in the world—how would we be able to focus *and* protect each other?

I frowned as I stood and grabbed my bottle, spraying the refreshing water into my mouth and then over my face. I really liked Delilah, but I also felt like I'd have to be cautious with this one.

"I'm hitting the showers, Hulk," Lars said as he grabbed his gym bag and started walking toward the locker room door. "Are you done here?"

"Yeah, I should probably head up too," I said, nodding and following him out.

Soon I was all showered up and ready to grab some breakfast. Making my way to the breakroom, I walked past the little hallway that led to Delilah and Edith's office. I hesitated for a moment, contemplating whether I should go see if she was in already. I didn't want to come off as stalkerish, however, so I turned back to the breakroom, pulling my premade protein shake and a paper bag out of the fridge. Sitting at one of the tables, I dug in to my breakfast and watched as Jordine walked into the room, holding a huge purse that was big enough to probably keep her whole life in.

"Morning, Avery," she said as she walked past me and started putting things in the refrigerator.

"Morning, Director," I replied, standing up to get her attention. "As you may have heard, we had a break in the McGregor case last night."

"I am aware, Jace," Jordine turned and faced me. Her piercing green eyes bore into me like chisels. "What do you want?"

"I just thought it would be fitting for agents Hadley and Banks to sit in on the briefing," I stated simply. I knew Jordine was a very straightforward woman and there was no point in beating around the bush. "Maybe not to engage the threat quite yet but to expose them to cases they may be handling soon."

Jordine sized me up, a finger unconsciously on her chin. "Very well," she said. "But please keep the briefing just that—brief; those girls have a lot to do to get ready for advancement and my day is already jam-packed. Your team can finalize any details with me tomorrow—I've already set it up with Jameson."

"Yes, Director," I said as I let her pass me out of the breakroom.

I finished my breakfast and walked down the hall to Delilah's cubicle. As I entered, Edith looked up from her report. Giving me a grin exposing a missing tooth, she used her eyes to point down under the desk.

Walking over, I found Delilah on the floor, crunched up in front of her chair as if she were in a game of hide-and-seek. Her face burned red as she looked up at me before scrambling out, smoothing her turquoise button up and flipping her braid over her shoulder.

"Hey Jace," she said, breathlessly.

"What were you hiding from?" I asked, trying not to laugh at the momentary site of someone so tall curled under a desk.

"Well..." Delilah said hesitantly, before Edith broke in from her little corner.

"As soon as Liles got here, Lars and Arthur came and asked her on a date at the same time," Delilah shot daggers at her, but Edith remained oblivious. "When Delilah tried to dodge the questions, they followed her up here till she got away from them by running to the bathroom."

Delilah looked embarrassed. I tried to push down the heat crawling up my neck. Those guys were going to get it later.

"Looks like your little date last night was enough to open the flood gates," Edith continued, looking smug.

"Well, I am the luckiest in the office to have gotten you first," I said, making Delilah blush and Edith squeal in delight. I tried to maintain a professional air because I had a reputation to uphold, but it was hard not to smile at Delilah's red face. "Please, ladies, I would be honored if you accompanied me to a briefing on Jameson's and my case. Jordine has already given the okay."

Edith scuttled around her desk frantically as I glanced at Delilah, who couldn't have looked happier. "Thank you," she whispered as I led them out of their cubicles and down the floor to the briefing room.

Once there, they made their way to the back seats of the room, but not before Delilah had grabbed my arm and given it a little squeeze. I smiled; if that's not a confidence booster, I don't know what is. Jameson nodded as I joined him at the front table, reaching him just as he opened the file sitting atop it.

"Remember your discovery about McGregor, yesterday?" he muttered, pulling out papers and laying them across the desk as more of our team made their way into the room. "I found where he's operating from this month."

"That's what you meant last night," I said, also keeping my voice down but letting my eyes wash over the people entering the room. Jordine came in close to last, accompanied by her guard for the day, Arthur Samson, the knucklehead that tried to ask Delilah on a date. My face grew warm as I turned back to Jameson, realizing I didn't know if she had said yes to him or not.

"And we're going to plan an infiltration," Jameson continued as the room grew expectantly silent. He cleared his throat and nudged me, nodding to the crowd of about ten people sitting in front of us.

"Okay everyone," I started, unsure why Jameson wanted me to do the talking. "Thanks for meeting with us today. We'll keep it short because we know how busy everyone is, but there has been another break in the McGregor Case."

Mutters from several people blew through the room as some looked relieved, others worried. I continued:

"Around three yesterday Jameson and I were collecting our intel on the subject, assuming that McGregor was transporting drugs overseas. Our assumptions were correct, and upon further investigation, we discovered that the main drug being transported is Ketamine."

More mutters followed as I looked around the room. "Ketamine is a fatal and highly addictive drug that can cause people to lose their minds before losing their lives. The quantity of these shipments is terrifying, as well as the rapid speeds at which they are leaving the Manhattan Harbor."

"We have to stop this immediately," Jameson chimed in. I moved around to the side of the table, so everyone's full attention would turn to him. I couldn't help but notice Delilah's eyes still on me, though. "Working on this case since January has been frustrating for the entire team. McGregor has been slippery, but last night after Jace told me his theory and showed me his evidence, I got on it as fast as I could.

"We followed any trails of Ketamine manufacturing and usage we could find, and I believe we have discovered the whereabouts of McGregor's headquarters. Also, after working around the clock and following all kinds of drug trails, I'm pretty sure I know when we can catch him there."

Some in the audience clapped while others remained looking skeptical. Jordine nodded her approval to us before quietly slipping out.

"We will assemble a small task force to engage on the dates we suspect McGregor to be in town," I continued as Jameson gave me the go ahead. "We plan on ending this case by the end of next week and putting McGregor behind bars." I sure hope Jameson agreed with that—I got caught up in the moment.

As the team began filing out, some approached us with congratulations. I heard a lot of complaints as well, though, and assured everyone that if they didn't want to be on the task force they could opt out. I was sure we would be able to get enough to fill a sizable force to arrest the crazy drug lord.

Delilah, Jameson, and I were the last in the room. Jameson patted me on the back and told me to meet him in the conference room in five minutes to finalize the plan. As soon as he left, Delilah rushed me, looking excited. She grabbed my arms and I held hers, looking into her beautiful eyes. I saw the admiration again and my heart skipped a beat.

"I want in, Jace," she said breathlessly. I smiled, but there was more than just admiration in her eyes; ambition resided there as well.

CHAPTER 3

Delilah

Dot came dancing around the legs of my piano bench as I pounded out a piece I had learned in high school. I didn't practice often, but when I had time, I loved to mess around on the piano my grandparents had given me. I usually had to take off whatever I had sitting on top of it though, because I would get a little carried away and knock things down with the force used to stroke the keys. It didn't happen often now that I had neighbors to worry about, but today was an exception.

It had been four days since Jace and Jameson got their mission cleared, four days since I begged to be on their team, and four grueling days of listening to Jace say he'd see what he could do. Jordine didn't seem to be too hot on the idea, but even she couldn't deny me outright; she just kept saying we'd have to wait till after my ceremony. But according to my calendar, which probably isn't too different from hers, my ceremony is exactly one day before they are planning on the infiltration. What better way to start off my career? I continued playing till my forearms started to hurt, getting carried away in my thoughts. I tried to stay a patient and humble person, but I felt like I'd proven myself enough to handle something like this.

At least Jace had my back. Ever since Wednesday he had been approaching Jordine about allowing me on the team. At first, I didn't think he would like the idea either, given how he had treated me on our date; the perfect gentleman. Men like him—and my dad—don't think most girls can handle themselves. But he proved me wrong; as soon as I asked he went straight to Jordine's office and vouched for me. I smiled as my fingers flitted across the keyboard. That meant a lot. Jace was sweet and sincere, attributes that I've come to realize a lot of men his age lack.

I'd gone on a date with Arthur Samson last night, another agent from the office. Did I feel guilty about it? If it led him on, maybe, but I'm pretty sure I stabilized that threat from ever happening. He had planned everything for the entire night, and I mean everything; I'm pretty sure rejecting his first advance for a kiss had thrown off his whole strategy. I wasn't rude; he just wasn't the kind of man I would want as my second-ever kiss. I don't think he'll be asking me on another date anytime soon, however. I don't mind; lately I've had someone else in mind for that kiss.

Speak of the devil, a knock came to my door. I wouldn't have heard it had there not been a decrescendo written in my piece at that exact moment. I jumped a little. Was it five already? Glancing at the clock and closing my piano, I realized I was even late to my own dinner party. Sunday had gone by so fast that I'd almost forgotten about it.

Running down the entry hall with Dot trying to lick my bare heels, I picked up a stray bobby pin from the floor. I pulled open the door, trying to look put together as I blocked my cat from escaping.

"Jace!" I said, smiling. The way he had obviously tried to do his hair, but failed, was adorable.

"Hey Liles," He smiled back, his hands full of grocery bags and a crockpot. "How's your Sunday?"

"Pretty normal," I said, trying to sound casual as I moved to let him in. "Can I help with something?"

He laughed. "I pride myself in bringing all my groceries in at once," he said as he made his way to my kitchen table. "I can handle this little bit, thanks."

As he set everything down, I tried to jump in and help where I could. He had offered to bring the bulk of tonight's meal when I had explained my idea of takeout. When he kept boxing me out of my own kitchen, I decided to just watch. His T-shirt was tight around his biceps—most likely an accidental fit, but I'm not complaining. His white skin contrasted against his dark hair, making me try and remember when he had lost his tan from last summer. When he had finally unloaded everything and tied the bags in a knot, he turned back to me. I tried to look like I wasn't blatantly staring at him that whole time.

He smiled again, his strong jaw throwing shadows across his neck. "Was that you? Just playing the piano?"

I blushed. I'd forgotten how much people can hear while standing right outside the door. I had to get my wits back; something about Jace made me feel less sarcastic and more innocent.

"No," I brushed it off, walking around the table to look in the slow cooker. "That was my roommate."

I avoided his eyes but could tell he was confused. "I didn't know you had a roommate," he said, uncertainly.

I laughed, looking up and shrugging. Realization dawned on his face as I took a whiff of the food simmering in the crock pot. "Mmm," I said, taking off the lid and wafting the fumes over the table. Whatever it was, it smelled delicious. "What did you make? I didn't know you were a chef! Usually guys just bring fast food."

"Oh, you have guys over often then?" Jace smirked as he bent down to pet Dot, who had been sitting at his feet as soon as he had stood still. It was a sign that she liked him. "Tonight, I prepared for you slow-cooker barbeque ribs, with a side of spinach and arugula salad and served atop my mom's world-famous mashed potatoes."

"You sound like you're from the *Food Network*," I laughed, pulling down plates and silverware from my cupboards. I probably should have done that before he got there but time had slipped away from me, as usual. Jace didn't seem to mind though, walking over and helping set the table. "Well, I prepared some mean raspberry lemonade for our beverage and brownies straight from the box for dessert."

He laughed again, making me grateful I didn't have a roommate. But then there was another knock on the door, and I tried not to look disappointed as I went to answer; I had invited them after all.

Jameson, Edith, and my neighbor Beau walked in, each carrying a side dish of their own. I had thought it would be fun to organize a get together now that my nights were no longer chalk-full of studying. I introduced everyone to Beau, a short man with a grisly chin, and we all took seats around my table. I had strategically placed Edith next to Beau, hoping to do a little matchmaking tonight—another hobby I had been missing out on.

"I still don't see why we couldn't have just gone to the club for some drinks," Edith said in a slightly crestfallen voice. If I wasn't sitting so far away from her I would've kicked her under the table; I didn't want to draw attention to my naivety. The truth was, I chose when I was nine years old, after watching my aunt struggle out of an abusive, alcoholic relationship, that I would never drink. Hence the juvenile game nights I was so inclined to —less temptation.

"Eh, it's good to get out of that scene every

once in a while," Jace said loudly, avoiding my eyes. "Jameson and I were just talking about how we needed a quiet night in, weren't we?"

"Oh yeah," Jameson said quickly, and I decided to ignore Jace's elbow in his rib cage. "Who needs the beer and the lights and the women when you can have a nice, home-cooked meal with friends?"

"For free," Beau added. I couldn't tell if he was being sarcastic, but I gave them all a grateful smile anyway as I started to dish out the food.

The ribs were even more delicious than they'd smelled, and Jace's salad added a nice green balance to the meal. I mean, everyone else's food was fine too, but this man never ceased to impress me. As we ate, Jace asked when I would walk for graduation, and that started everyone on the conversation of how grateful they were that they were no longer in school. Jace remembered details from our last dinner that I'd forgotten I had even told him, bringing them up when there was lull and letting everyone say their opinions on it. It was impressive. I secretly prayed that he was not just a jerk using strategic flattery to get me. It didn't seem that way, but a girl had to be careful, and I tended to be overly cautious.

Jameson's phone rang about halfway through dinner, and as he answered Beau asked politely if he could use the bathroom. Both men got up from the dinner table, and Edith, bless her heart, stood saying she needed to make a phone call as well and went into the other room.

"So," I said quietly, feeling guilty for bringing up work but hating to be left in the dark. "Has Jordine said anything about the McGregor mission?"

Jace set down his fork, looking carefully at me over his glass. "Not about *that* case, no," he said nonchalantly. I folded my arms across the table.

"Has she said something about another case?" I asked, trying to read his facial expressions. For an FBI agent, he wasn't very good at keeping secrets. Or was he letting me see through him?

"Well," he said, slowly wiping his mouth with his napkin. He was stalling. "I'm technically not supposed to say anything, seeing as you'll be asked tomorrow morning..."

"Spit it out, Avery," I picked up my fork and pointed it threateningly at him. He tried to look offended.

"I have a first name, you know." Holding his hand to his chest in a very feminine manner, Jace put on a pouty face. "I would think this being our second dinner together you would have taken the time to learn it."

I rolled my eyes, putting some mashed potato on the fork and flicking it at him. My silverware may not be the best in the state, but it was the perfect flimsiness for flinging food. He dodged, letting it fall to the floor, where Dot hastily cleaned it up for us.

"All right, all right!" he said, dropping the act. "Lars' team cracked another case, a smaller one but still a pretty big feat. Jordine has been messing with the idea of letting you join their task force to tackle the threat, before your induction ceremony."

I couldn't hide my excitement. This was no McGregor, I could already tell, but at least she was trusting me with something, and so soon. Jace seemed satisfied with my reaction.

"You'll find out all the details tomorrow," he said as Jameson and Edith returned, a questioning look on her face and an oblivious one on his. "But I was asked to join the force as well, and I'm looking forward to working with you in a combative situation." Jace added quietly as Beau took his seat once more.

I blushed at the compliment, trying to hide my red face by pulling my napkin up to my lips, but I think he saw it because he smiled shyly and turned back to his food. If he was just trying to use me, he was doing a bang-up job of making it seem real. His food was impressive, his personality sweet, and his looks were just the cherry on top. How in the world would I keep from falling for him? I mean, I guess it isn't like he's a complete stranger, since we've been working together for so long. I tried to hide my thoughts through the rest of the meal, but I'm sure they showed plainly on my face as he offered to help me with the dishes.

"I do them every day," I said trying to lead him over to the couch with the rest of my guests. "Jace, really it will take me two seconds."

"Yes, but you do *your* dishes every day," he said, dodging around me and starting to clear off the table. Edith smiled knowingly while Jameson looked at my bookshelf. "This is partly my mess. So, I will dry. No one likes drying."

He was right, that was my least favorite part of the chore. And seeing how I didn't own a dishwasher, I was grateful for his offer to help, even though I let him grudgingly. While Edith, Jameson, and Beau visited in the living room, Jace and I whisked through the dishes. At one point, he pulled out one of the wooden spoons I had just cleaned and used it to flip soap into my face as I was washing the crock pot. As I tried to keep my hair out of it, I flipped soap onto his chest with a spatula. We went back and forth for a minute, getting more animated with each flip, trying to outdo the other while still hitting our targets. I had never had siblings, but I imagined doing dishes with them would be something like this. Except for the fact that I had a crush on the man trying to convince me I'd look great with a soap beard.

After we finally got dinner cleaned up, and the mess we made while trying to clean up cleaned up, we joined everyone else in the living room. There were still spots open on the couch, as Edith and Jameson had been so kind to take the floor. It swallowed us up, just as it had the last time we sat there, only this time, Jace sat much closer to me. Goosebumps erupted on my arms as I recognized the lack of space between us, but I still had my guard up; there had to be something wrong with him. Could any guy be this perfect?

"So, I hope you weren't planning a rematch of cards yet," he said sheepishly as Dot jumped up into his lap. "I haven't practiced much since you destroyed me last time." He added behind his hand to everyone else, "She doesn't lose."

They all laughed. I smirked. "Don't worry," I said, grabbing the remote from the coffee table. "I thought today we'd try your skills at something else."

"I think the two of you are a bit too competitive to be holding game nights with us mild-tempered folk," Jameson laughed.

"I don't know," Edith shrugged. "I like to see people tear each other apart. Figuratively, of course."

Jace flexed, "Well if we're wrestling I know who'll win."

Jameson rolled his eyes as I pulled out my old Nintendo 64. Jace's face brightened immediately. "Oh, you don't want to challenge me at this."

"Worried you'll lose again?" I stuck out my tongue as I passed out controllers.

Just then Beau stood. "Hey, I can see ya'll have enough people to play, and I am horrible at video games, so this may be my time to go."

"We haven't even had dessert," Edith stood as well; I knew she had gotten her hopes up, no matter how badly she tried to hide it.

"Much obliged, little lady, but I've got to be up early tomorrow morning," Beau headed to the door. I didn't feel too bad not walking him out seeing as Edith was taking up that duty. "Janitorial duties, you know how it goes."

As they walked out, we started the game. "Scared, boys?"

Jameson snorted as Jace leaned in closer.

"More worried you'll never talk to me again," he said, sitting on the edge of the couch. "I played this for eight years straight as a kid."

Jace was right. My competitive side got the better of me, and the fact that he beat me at almost every video game we played made it hard to continue sitting so close to him. He was a professional. It didn't matter if we were racing, fighting, or just decorating cakes; he won every single time. By the end of the night, I was slowly counting to ten to control my breathing.

"You're kind of a sore loser, aren't you?" he teased as we sat back into the couch, finally turning the game off. Jameson and Edith joined us on the couch as well, having had enough of the floor. Jace stroked back a stray hair from my face. There was no way I could be mad at him.

"I can get a bit competitive, yeah," I said.

Jameson laughed, "You joking Rapunzel? You got second place in every game."

"Seriously," Edith's shoulders had slouched ever since Beau departed. I felt bad, but I got the feeling she was dodging a bullet since he'd decided to leave right when the fun began. "It was like Jameson and I weren't even here. Speaking of, I really should head home."

"It is pretty late," Jameson stood. "I've got some stuff that needs to get done before work tomorrow, and I unfortunately am not the best at getting up on time, so I'll have to do it tonight."

We all stood up together, and I helped them gather their dinner supplies, leading everyone but Jace back to the door.

"Thanks for coming guys," I called after them as they walked out. "We'll have to do it again soon!"

"Next time, I plan!" Edith called back. I laughed before turning back to find Jace standing at the end of the hallway.

"Liles," he said, walking over to me with his crockpot under one arm. "Thanks for being normal. Not rushing anything. I mean," He looked embarrassed, like he couldn't find the right words. "I've never spent so much time with a girl where all she wanted to do was... challenge my gaming skills. It's been refreshing."

I smiled. Glancing down to his lips, I had to catch myself. He'd just told me he liked slow, and my front door was wide open. What was I thinking?

But before I knew it, his arm was around my waist, pulling me closer. I didn't try to stop it as our lips touched, my hands on his chest.

And then it was over. As quick as he had come, Jace was pulling away from me. He smiled, thanking me again before walking into the hall. I closed the door behind him, sinking to the ground and holding my heart. I hadn't felt butterflies like that since high school.

* * *

"If you could study any specific part of the human body," Edith said as she held my punching bag for me, "what would it be?"

I took two swings and then dove to the side as she pushed it back at me, using the momentum to aim a swift kick to the center. "The brain, of course," I said as I pulled back and released a combination of fists and elbows onto the pockmarked bag.

Edith laughed, switching places with me to take a few hits. "Why the brain?" she asked as I held the bag steady for her to practice her quick jabs.

"Why not?" I replied, watching her body steadily. Edith was always fast, but if she got too carried away her form would get sloppy, and that would be a perfect time to push the bag out at her. "It's amazing how it works, and how just one little thing can turn it from fully functioning to fully not."

"I see your point," she said, not looking up but tirelessly continuing to jab and weave. "But I guess I just thought you would be more interested in the muscle development, or pulmonary vessels."

I saw my chance; pushing the bag out as she took a false step, I knocked Edith to the side. "You're just saying that because I'm a big person. There is more to me than just this." I flexed my arms, showing off the toned muscles I had worked so hard to get.

Edith walked over to the benches to grab her towel. "Cheap shot." She squirted water into her mouth and offered me some as well. "No, I just know how much you like to work out."

"I only like it because it keeps me doing the things I love." I walked beside her as we entered the women's locker room. "I wouldn't be able to go on backpacking trips without an hour and a half a day down here."

She continued to ask random questions as we showered, changed, and headed to our desks. And quite unremarkably, the conversation turned to Jace.

Sitting down in my chair and pulling a file from my cabinet, I took a sidelong glance at her. "What about him?" I tried to ask nonchalantly.

"I left early last night for a reason," I could tell all the meaningless talk this morning had been leading up to this. "And Jameson thankfully caught my drift. I did that for you, so, did anything happen?"

I tried not to smile. I was excited to tell someone about our kiss, but did I really want it to be Edith? She wasn't exactly a one-key safe. Anyone could get information out of her if they asked the right questions—another reason that made me wonder how she was an FBI agent.

She must have seen right through me, though, because she squealed and wheeled her way over to my chair, grabbing my hands and giving me that toothless grin. "Tell me all about it!"

"It was just a kiss," I said amid her giggling

and shaking. "Right before he left, he grabbed me and kissed me. It was pretty fast, but..." Now that I was talking about it, the excitement of last night seemed real again, even though it was such a small gesture. "He really seemed nervous, like he didn't know what I would do."

"What did you do?" Edith asked breathlessly, her hands now on her own heart. I felt like I was the star of her favorite Bachelorette season.

"I kissed him back." Thinking about it made heat rise in my cheeks. "He did it fast, but it was really cute, and I just wish I could find something wrong with him because so far he's just been perfect." The words came out all at once, and I had to stop myself from laughing. "That probably sounds ridiculous."

"That's not ridiculous, Liles," Edith said, straightening up with a completely somber face. "Women have to be careful, nowadays. You never know a man's true intentions. But girl," She took my hand again, a mischievous sparkle in her eye. "I honestly think he's sincere, the way he looks at you. But if he does have any problems there's no way he could hide it from me. I'll dig till my hands bleed to make sure you don't get hurt."

"Oh," I said, worried I had awakened a monster. "I can handle myself. If he is just doing these sweet things to use me, I'll find out soon enough."

"But before you fall for him?" she eyed me suspiciously. Of course, I had already fallen for him. But I wasn't going to let anyone know that yet.

Just then, there was a knock on the wall next to our cubicles. We looked up to see Jace and Lars standing in the doorway. Obviously Jace had not told Lars anything about last night's events, because Lars winked at me with a stupid grin on his face. I tried to act like I hadn't seen it, looking instead to Jace.

Our eyes met, and I knew at once something was wrong. He almost looked pained, but he still smiled at me. I gave in to the tingling in my stomach as I watched him.

"Ladies," he said, continuing to look only at me, "Jordine is ready for you in her office. We have got some great news, for the both of you." Only then did he break eye contact, swiftly giving Edith a quick nod before pushing Lars out of the doorway. "And we are your escorts."

Edith took the hint, bolting from her chair to get to Lars before he could say anything. Looking slightly crestfallen, he glanced back at Jace and I as they walked away. Jace waited in the doorway for me, watching as I slipped out from behind my desk and walked toward him. He didn't say anything, though, so when I reached him I grabbed his arm.

"Are you okay?" I asked, looking back into his eyes.

"Sorry." Jace guided me out of the office, and we started to slowly walk to Jordine's. "If last nights, um, events were, uh, uncalled for." He snuck a nervous glance at me.

"Don't be sorry," I said, trying to give a sincere

look, "I didn't really mind." The smile that appeared on his face was so relieved it made me giggle. But then he ruined it all as he continued:

"I don't know if we should do this, though," Jace's eyes fell to the floor. "I mean, we're colleagues in a pretty dangerous field."

I'll be honest; my initial reaction was to punch him. "You don't want to date me?"

We reached the open door of Jordine's office just then and both tried to conceal that anything had just passed between us more than a handshake. I felt a sting behind my eyes I hadn't felt in a long time and pushed it down; we will definitely be discussing this more as soon as we're alone together again.

Jordine's office was the biggest on the floor, but there were probably about fifteen people standing inside it, making it feel quite cramped. I recognized only a few apart from Lars, Edith, and Jordine; in the corner I saw Maurine Flitter, a brawny woman with close to no eyebrows; standing near Jordine's desk stood Blakely and Ferguson (I didn't know their first names); and sitting in a chair right beside the door was Kenneth Stanley, the oldest operating field agent in the office. Everyone else was probably members of Lars' team, whom I hadn't had the chance to work with yet.

Closing the door behind us, Jace gave a nod to Lars, who was standing on the opposite wall next to Edith. Edith had struck up a conversation with a woman who had to be no taller than five feet. Lars crossed the room to Jordine's desk, speaking in low tones to her as the room began to quiet down.

Jordine cleared her throat and the entire room went silent. I have always wondered what this woman did to deserve the respect she got around here. It was impressive.

"As you all know, Lars and his team have made a break in the most recent Cyber Attack on the Pentagon, code named CAP." Many people nodded around the room. This was news to me, but of course I wasn't at the same level of clearance as these people. Yet.

"Their team has followed the trail of this attack for two months now and have developed a theory as to where it's originating. They need a small task force, no more than six people, to infiltrate and exterminate." Jordine made eye contact with me before continuing, giving the faintest nod. "I have hand-picked two of our newest and finest to be part of the team, and we have had one volunteer already. It goes without saying that Lars will be leading the endeavor, which leaves two spots open. I have called you here to finish assembling the team and give any final information for this to be carried out."

"Is this them?" Stanley asked from his chair, his voice a gravelly baritone as he pointed in mine and Edith's direction.

"Yes, Kenneth," Jordine said, walking around her desk and addressing the rest of the room. "For those of you who don't know, this is Delilah Hadley and Edith Banks. They will be our newest special field agents starting Thursday, but we wanted to give them an idea of what they were getting themselves into." There were chuckles around the room as everyone acknowledged us.

"Count me out, then." Stanley stood and made his way to the door slowly. What a sexist old —, "If you need that kind of speed and agility, this is not a mission for an old guy like me."—oh.

Jace laughed as he patted the old man on the back, opening the door for him. Maurine started toward the door as well, quietly stating that her kids had recitals all that week, so it was no good for her anyway. Before anyone else could opt out, however, the short woman Edith had been speaking with and a slightly overweight man with a mustache volunteered. Jordine excused the rest of the room, keeping the team together as others filed out.

Jordine went back behind her desk as she addressed Lars, "You and your team should get acquainted if you are to work together. We rarely do this, but I figure most of you have operated together enough to know what you are doing. If you need any other approvals please bring them to me; other than that, I expect this entire thing to be done by Wednesday morning, according to the time frame you gave me."

"Of course, Jordine," Lars said, his voice slick with flattery. I swallowed the gag welling in my throat. "My timeframe was accurate, and we'll be carrying out this infiltration tomorrow night. I'm sure everything that needs it has already been approved by you, but I will triple check my files once back at my desk."

Jordine gave another curt nod before sitting back in her chair, dismissing us all from her office. As we walked out, the mustached man held out a hand to me.

"The name's Hauffer. Gordon Hauffer, but you can just call me Gordo." He shook my hand vigorously, his thick German accent slightly surprising. "I'm the personal getaway driver." He patted his stomach affectionately. "Haven't seen the action up close and personal for a while now, and I'd like to keep it that way."

After introducing myself, I turned to find the short woman staring up at me. She had fiery red hair and eyes shaped like almonds. She smiled, revealing sharp canines. "I'm Paula Gray." She was more than a foot shorter than me, yet her voice was booming and unapologetic. "I specialize in our technology department. I figured a case involving cyber tech would be one they'd need me in."

"Okay guys," Lars interrupted, walking around us to tighten the circle we were already in, "Please meet in conference room 4B at 1:00 today, to go over details of what my team discovered, as well as to devise an attack strategy." He looked nervous, the confidence he showed in Jordine's office melting away with each word. "I have compiled a list of possibilities, but I want everyone's opinions on the best way to tackle this one. Thank you all for being willing to work on this with us."

Everyone agreed and went their separate ways. I hung back, standing beside Jordine's open door. Jace was beginning to walk away when he caught my eye.

"Liles," he said, coming closer so that I could hear as he talked softly, "I don't know how well she'd take you asking personally to be on my team."

I tried to look innocent. "I wasn't going to. . ." I shut my mouth at the look he gave me. I wanted to kiss him again so badly, but I scrunched my eyebrows, irritated. "Okay, you caught me," I said, walking away from her door with him. "Have you already asked her today?"

"Not quite. The whole office has been buzzing about Lars' news, and I didn't want to steal his thunder. He's never led an attack team before."

We rounded the corner, walking down the small hallway toward the sound of Edith's voice. I stopped and turned to him, my arms folded across my chest. He raised an eyebrow.

"I will ask her after our meeting with Lars, okay?"

"I would really appreciate it," He moved to continuing walking, but I blocked him. "But I think there's something else we need to talk about?"

He sighed. "Look, I would love to date you—"

"Hey me too, but about you. So, what's the problem?"

"We work for the FBI," Jace spread his hands exasperatedly. "First of all, I'm pretty sure it's against the bureau's HR rules to have interdepartmental relationships. And then what happens if one of us gets hurt? Or too distracted to do our jobs right?"

His career was important to him. I get it. I guess we had only been on one date if you don't count the night he actually kissed me. I suppressed the angry lava in my stomach.

"Fine." I turned away, leaving him with his mouth hanging open as I headed back to my desk. I didn't want to lose a friend over my over-eager feelings, and I knew if I stayed I'd say something I'd regret.

CHAPTER 4

Jace

I watched as Delilah strapped her gun to her waist. She looked completely comfortable with the firearm, but she still glanced over at me with nervous eyes. I gave an encouraging smile. Regret filled my stomach like helium as she looked away without so much as a twitch of the mouth.

We sat together with Lars in the empty office. The clock had just struck 8:30, and we waited there to rendezvous with the other members of the team. Lars was wringing his hands, glancing at the clock every few minutes. We had scheduled to deploy around nine, but of course I wanted to be early. And this was the first time I had seen Delilah early for anything.

I wished Lars wasn't there. I wished I could talk more with Delilah just one on one, kiss her and feel her soft skin. But every time I thought about it I'd get this horrible feeling, like something inside me knew that something would go wrong if I acted on this urge. It's not like I broke up with her—we weren't even officially dating. I'm pretty sure I was the one suffering, however, because she had completely distanced herself from me since yesterday. I had to keep trying to convince myself of the reasons not to date her, which were strictly only the ones I had reluctantly confessed. I mean, Delilah even looked beautiful in her Kevlar vest and slacks, her dark hair laced back and forth down her back. If her gun wasn't lethal enough, I figured she could always whip someone with that heavy braid.

We sat in silence for a while, mainly because of the nervous tension in the air. I felt completely at home, however this being Delilah's first mission and Lars' first lead, the atmosphere was still heavy. I had thought about trying to lift some moods with a joke, but then decided it would be better to keep everyone's minds on the mission. Including mine; I had to keep reminding myself that my job wasn't to protect Delilah; she could do that herself.

Edith and Paula walked in, laughing and both holding Starbucks cups. I was surprised at Edith's ease; this was her first mission as well after all. Looking around, she set down her cup. "Why all the long faces, guys?" she asked, making Paula giggle again.

"I'm sure they are just nervous," Paula said, walking around to Lars and giving him a pat on the back. "I remember my first mission. Course, I've only had to be in actual combat like twice."

The plan was for Paula and Gordo to stay in the surveillance van while the four of us surrounded the old warehouse where Lars had tracked down the hackers. The strategy for the night was stealth; I don't know Edith super well, but I did slightly worry she might ruin it. The threat was only supposed to be two or three suspects, however, and that made me feel better about our little tag team.

"This isn't my first mission," Lars defended, standing up and walking to the windows. "I just hope this goes smoothly. No accidents."

I knit my eyebrows together, looking down. I could understand why he was so worried. He had been the backup lead on a mission against a suspected terrorist operation a couple of years ago, and his team lead was shot in the first five minutes of the altercation. Lars himself barely got away alive, leaving with a broken leg and a bullet in his shoulder. From what I'd gathered he was scarred from it, but I highly doubted tonight would be anything like that.

Gordo swaggered in after another minute passed. "Hello everybody," he said, winding around the cubicles to make his way to us. "Am I late?"

"Five minutes early, Gordo," I said, tapping my watch. "Right on time. Lars, are you about ready?"

Lars turned to face us all, an artificial grin on his face. "All right team," he said, clenching and unclenching his fists. I wished I could just tell him to relax, but I didn't want to embarrass him. "Tonight, we've got surprise on our side. Let's go over the battle plan, then quit wasting time and take down these computer nerds."

"I resemble that comment," Paula muttered, earning a giggle from Edith. I smiled, grateful that at least some of us could stay positive.

Ignoring them, Lars continued, "Hauffer, Gray, you stay in the van, just close enough to tap into any possible security. Banks and Hadley are to proceed through the front of the warehouse while Avery and I sneak in the back. Hopefully, if there are more than just a couple nerds behind some desks, we can surprise with an attack from both sides. Remember, the thought is to enter peacefully; Avery and I are just there for insurance. If it turns nasty, Banks and Hadley are to make for the computers with the USB's Paula will provide to wipe any memory while Avery and I work for the arrest. Everyone got it?"

I nodded, watching Delilah out of the corner of my eye. She was folding her arms across her chest, a determined look on her face. It was fascinating to see such a beautiful, carefree woman look so intense. But then I remembered the way she looked at me after I told her we couldn't actually go out, and my shoulders sagged.

"Well, enough review." Lars clapped his hands and started heading out, everyone falling in step behind him. "Let's take the test."

The ride was long and crowded, especially sitting in the back of a cramped van with three other people and a set of computers. I did enjoy the fact that Delilah sat next to me, even if she was stiff as a board. I shook my head and hands, closing my eyes and getting my head back into the game. This was not a date; we were not dating.

Finally, we stopped just a couple yards away from a tall gray building with power lines stretching over the top and loading docks lining the side. There were a few dark windows in the front, and aside from the black SUV sitting outside one of the docks, it looked virtually abandoned. Graffiti littered the building's walls and a large quantity of trash in the front blew around in the wind.

"Pleasant," Paula whispered as she climbed into the back with the rest of us, turning on some of her computers piled up against the wall of the van. The space became even more cramped as Gordo tried to climb back as well, making the whole van rock as he squeezed his way out of the driver's seat.

"Maybe you should stay there," Lars said, his voice tight. "Just in case we end up needing a quick getaway."

Once Paula had pulled everything up and done some ridiculously speedy typing, she gave the okay for us to go. She put on a headset as we all put in our earpieces, making sure it all worked. Delilah looked excited, like she hadn't thought this moment would ever come. I smiled at her, wanting to just sweep her off her feet right then, but knowing I couldn't. She finally smiled back and the tension in my back released.

"Okay everyone, remember," Lars said as Gordo opened the back door for us to start piling out, "Banks, Hadley, keep your bearings so at any sign of trouble you can give Avery and me your exact location. We'll be searching the back."

"See you inside," Delilah saluted as her and Edith started walking across the street to the front of the warehouse.

Instead of crossing diagonally, Lars and I went straight ahead, reaching the sidewalk and cutting through the empty parking lot to the left of the loading docks. Paula's voice came into my ear. "No cameras as far as I can see. Security system rigged on front door and loading docks."

"KZ8 T25," I whispered as we passed the SUV. "Run the plate."

"Stolen," Paula said after a few minutes. "Ladies, security is disabled, you're good to go."

"Figures," Lars whispered. We heard the heavy knock on the door just as we peeked around the corner to the back. There was one back door, no windows or other loading docks in sight. We were hoping Delilah and Edith could just make a civilized arrest, but if anything turned ugly Lars and I would be ready to break in the back for a sneak attack.

"No answer," came Delilah's voice. "And no lights inside. Permission to break and enter?"

"We've got a warrant," Lars replied, nodding to me and standing to the left of the door. I stood to the right, waiting for the signal. We heard the crack of drywall echo across the street, along with some crumbling static through our earpieces.

A second later Edith's voice entered the frequency. "All clear in the front. Layout seems simple, a connection of outer hallways all leading to the north side of the building, as well as to an open area in the middle. My guess would be they're in the middle."

"A good guess," came a new voice.

"They hacked our frequency," Paula's voice was breathless as we heard frantic typing and clicking in the background. A rusty static built in the earpiece, making it seem like it was all around us. "We're timing out in three minutes."

And then we heard the gunshot. Lars gave the sign and together we kicked down the back door, wood splintering. Checking around the corners before entering, Lars and I moved into the dark hallway, pulling flashlights from our belts. I agreed with Edith; this was a simple layout, we just had to get to the North side. "Banks, Hadley, you good?" Lars whispered.

"All good here." Relief flooded through me as I heard Delilah's voice. "Edith just panicked and shot this guy in the leg. I staunched the bleeding and got him handcuffed to a pipe."

"Make for the north side," Lars whispered as we made our way down the hall. "Paula, watch that SUV and the South exit as well."

There was a gap in the inner wall of the hallway. The gleam of the city lights streamed in through the broken doorway, but it remained fairly dark as we neared the break. I signed for Lars to slow, stepping slowly toward the gap. If I were a criminal avoiding arrest, I'd attack from a virtually nonexistent hole in the wall, too. Flattening myself against the inner wall, I took another sidestep toward the branching off hallway. The sound of a gun cocking behind us stopped me dead in my tracks.

Lars and I both swung our flashlights and guns toward the sound, illuminating a tall and thin young man pointing a pistol at us. "Don't move," his voice was squeaky but level. "You're outnumbered."

His voice may have been calm, but his hands were shaking. This was no bodyguard. This was a decoy.

A heavy blow hit the back of my knees, making me tumble forward as Lars charged the kid with the pistol. There was no gun shot as I watched him grab the gun from the boy and lurch his arm back with a sickening crack. I rolled on to my back and jumped up in time to catch the arm of a much huskier man in black coming down on me. The kid howled as the man tried to wrestle the gun from my hands, pushing and pulling my arms like we were fighting over a toy. These guys were obviously not trained to be guards, which meant we weren't close enough to the center to be bothered with yet. I pulled the gun back toward me, using the big man's forward momentum to kick out his foot and elbow him in the face.

He fell to the ground, holding his bleeding nose. Lars sprinted over and grabbed his arms, forcefully locking them in handcuffs behind his back. I glanced at the kid, who Lars had knocked out and now lay unconscious on the ground.

"Looks like you're horribly out-skilled," Lars said as we started toward the north side again.

We made the unspoken decision that stealth was no longer on our side, seeing as they had infiltrated our radio, so we moved forward more quickly and less cautiously.

Rounding the corner to what we thought was the north side, the winding hallway with six or seven other hallways branching off in both directions made it apparent we were in some sort of maze. That explained the smug voice on the radio; there was more than just one way through this warehouse.

I wondered if Delilah and Edith had run into any more trouble yet. There were no more gunshots ringing through the warehouse, but the silence was even more deafening. Where was everybody? Was the kid bluffing, or were we really outnumbered?

"We're offline," Lars whispered behind me, taking out his earpiece and setting it in his pocket. "They broke the connection. Think Paula will get it back up?"

I nodded. "I'd keep that earpiece in, if I were you; Paula Grey knows her way around technical interference."

We continued walking forward, illuminating each hallway that lead to the north with our flashlights while giving a wide berth to the ones leading to the center of the warehouse.

As Lars readjusted his earpiece, a short figure

came barreling out of an inner hallway, knocking him into the opposite wall. “Freeze!” I yelled as the man made to grab Lars’ throat. No guns, really? Did they not realize we were the FBI?

The man raised his hands behind his beanie covered head, slowly turning to face me. His smile held a single gold tooth, and his eyes glinted in the beam of my flashlight. There was only one explanation for the smug look on his face, the trigger-shy teenager and the untrained bodyguard; we were on the wrong side of the warehouse.

“They’re distractions,” I said, pulling out my own handcuffs. “We need to make to the middle or south side of the warehouse.”

“That explains a lot,” Lars replied as we made our way down the hallway the man had come through. There were no branches off this hallway, just doors to rooms and a right turn up ahead. “What kind of warehouse is this?” he murmured to himself.

“I thought you would have researched more. Who doesn’t know the layout of the building they’re infiltrating?” I accused, reaching the turn and carelessly going around it. Thankfully there was no one hiding in the shadows to spring out at me because my frustration was overcoming my caution.

Lars didn’t reply, and I knew I couldn’t blame this on him. Maybe he had researched it and found the old blue prints. The place wasn’t new, but you could tell some renovating had been done. I was just worried about Delilah—and Edith too, I guess.

"Sorry," I muttered, taking another turn to the left this time. "Let's just find the main op and finish this."

There were no doorways in this hall, just a long stretch ahead of us. There was a different source of light filtering down the walk, however, so Lars signaled for our lights to go out. Switching off my flashlight, my eyes adjusted and saw light from outside mixed with an artificial glow emanating from a huge opening in the right wall of the hall, about ten yards down.

"They're trying to make a getaway," I whispered as we slowly approached the opening. There was no possible place someone could attack us here but from the front or back, so letting Lars lead, I put my back to him and watched the way we had just come.

Lars finally stopped just shy of the opening. I kept facing the other side, waiting for his synopsis of the situation. Leaning forward, he kept his voice low, "There's a giant garage door with a tractor trailer backed up to it. Three bolt-action rifles, two on either side of the trailer facing out, one facing in," He sounded disappointed. I bit my tongue, thinking how in the world he missed the giant entrance on the south side of the building. "Two other guys with shotguns spaced in between and three men loading the truck with computer parts. A couple metal crates to the left of this opening, and another opening on the east wall."

We agreed silently on the plan of action. The

rifles being more of a threat, we'd need them taken down first, and then we'd deal with the others. "How hefty are the crates?" I asked, thinking of how fast we would need to pull this off.

"Probably not hefty enough to withstand a shotgun blast." Lars sounded decisive, like he was thinking of turning back. I pulled out my other gun, cocking both in either hand.

"Then we'd better do this fast," I said, checking one more time behind me and then nodding to Lars. "This isn't what we expected but it's still possible. We just have to stop the trailer."

Lars nodded, cocking his own gun and closing his eyes. I let him take a breath, taking my own as well. At least, judging from the absence of more gun shots, Delilah and Edith may have gotten out. A buzzing came back into my ears as we stood together, making it apparent Paula was getting the radio back up. I took my earpiece out though; if we were going to do this successfully, we couldn't risk someone on the wrong side hearing our plan.

"I'll go for the two on top as soon as you take out the one closest," I said, trying to imagine the scene play out in our favor. "Get behind the crates after your shot and pray their loaded with something dense enough to keep those shotguns out."

It was a makeshift plan, but good enough. I had a better long range shot than Lars, and he was quicker on his feet.

We nodded to one another before Lars rounded the corner, taking quick aim and pulling his trigger. As soon as I heard the body hit the ground I moved forward in time to see Lars sliding across the floor, picking up the rifle as he scrambled for the crates. The surprise seemed to work, everyone was turning in what seemed slow motion. I moved forward, my guns trained on the second and third rifle-bearers as they hefted the firearms into position. The shots were easy—they had on Kevlar, but their heads were uncovered. Both dropped to the floor as the deafening sound of a shotgun echoed through the warehouse.

Diving for the crates, I knew they wouldn't keep out the blasts for long. They were not a strong metal and judging by the sound of me knocking into the nearest one with my shoulder, they were hollow.

"What now?" I asked Lars, watching him fiddle with the rifle's bolt. Another shotgun blast rang through my head as the farthest crate to the left was moved a foot or two back from its original place.

There was another shot, but this one didn't hit any of the crates. Peeking over, I watched in horror as Edith charged into the room from the east opening, leaving a fallen shooter in her wake. With his back turned to us, the second man with a shotgun was aiming carefully at her. I vaulted over the crate I was hiding behind, forgetting my guns and lunging for his legs. I reached him just as he pulled the trigger, sending his shot awry as we tumbled together. I heard Edith scream as I wrestled with the guy, looking up to see her writhing on the floor in pain, holding a bleeding leg.

Delilah was running to her at a full sprint from the same opening, but when she reached her she didn't stop. The men loading the trailer had stopped now, two of them advancing toward Delilah and the other attempting to close the semi's door. None of them had weapons, thankfully, but all had the build of professional football players.

The man I was wrestling knelt on my legs and put me in a headlock, slowly closing off my airway. I watched as the first man reached Delilah, going for what looked like a routine football tackle. At the last minute, Delilah dropped into a squat, the man's upper body bending over her back awkwardly. Using her sheer leg strength, she pushed her body up and over, using the man's momentum to throw him onto his back.

Lars came from behind, and I heard a sickening thud as the man's arms around my neck slackened, his body falling limply to the ground. Lars didn't wait around, however, and sprinted to Edith, tearing off his vest and ripping his shirt to put over her wound. I stood and ran to Delilah, who was dodging around the second big guy. She made eye contact with me before unstrapping her gun and flinging it at me with the force of a shot put. I caught it just as she crossed the man over, making for the tractor trailer. I saw the glint of her knife as understanding dawned on me. Running to the man giving her chase, I cocked the gun and steadied my aim before pulling the trigger. His hands inches from Delilah's heels, the man fell to the ground with a crash.

The last guy was already in the driver's seat of the tractor trailer when Delilah reached the truck. Running low and hard, she slit the back two wheels and then dove for the front on the passenger side, stabbing another wheel with her blade. The air quickly spilled out of the tires in a hiss, and Delilah made her way to the driver's side door as the man tried to step on the gas. The tires groaned and sluggishly rolled forward a couple feet before sinking to the ground.

Reaching the door, Delilah pulled it open and dragged the driver out by the scruff of his shirt, leading him back in as she pulled out her cuffs. "Is she okay?" she asked, coming toward Edith with the first look of concern on her face I had seen all night.

"It just grazed me," Edith gasped, sweat and tears mixing on her face. "That was my fault."

"She's losing a lot of blood." I squatted down and examined her thigh. "We should get her to the hospital."

Delilah and I slowly made our way back through the warehouse, grabbing the four men we had left in the halls and bringing them all back to the main hutch, where Gordo was backing up his van beside the dilapidated truck.

"Carson Steele," Lars said as we gathered the surviving criminals into our van. He addressed the man Delilah had pulled from the semi, whom I now recognized from the reports that became public about ten years ago. "Ex-convict for leaking information from D.C. Should have known."

Steele spat on the ground as we shoved him into the back of the van with the others. Paula walked around the lifeless bodies, covering them with sheets. After we finished here, she and Gordo were to drive the survivors to the station while the rest of us waited for an escort and ambulance we had phoned in. I originally thought we could just take the stolen SUV but learned Delilah had slit its tires for good measure.

Edith lay beside one of the crates, her breathing and bleeding slowed to a stable point, according to Gordo. Delilah sat beside her, holding Edith's hand with her eyes closed, as if she were praying. The ambulance and FBI issued vehicle arrived within minutes of the van departing, and they loaded Edith up in no time. Lars insisted he ride with her, arguing that he was her superior in the FBI, she was shot on his mission and he was the closest thing to family they could find at this point. He eventually broke them down, and after flashing his badge about a hundred times was allowed into the ambulance with her.

Delilah and I told them we would meet up at the hospital before sliding into the backseat of the black Camaro. More FBI agents and a few cop cars were pulling up to the warehouse as we were leaving, there to gather the remaining evidence and bring it in for prosecution.

In the backseat of the car, Delilah put her head on my shoulder. No matter how hard I tried, I couldn't help but like the feeling.

"First mission..." she whispered, sounding much weaker than she had earlier. "A bit more than I was expecting."

"A bit more than we all were, I think," I said, keeping myself from stroking a stray strand of hair back behind her ear. A silence followed as the car hummed onward.

"I hope Edith will be okay," her voice was even quieter this time, like she was about to pass out. She must be as emotionally exhausted as she was physically.

"She will be," I said, looking out the window as city lights began to flash by again. We were almost to the hospital already.

* * *

"I cannot allow it, Avery," Jordine said flatly as she sat behind her desk, looking up at me. "She simply does not have enough experience."

Jordine had just gotten back from the hospital to congratulate Edith, who was bedridden for the time being as they had to fish out what they expected to be at least 6 BB's in her leg. Jordine had congratulated the rest of us in front of the office earlier today after giving Lars a harsh lesson on reconnaissance. Everyone had left the office but us, and I was determined to have Delilah on my team after seeing her in action... plus, she probably needed some good news.

"Enough experience?" I asked incredulously. "Jordine, she just saved a doomed operation on her first assignment! Sure, she hasn't been in the field much, but she has the knowledge of a weathered agent. You should have seen her keep her head after Banks got shot." I reverently placed the gun Delilah had thrown to me the night before on the table. "She even avoided killing anyone."

I knew Jordine had a soft spot for those who valued life. I needed to pull some heart strings to get this to work. "She hasn't even been officially sworn in." Jordine sighed her frustration, splaying her hands over her desk. "There's absolutely nothing I can do till that happens anyway."

"So, make the decision now, just don't give the order yet." I set both hands on the table, looking into those bright green eyes. They looked tired. "My operation doesn't take place till a day after her ceremony anyways."

"I don't know Avery," she broke the eye contact, rubbing her hands down her face. "What if something like this happens again and I have another brand-new agent thrown in the hospital?"

"Dang it, Jordine!" I said, slamming my fist on the table. She looked up at me again, her stern face flashing a warning. I decided I should be a bit more tactful. "I'm leading this mission. I have worked tirelessly setting my plan into motion and I have done all the possible research I could. I am the most cautious man you know."

Amusement lit up her face slightly. "Are you

asking this to show Lars up? Show you know how to handle a tough mission with new agents?"

I rolled my eyes. "Look…" I stood back and pointed out the window. "If it wasn't for Delilah, Carson Steele would still be at large with all the information he had leached from the Pentagon. She kept that from happening, not your two seasoned agents who were leading the mission."

Jordine studied me thoughtfully. "Fine," she said after at least one full minute of silence. "But if something happens to her, so help me Avery, you won't lead another mission for a year." She stood and made her way to the door.

"Six months," I pressed, following her out of her office as she shut off the lights and closed the door. "You know you can't go without my team that long."

She shook her head, making her way to the elevators with a smirk on her face. "Watch yourself, Avery."

CHAPTER 5

Delilah

I stroked Dot, watching the clock. Dad would be arriving any minute, and I had promised to take him to dinner once he got here because heaven knows I can't cook. I had cleaned the entire apartment, done all my laundry, and even baked more boxed brownies. I was excited to see him, but I was also very distracted. Edith was still in the hospital, and our ceremony was tomorrow, let alone the fact that Jace had texted me a single message saying we needed to talk. Everyone knows that is never a good thing, and the fact that he had already dashed my hopes of dating him earlier last week, this was probably something worse.

I had done my hair today in honor of my father coming; it had taken almost two hours to get it in the wavy curls now cascading down my back. I wore a plain black dress, hoping to uphold his standards. I had insisted on picking him up at the airport, but he told me that he could catch a cab and be here quicker than I could say "okie" without wasting a dime of my gas money. I had also tried to convince him that he could sleep in my bedroom during his stay, but he wouldn't have it; therefore, all the blankets and pillows I've ever owned now rested in a pile on the couch. I hadn't pulled out the hide-a-bed yet, though, in fear of making my apartment look cramped on first impression.

There was a gentle knock on my door and I stood, smoothing out my dress and checking my reflection in the mirror on the wall. I always thought I looked more like my mom, but my dad had blessed me with his Native American facial structure. As I opened the door, the man standing outside it looked much older than my dad. Of course, seeing how my parents never bothered to learn Skype, I hadn't seen him since I moved to New York, but that was only a year and a half ago. He had long gray hair pulled back into a ponytail under his white Stetson, which contrasted beautifully with his dark skin. His button up was tucked into a huge belt buckle with a bull etched into it, and his dark boots had spurs poking out of holes in the bottom of his jeans.

"Dad," I said, reaching to wrap my arms around his neck, which was a couple inches shorter than my own. My mom was about three inches shorter than him; they were both an average height, but I think I got their genes put together and received all the height in the family.

"Liles," he put down his bag and hugged me tightly.

His arms were strong and as he pulled back to put his hand on my face, I felt the rough calluses I was so accustomed to. I hadn't realized how much I missed them.

"You look beautiful!" His accent was not as thick in person as on the phone. His eyes had a sad slant to them but were full of light.

"You look old," I joked, grabbing his bag and leading him into my apartment. He chuckled, closing the door behind him.

"Is that Dot?" he asked as the black cat came bounding down the hall with her tongue hanging out. "She got fat! What are you feeding her?"

"It's more like what she's feeding herself," I said, walking into the living room and dropping his bag on the couch. "She cleans up whatever I drop on the kitchen floor. It's nice though, I don't have to sweep often." I shrugged as he laughed again. My dad's laugh was deep and grindy, but mirthful all the same.

"So, this is the place, huh," he looked around with his hands on his hips. My dad was not a very judgmental person, but I still cared what he thought. "Do I get a tour?"

"Of course," I took his tough hands and showed him around the front room, explaining the hide-a-bed and offering one last time for him to take my bedroom instead. He declined again, of course, and I led him through the kitchen, explaining everything there was his to eat, as well as how the bathroom was free game unless I was in it. As I brought him into my bedroom, my phone lit up on my dresser. I tried to ignore it, but he saw too.

"Do you need to get that, sweetheart?" he pointed to my phone. He didn't look offended or sad, though, and I was reminded again of how much more understanding he was than my mom.

"Oh no, I already know who it is," I said, peeking at the beginning of the message as I slid it out of view. It was from Jace and all it said was "Tonight." I tried to take a deep breath. What now?

My dad studied my face when we got back to the front room. "Boy issues?"

I tried to look offended. "Oh father," I said. He hated it when I called him that. "You should know all I do is work! I have no time for boys!" Hooking my arm in his while grabbing my purse with my other, I led him to the door again.

"Sure, Liles," he replied, a little too knowingly. "But you'll never convince me a gorgeous girl like yourself hasn't been on at least one date in the Big Apple since you arrived."

I blushed, laughing and trying to convince him there was nothing serious. I respected my dad but seeing as Jace didn't want anything to do with me, I was willing to lie to avoid the shame of probably having the shortest-lived relationship in New York. I tried to turn our conversations anywhere other than men as we hailed a cab to the city. Thankfully, all the lights and crazy people were enough to distract even my curious dad from asking any further questions.

I took him to the same place Jace had taken me, the *Blue Hill.* My dad loved burgers as much as

I did; I suppose that's where I got it from. The taxi dropped us off down the hill from the restaurant and we walked arm in arm up to the front door. We had officially two hours to finish our dinner, which gave plenty of time for us to chat while we ate, thankfully.

The waiter greeted us and led us back to the exact booth Jace and I had eaten in during our first date. I tried not to think about it. As we ordered, my dad asked me about my finals and when my diploma would be coming (I chose not to walk at graduation because that would take time out of my workdays). It was a pleasant conversation, but very light, even for my dad. He wasn't a very talkative man, but when he wanted information, he knew how to get it. Another trait I guess I had inherited.

It was when our food finally arrived that he laced his fingers above his plate and looked me in the eye. "What happened, Delilah," he leaned forward slightly. "I can tell something is wrong."

"Dad," I tried to say lightheartedly. His face grew stern. "Oh alright," I gave in, putting my hand on top of his to show my sincerity. "I've just got a lot on my mind. I finished my first mission the other night and it was a bit more intense than I expected it to be."

"What happened?" He picked up his quadruple patty buffalo burger as he asked, apparently satisfied that I was finally filling him in.

I explained how there was heavier artillery than we had anticipated and one of my friends had been shot in the fray. His face was calm as I relayed the story, and it made me feel less tense by the minute. My dad's aura was a contagiously relaxed feeling and helped me in coping with the previous night's events. I picked at my fries while I told him how the night ended with Jace and I parting after making sure Edith was comfortable in the hospital.

My dad wiped the corners of his mouth with his napkin, then leaned forward and grabbed one of my hands. "I'm sorry your friend was injured. Sounds like you did an outstanding job at keeping your head, though. That's my girl."

The pride was prevalent in his voice as he squeezed my hand. I blushed, unsure of what to say. The truth was I didn't keep my head; I wanted revenge on those crazy men for attacking my partner. That is the only thing that inspired my mad dash to slash the tires. The only time I did keep my head was when I held back from beating them senseless once we got them all rounded up.

My dad leaned back, taking a drink of his coke. "So, who is this Jace fella?" He asked it nonchalantly, but there was a slight twitch in the corner of his mouth.

"Just the criminal profiler at the bureau," I tried to sound just as cool, refusing to give chase to the butterflies that rose in my stomach when I heard his name.

"Come on, Liles," dad folded his arms across his chest. "Every time you said his name in your story, your face lit up and your voice grew soft. If that isn't love, I don't know what is."

I gave my dad an incredulous look. He knew everything! Even when I hadn't lived with him for a year, he could still read me like an open book.

"Okay, so we've been on one official date," I said hesitantly, trying hard to discredit the knot in my stomach. "But I don't think it will turn into anything serious. We just enjoy each other's company."

My dad laughed, plopping a fry in his mouth as he did so. "Delilah, don't you know that's how a relationship starts? You enjoy the company you're in, so you want it more, and then the feelings grow physical—"

"Dad!" I cut across him. I did not need a biology lesson tonight. "I know how it works! I just don't think he's all that interested in me." I left out the fact he had hardcore turned me down after leading me on.

"But you *are* interested in him," he sighed with a smug smile on his face. "And I'll be damned when I see a man who can decline the affection from a woman such as yourself. My, when your mother and I first met. . ."

He trailed off, a pained look scattering the smile previously playing on his lips. I couldn't let him think about mom, not when it made him this upset still. I switched subjects as fast as I could.

"Did you like the buffalo meat they had?" I asked, nodding to his now empty plate. My dad wasn't a chubby man, but he could eat anything and everything he wanted.

"Not too bad, not too bad," he tried smiling again, but this time it was a little more strained. "Could have used a bit more sauce though," he whispered as the waiter came to collect our plates and offer dessert.

Once again, we both declined, being too full to eat anymore. We made our way out to the street a bit slower than on the way in, my dad taking in all the exotic lights and sounds of the city. He had always lived at least seven miles from the nearest Walmart, so I was sure this was a delicate sight to him. And I was sure he would get to the point where it was too much, probably just before his visit ended. I personally loved the crazy city, especially at night.

As we caught a ride home, my dad requested the radio to be tuned to the nearest country station. Surprisingly, the driver obliged. Judging by the amused look on his face when we first hailed him, the cabby enjoyed having country folk in the back of his car. It again reminded me of my date with Jace, and how he hated country music. I wondered if he would be so bold as to plug his ears if he were with us. We made it home quickly for how busy the streets of New York City were at night, and my dad followed me up the three flights of steps to my apartment.

Dot came running to greet us as I pulled open the door, almost making it into the hall before I blocked her way with my foot. My dad helped me pull out the hide-a-bed and then excused himself to the bathroom. I dressed the bed for him, setting the blankets and pillows in the most comfortable way I could imagine to make the rickety thing a bit more bearable. Pulling out my phone, I sat down on the foot of the bed. The text I had seen from Jace was the last I received. I decided it would be rude to just ignore him.

You can come tonight if you want. My dads here tho so I can't talk long.

His reply came within seconds: *See you soon.*

I sighed, trying to keep my face calm as my dad came back into the living room.

"Now that almost looks like a normal bed," he marched over to the bed and sat down with a flop. "Very comfortable, though!"

I smiled. "Hey, someone may be coming over soon, just with more news about Edith," I tried to sound normal, as if my heart wasn't about to be crushed even more. I couldn't help but think Jace was just coming to embarrass my feelings even more, though that was a pretty irrational thought considering how thoughtful the guy is.

"Well don't let me ruin your plans for the night," my dad said lightly. Thankfully he was not paying that much attention to me now as he started taking a robe and some other toiletries out of his bag. "You alright if I use your shower then?"

That would make it substantially less awkward, my dad out of earshot while my weekend boyfriend dumped me—again. "Of course," I walked into the kitchen to grab a glass of water. "Just don't turn the faucet too hot too soon; it takes a minute to warm up."

I walked to my bedroom, sipping my glass of water and kicking off my flats as I crossed the threshold. Glancing in the mirror above my dresser, I noticed some smudged mascara under my eye. I didn't care if Jace wasn't interested in me—I would look my best, just to show what he's missing out on. I realized I was jumping to conclusions again as I heard the shower water turn on. Wiping the smudge with a tissue, I checked my hair to make sure the curls had stayed fairly buoyant. My hair was heavy enough to straighten them out but judging by my reflection I still had about an hour and half before they'd completely disappear.

Before long there came a knock on my door, much sooner than I had anticipated. I walked resolutely forward, trying to keep my composure. Maybe he's not coming to talk more about our non-existent relationship. Maybe he just got some sad news about a grandparent and he needed someone to talk to. I prayed it was the latter as I opened the door.

Jace walked straight into the apartment, closing the door behind him and making me take a couple of steps back. "Hey Liles."

"Jace," I studied him, his face full of excitement. "Why did you need to speak with me so badly?"

"I have some great news," he shrugged, and his arms moved awkwardly as if he wanted to pull me into an embrace but couldn't. I kept from rolling my eyes.

"What is it?" I leaned back against the wall as Dot came jumping onto his shins. I couldn't help but smile as I watched Jace bend down and stroke her before looking back up at me.

"Wait," looking around, Jace pointed down the hall. "Where's your dad?"

I had totally forgotten my dad was there until I realized I could still hear the water running. He was going to rack up my water bill with this shower.

"He's in the shower," I took a step toward him, wanting this over quickly, "but really, I need to know why in the world you needed to speak with me so badly. It's been driving me crazy all night."

Jace looked me in the eye and a smile played on his plump lips. I had to keep myself from leaning forward and kissing him. I scrunched my eyebrows, trying to be annoyed instead. He took a deep breath.

"First, how are you? After last night, I mean," he looked genuinely concerned. I sighed.

"I'm okay. I'm more upset than anything that I didn't act faster," I considered his muddy eyes, thinking of how I could convince him. "I know she'll be alright, but still."

"Don't go blaming yourself," he wrapped his arms around me, completely flattening my hair. I tried to hold back, but soon I felt as though my body could melt into his, I was so relieved that he was willing to hug me. "She rushed into that fire, and Lars didn't do proper reconnaissance. Edith was just a victim of the circumstance."

"I'm fine," I said, pulling back and looking back to his face. "Will you tell me what's up now?"

He smiled, his hands squeezing my shoulders. "You're in," it took me a minute to register what he was saying. "On the McGregor case, Liles, you're in. Jordine is asking you after your ceremony tomorrow to join my team."

I let my hands clap to my open mouth. This was huge news; I barely noticed the shower water turning off. Jace's smile was ear to ear and his excitement spread through my entire body as if it were contagious. I jumped up and down a couple times before barreling into his chest, not able to contain myself.

"Did you—?" I asked, my voice muffled because my face was buried in his shoulder.

"I'm pretty convincing," He had a hand in my hair, his voice quiet and gentler than I had ever heard it. "You look beautiful, by the way."

I pulled out of his shoulder and held his neck as I kissed him—I didn't care what he had said earlier. Apparently neither did he as his hands rested on my hips. Then a voice from the end of the hall cut between us like a knife.

"Enjoying each other's company, eh?" We broke apart quickly to see my dad standing at the end of the entry hall in his fuzzy blue robe and slippers. A sly smile was on his face that made me wonder just how long he had been there.

Jace cleared his throat. "Mr. Hadley," he

started forward, his hand outstretched. I tried to hide my face as my father reached forward as well.

"It's actually Cornsilk," my dad said, chuckling and shaking Jace's hand vigorously. "Liles took her mother's name seeing as it's a bit more, ah, common. Call me Emmit. You must be Jace."

Jace looked confused. "How did you know my name, sir?"

"As much as she tried not to," my dad smirked at me as he turned his back to us. "Delilah told me all about you. Don't let me ruin the fun, though. Enjoy your night, kiddos."

Jace returned to me, shaking his head. "Your dad is pretty chill." He stood awkwardly in front of me. I brushed my disheveled hair out of my face, completely at a loss at what just happened between us.

"I guess he is," I said, silently marveling at my dad's level-headedness. I was his only daughter, after all.

* * *

"You completely lied to me."

"No, I didn't... I'm still confused as to his feelings for me..."

My dad watched as I cleared away the remainder of our lunch. "I don't understand what the hold-up is; you're perfect. He probably knows he isn't worthy."

I laughed. "Dad, let it go. I'll figure him out

soon enough. Plus, I came clean about everything before bed last night."

"Ppfft, came clean? I caught the two of you making out!"

It was two days since my dad had come into town and caught Jace and I kissing in my entry hall. He had been teasing me ever since, even finding the opportune moment during my swearing in ceremony yesterday to give Jace a hard time as well. I had never seen Jace blush before, but my dad must have said something to embarrass him, because as they passed one another walking out, Jace's face had turned the color of a radish.

"Okay, okay," I walked back over and put my hands on his shoulders. "You caught us. But I know you like him already. I just have to figure out if he likes me."

"I still don't believe there will ever be anyone good enough for you, Liles," he stood and walked into the living room. "But so far he has impressed me. But not, at the same time, since he's smoochin' ya and you don't even know if he likes you. Yuppie rubbish."

After the ceremony yesterday, Jace drove dad and I to the hospital to visit Edith. She was doing well, even though the surgeons still hadn't removed the sixth BB due to its delicate position in her quad. Unfortunately, her ceremony had been postponed to next week, given she wouldn't be discharged from the hospital till they extracted the last one. My dad was a bit uncomfortable with the visit, given the fact that Edith is basically a carbon copy of my mother in personality. It was fun to take him out and show him off though; I was very much a daddy's girl.

Jordine had then called to assign me to Jace and Jameson's mission, which my dad was thrilled about. He didn't care that he was leaving in just a couple days; in his words, this was "huge for someone my age to be operating with such a seasoned team," and "it would be worth less time with his baby to see me succeed in my career."

Today was the day of the mission, and Jace was coming to pick me up at 4:00, because I had requested the day off when I heard my dad was coming. We figured carpooling to the office would make it easier if my dad decided to use my jeep while we were out, plus then the mission wouldn't be waiting on public transportation. It had been raining on and off all day, so my dad and I had spent the majority of it inside my apartment. We used a lot of the time to visit, as well as to play card games and make food. It was fun to be around him again, but I was excited to get away for a bit as well, mainly because of the opportunity this mission would give me in the bureau. But also, maybe because I would get to be with Jace again.

When the knock finally came, my dad snorted from the couch, making Dot jump from his lap. "That boy must be the most precise person I have ever met," he called after me as I walked to the door. "He was even earlier than we were yesterday!"

My dad was a pretty punctual person as well, which was another supposed reason my mom left him; she was late to everything. My sense of time was definitely inherited from her side. We did manage to make it ten minutes early to the ceremony yesterday, however, and of course Jace was already there when we arrived.

Pulling open the door, I saw Jace standing on the other side. He was not fully equipped in a bulletproof vest and his weapon belt, but he still looked ready for action. He smiled when he saw me but made no move to make contact.

“You ready to go?” I closed the door behind him as he walked into my apartment. “Hey Emmit,” Jace’s back seemed to straighten as he made his way to my dad, shaking his hand vigorously.

“Jace,” my dad went to stand, but Jace shook his head and patted his shoulder.

“You’re good, sir,” he looked to me, “We don’t really have much time. The rendezvous is coming up on us fast, and we’ve still got a couple other agents to meet up with first.”

“I just need to grab some things from my room,” I nodded and walked back to my bedroom, pulling on my backpack that had my own vest and gun in it. Grabbing a hair tie, my phone, and my keys, I walked back out to the chatting men.

“All ready,” I bent down and kissed my dad on the cheek. “I don’t know when I’ll be back, so if you go out just remember the spare key is hanging just inside my bedroom.”

Jace said a cordial goodbye as we walked back to the door. "There's food in the fridge if you decide to stay in," I called behind me, "And the TV remote is on the piano."

I heard my dad curse at me as I closed the door behind us "I am an adult, woman." Jace chuckled as we made our way to his car.

The ride was long but fun. To avoid any suspicion from the opposing forces, we had set up designated rendezvous points for each group to meet before going to the area of attack. We met up with several other agents in the parking garage of our office building, all of us piling into a large black van. I felt more at ease as Jace laughed and made jokes with the other agents. I started to feel caterpillars in my stomach, though, as I remembered that we were about to go bust not just any drug lord, but *the* drug lord. If Jace got hurt, or worse, what happened the other night between us could come to a quick end without even really beginning. For the first time, I was beginning to see why he wanted to avoid a more serious relationship with me; this was all very distracting.

Soon another dark van pulled up beside us, as well as a black sedan behind. The conversations in the car came to a stop as we saw Jameson sitting in the passenger seat of the boxy car. He nodded, and they passed us, merging into our lane amid the congested cabs and then taking a right. Jace followed with the sedan closely mimicking the maneuvers behind.

"Here we go," Jace said as we pulled off the road in front of a tall chain fence, beyond which were what had to be thousands of metal shipping crates. He reached over and squeezed my arm before pulling out an earpiece while the other agents filed out of the van. "Remember the plan?" he started getting out as well.

I followed, taking comfort in the fact that about 15 men and women were now exiting the van and sedan, about 50 yards down the fence from us on either side, almost out of sight beyond the borders. The agents from our vehicle were scattering along the points of entrance lining the fence in either direction. This was a lot more put together than my last mission. I nodded to Jace, pulling on my vest and taking out my gun. Pulling my earpiece out to examine it, I really hoped these guys didn't have a hacker too.

Jace and I moved silently through an opening in the fence, reflecting the same actions as all the agents on the task force, waiting for the signal from the first responder. The woman was called Birdy throughout the office, and I didn't know much about her other than she was a tall and slender African American with dreadlocks to her shoulders. She was to take her team of three into the first row of shipment crates, then give the go ahead to the next team who would take the next row. According to Jameson's research, the main operation was happening in the middle of the crates, several miles in from the road and docks.

Team after team made their way into the maze of crates. Overhead, the sky was a leaden gray, making it seem darker than usual for the time of day. I could hear the crash of waves off in the distance, making me grateful there wasn't the extra distraction of rain pouring down over our heads—yet.

Finally receiving our cue, we walked back to back into the row closest to where the bureau's car was parked, random people's voices coming into our ears as each row was cleared of activity. Apparently, Jameson had done his homework, because the directions he had given us to navigate the crates were as simple as finding a terminal in the airport; lots of turns and backtracking, but all in all, continuously moving forward. According to Jace, Jameson had interrogated a shipment captain who frequented this dock regularly, and it seemed to be paying off. So far there were no random gunshots or men in black jumping on top of us, so I started to believe this mission was definitely on another level than my last.

"Hold," eventually Jameson's voice was heard over the earpieces, after we had been walking for at least an hour. I held my gun low, keeping it cocked and pointed down. I had been facing in the direction we had come the entire time, and by now all the crates looked the same. I wondered if we'd be able to find our way out of this.

"If there is a 'T' before you, you are on the edge of the main," his voice was quick and quiet, as if we were playing a huge game of hide and seek. "Once you reach this point, lead is to proceed with caution to the left while a guard is left behind."

Jace and I continued moving forward. Apparently, we hadn't reached it yet. Men began to yell nearby, and a couple gun shots sounded up in front of us. "There's the break," Jace said as we pulled level with a 'T' in our path. He turned to me, moving forward but then stopping. "Remember, only come if you hear the distress call on the line," he tapped the earpiece. "If not, watch for anyone that shouldn't be leaving."

He turned his back on me and took the left turn. I felt vulnerable, standing with my back to the way we had come. If someone was going to attack me, they could literally come from above and I wouldn't see them till they were right on top of me. So, I began to pace. I stalked back and forth between the two crates forming the stem of the 'T', looking right, left, up, then right again. I was not going to be snuck up on—I had been trained for this. I didn't really need to think as I listened to the orders barked over the radio in my ear, hearing people's voices as well as frequent gunshots echo off the metal crates around me.

Judging by all the racket, I figured there had to have been at least an equal amount of people on the other side of those crates as there were on our side. It started driving me crazy, just pacing back and forth while all the action was a crate or two in front of me. Maybe they did this on purpose; I'm the newest agent, so I should stay where they can hold me in reserve, only use me if they absolutely need it. The thought made me angry until I realized every other team also had one guard stationed in the exact same position I was. I kept reminding myself this was just the strategy, not a ploy to keep the newby out.

The clouds kept the sky dark as more and more shots filled the air. I heard Jameson's voice most prominently in my ear, but occasionally I heard an order from Jace, and my heart would skip a beat. As long as I could hear him every now and then, I would know he was okay. At least we had the element of surprise, and there didn't seem to be any heavily armed men in the vicinity. I looked up at the crates to my left. If I got on top of them, I could keep a full view on my branch between crates, along with a clearer shot of the branch running horizontally across it that Jace had run into. During the briefing, they hadn't outlined *exactly* what position we were to stay in, so I figured I was okay to proceed with my plan. It was more efficient then pacing back and forth, anyway.

After making sure my gun was on safety and securing it in my belt, I started scaling the bumpier part of the crate. I was not on the side where there was a ladder, unfortunately, or it would have made it a lot easier. The metal was slippery and there was virtually no place for a foothold for the first couple of feet. Relying only on upper-body strength, I eventually placed my foot where I had placed my hands a moment before.

Rolling on to the top of the crate, trying to keep low, I had to remind myself I had gone to the crate on my left, meaning I needed to keep an eye on my right-hand side. Looking around, I saw what seemed to be thousands of other crates all around the one I was on top of, and I saw two or three other people on top of their crates as well. Staying low, I pulled out my binoculars, looking at each person in turn to make sure I recognized them. Satisfied, I continued to keep watch on my branch.

It was much windier on top of the crate, and the shots seemed only a few feet in front of me, although I couldn't see over the next two crates straight ahead. I was getting frustrated over the fact that I really had no idea what was going on when Jameson's deep voice seemed to ring through my brain.

"McGregor, Avery, not ten feet to your left."

"No shot."

"Me either," Jameson sounded strained, as if someone was holding on to his neck. "He's running."

"On it." Jace's responses were short and breathless, like he had been running a marathon.

Hearing the cacophony of gunshots and yelling from below, I counted the seconds as I waited to hear Jace's voice again. I prayed we weren't losing lives out there as something else reached my ears. Footsteps; a pair of running footsteps.

Glancing down, I saw a figure in a brown leather jacket and jeans come sprinting around the corner of the 'T', heading straight for my branch.

Seconds later, Jace came hauling around the same corner, blood glistening in his hair. He must have gotten hit on the head.

I crouched, cocking my gun and following McGregor with it. As soon as he would turn the corner into my branch, I'd have a clear shot of his head. But he didn't make it there. Jace sprung from at least five feet behind the man, entangling McGregor's legs with his arms. He fell roughly to the ground but quickly turned over and kicked Jace in the head. Twisting out of Jace's arms, McGregor got to his feet as Jace pulled out his gun, still on his stomach.

My shot was gone, they were too close, and I was too high; I was no sniper. If I missed I'd hit Jace. I watched, frozen for a moment, as McGregor grabbed Jace's gun arm, pulling it perpendicular to his body and kneeling on Jace's shoulder. The gun went off, but he was standing too far to the right. And then McGregor made a quick but hard jab to the back of Jace's elbow.

The crack that echoed up the crates shook me out of my reverie. Jace's cry was short as the man pulled the gun from his hand and cocked it again. I jumped off my crate, letting my legs buckle and rolling on the impact of the ground.

Training my gun on the brown leather jacket, I shouted: "Freeze!"

I immediately regretted my decision to call attention to myself as McGregor, with alarming speed, turned and fired at me. I jumped behind the corner of the crate to my left, into my original branch, then moved back around it and fired twice at McGregor, who was now running in the opposite direction. He turned into the next opening to the right.

I sprinted forward, stopping momentarily to check on Jace. I saw his gun on the ground with the action open. It was out of bullets.

"You good?" I asked, crouching to put my hand on his back. He still had his face to the concrete.

"Yeah," as soon as I heard his answer I stood and started running. I heard him calling after me, but I didn't stop. McGregor was going to pay.

I skidded around the corner into the next branch of crates, seeing the brown leather jacket a couple yards down it. He was already puffing, and I had longer legs. This was cake.

I sprinted towards him, training my gun on his back but not wanting to chance stopping long enough to get a good aim. If I took too long he could turn down another row of crates and my shot would be gone, again, and he'd be farther ahead. I holstered the gun, focusing all my attention on catching up to him. I put my hand to my earpiece.

"In pursuit of McGregor," I said shortly.

There were many responses that sounded over the frequency, but Jace's was the most prominent as I followed McGregor around the edge of another branch of crates.

"Delilah don't," I heard him gasp out the

words.

"Jameson, Avery's near the south side of the shipment crates. He's incapacitated and needs assistance."

I wasn't going to say anymore. I didn't need help and I didn't need instructions. I knew my job.

McGregor was faster than he looked. I kept within close proximity of him, but never close enough. My heart pounded in my head. We finally broke out of the maze of crates and McGregor jumped through an opening in the fence.

I closed the distance between us as we passed buildings and jumped through people on the street. I tried to grab him around the upper body, but he turned sharply into an alleyway. I shot past it, my legs quicker than my head. Backtracking, I turned into the alley and stopped, trying to see through the thick fog.

Wait. *Fog*?

I glanced behind me. No fog clouded the street. Facing forward again, a shadow moved through the dense haze, not 10 feet in front of me. Pulling out and cocking my gun, I stalked forward. The fog tickled my skin, like the mist was moving through it and into my body. I shivered, squinting to try and pull the shadow back into my sight. When I had seen it, it hadn't been running, so it couldn't have gotten too far ahead.

The tingling feeling began to burn. I almost dropped my gun, the sensation was so abrupt and overwhelming. There was nothing visibly different about my arms, even though it felt like they were on fire—tears formed as I struggled against crying out. Without warning, a gas mask appeared, floating inches from my face.

My gun flew out of my hands. I heard it skid across the concrete as fuzz overcame the feed in my radio. Thinking quickly, I swung my knee up and forward, making contact with what I assumed was the owner of the gas mask's leg. I heard a grunt as the mask lowered, but the wearer recovered quickly. Strong hands grabbed my shoulders as I struggled to grab the mask. I kicked forward, trying to hit something—anything. Finally, my foot found a chest and I was released. I went low to tackle them, but they caught me there and used my momentum to side step and push me into the opposite wall.

I caught myself with both hands against the brick, swinging around and punching them in the gut before grabbing both sides of the mask. *Why were they wearing it anyway? Maybe because this mist burned?* A fist caught my cheek, the other my ribs. I heard a crack and felt pain shoot through my abdomen. As we wrestled, I noticed that the brown leather jacket had disappeared. In fact, I couldn't see anything but black cloth.

This was not McGregor.

I started feeling light-headed and weak as I finally got the attacker into a headlock on the ground. With my knees on either side of him, pins prodded my lungs. The fog solidified around me—though my eyes said differently. My grip loosened, but I knew I was still using the same exertion as when I had pulled him into the headlock. Panicking, I worked to tighten my hold, but my arms felt like lead. What was happening to me?

That's what the attacker had been waiting for. My arms were yanked painfully forward, lurching me onto my back. I tried to stand but could only roll over. Every limb in my body reacted like jelly, as if the bones and muscles had been removed. I tried to cry out but couldn't even open my mouth, the ground clamping my jaw shut. I watched his boots step toward me as I realized I had been drugged. He picked me up and threw me backwards.

I felt the brick on my back before it hit my head. Then everything was black.

CHAPTER 6

Jace

Sitting beside the hospital bed, I adjusted my sling to a more comfortable position. I watched silently as Delilah's chest slowly rose and fell, the short puffing sound of her oxygen the only noise in the room. Her dad would be here any minute, and he would need an explanation. The only problem was, I didn't have one.

I tried to stop her. I tried to stand and give chase after McGregor had broken my elbow, but I couldn't because of the loss of blood from my head injury. She didn't listen when I tried over the radio. She must have thought she could handle him. But she hadn't researched him like I had; she hadn't seen that he has ins and outs throughout the whole city with a network of mobs and gangs working for him. I knew as soon as he could exit that shipment maze, he could get away. The one thing I didn't get was why Delilah was still alive.

I was grateful for it, of course, and I had already taken full blame of the accident when Jordine had demanded the report. It was my fault McGregor got away, and my fault for making a dumb move and getting myself broken. But McGregor was a ruthless man; if he didn't kill you, it was only because he'd have found a use for you as a hostage. I thought Delilah's fate was the latter as we combed the streets for her and was surprised to find her lying unconscious in an alleyway, rain mixing with the blood trickling down her neck.

I was at a loss for words as Jameson and I helped load her into the ambulance. I was in shock, not only from my own injuries but from seeing her lifeless body down the wet alley. I thought she was dead when I first saw her, and that was the only thing that could explain why she wasn't taken. But she must not have met McGregor himself in that alley; he would have made sure she was dead before just leaving a body behind. McGregor's men must have thought whatever they did to knock her unconscious was enough to kill her.

I reached up to rub my head till I remembered the newly sewn stitches embroidering my brow. Jordine had already banned me for the next sixth months to a desk job, keeping true to her promise. I didn't care though. I just wanted to make sure Delilah was okay.

It was hard watching over her. I didn't like seeing her head wrapped in bandages, her face swollen and bruised the way it was. The doctor had diagnosed her with a cracked rib as well as a coma caused by a traumatic head injury. They also deduced that an unknown toxin could be contributing to the coma as well; blood tests were being run now to see what toxin it was. I figured whoever she caught down that alley must have thrown her against one of those brick walls, because that is the only blow heavy enough to induce the coma. I only prayed that the toxin wasn't ketamine injected into her system once she was out.

I tried to calm my breathing. Consuming such a heavy drug under such strained bodily circumstances would surely have been instantaneously lethal. Maybe that's why they left her behind; they knew she'd die eventually. I kept an ear open to the machine monitoring her heartbeat as a nurse came in to update her vitals on the whiteboard hanging on the wall. As far as we knew, she had been unconscious since before we had found her, which was about three hours earlier. Following our report to Jordine, we contacted her parents. A voicemail and been left for her mother, but her father had answered.

Jameson came in and handed me a cup of black coffee. "How you holdin' up, Jace?" he put a hand on my shoulder.

I didn't want to talk to him. I didn't want to talk to anyone.

"Just trying to figure out what to say to her dad," I said, looking over at Delilah. Even with a black eye and cut lip, she was beautiful. I wished she would open those sparkling eyes. Regret pinched my stomach as I remembered trying to cut things off with her.

"He has to understand," Jameson pulled up a chair beside me. "It wasn't your fault."

It was, though. I knew Jameson knew it, and I knew Delilah's father would know it too. I made such a stupid move jumping into McGregor's legs instead of just shooting him. At the time, I was thinking bringing him in alive would be more beneficial to the bureau for interrogation purposes. If only I had sent a bullet through his skull when we leveled in that branch. He was the reason Delilah now lay bruised and unconscious beside me. I scowled, squishing the still full paper cup and spilling coffee all over the floor.

"Sorry," I muttered, as the nurse rushed over and started wiping up the mess. She didn't say a word, just nodding as she threw her paper towels away and exited the room.

"It will be okay, man," Jameson stood to leave. "Are you staying the night?"

"I probably won't leave her side till she wakes up," I looked up at him. "She has to wake up."

Jameson nodded but didn't say anything as he left the room. I knew he doubted the chances of Delilah living through this. I was grateful for the silence again, alone to think up a plan. Once I made sure Delilah would live, my next step would be to track down McGregor. He was going to pay for this.

Several minutes passed before I heard the footsteps of a man in spurred boots. I looked up, trying to gather my thoughts of what had happened into an intelligible explanation. A nurse led the

Cherokee man into the room. I stood as she left, closing the door behind her. Emmit stood speechless in front of the closed door, staring at his daughter's comatose body on the bed. I took a step forward, unsure if I should launch into an explanation or give him a moment to see his daughter. Emmit turned slowly.

Then, like lightning, he grabbed the neck of my shirt and swung me around, slamming me into the door. The impact tingled down my casted arm as I held up my good hand. I had seen worse reactions; I was the only one in the room, as well as the one responsible. I was surprised the cowboy hadn't pulled a gun on me.

The sad eyes considered mine, tears welling up in the deep corners. His mirthful gaze had fled, and his wrinkles seemed deeper than when I had first met him a couple of nights before. He held my collar tightly, his fists inches from my chin. His strength was surprising for what I only guessed was his age. I didn't say anything or try to break free. I'd let him do what he had to.

After several seconds, he blinked, and a tear rolled down his leathery cheek. He looked down, his grip loosening as his shoulders shuddered. He turned away from me to face Delilah again, and I waited. I was not going to jump into my excuse of an explanation while the man grieved. He walked to the edge of her bed, putting a hand on her covered leg. I respected the prominent love showing from his face; it was old and knowing, as if he had seen this happen before.

Emmit glanced at Delilah's vitals whiteboard before turning to me once more. "She didn't listen, did she?"

The question surprised me. Rethinking my whole explanation, I tried to find a way to avoid pinning the blame on Delilah's choices.

"It was my fault, sir," I motioned for him to sit down. He obliged, placing a hand on Delilah's as he sat. "I made a wrong move. She had no choice but to act."

"Don't sugar-coat it for me, Jace, please," his eyes were on his daughter's face again. "I need to know exactly what happened."

I sighed before launching into the story. I gave a play by play of the events of the evening, doing my best to make Delilah sound heroic and smart in her choices. But when I got to the point where I had lost sight of them, I couldn't speak anymore. The reality of what happened hit me. Delilah's eyes were full of revenge when she went after McGregor, and nothing more. She didn't go after him because of the mission; she went after him because of me.

Emmit, who had been watching Delilah the entire story, turned to me when I paused. "You don't know what happened next, do you?"

I adjusted my sling again. "I yelled after her to stop, and then tried persuading her through our radio. The last words I heard her say were that I needed help." I stopped myself. She was right; I had never felt so helpless in my life.

Emmit nodded. The scenes of what could have happened after I lost sight of them had flashed through my mind ever since we found her, and I'm sure Emmit was doing the same thing.

"How did you find her?" he spoke softly, taking his eyes off me and glancing to his boots.

"We used the radio she had in her ear," I pulled mine out of my pocket to show him. "They were developed with a tracking system earlier this year to better help monitor agents on missions. We pulled out our computers and could pinpoint which street she was on. Unfortunately, they don't have exact markers on them yet, so we still had to search for a minute."

Emmit said nothing. I assumed he didn't want to know that she was a bloody and broken mess when we found her, so I kept my mouth shut. I would only continue if he asked questions.

"When Liles was five," he said, leaning back in his chair and closing his eyes. His hand was still resting on Delilah's. "She was fascinated with fire. A natural pyromaniac, if you ask me."

I waited. I learned a while ago that many people cope in different ways. Emmit must find something comforting in the memories of his daughter.

"One morning, when I was at work and her mother was doing the dishes, Liles somehow got her hands on the matchbox."

He breathed slowly as he said the words, like he was reliving the memory slowly, thinking hard to remember what had happened.

"We had banned her from it probably about a hundred times. But all she cared about was the pretty dancing flames that those matches could bring. Believe it or not, my five-year-old thought if she could get those flames on her shorts, they would make her dance too."

"She lit herself on fire?" I asked before I could stop myself.

He opened his slanted eyes and gave me a sad smile. "Poor thing nearly burnt the field in our backyard down before she realized she had to get out of the tall weeds and into the pond. I'm glad you haven't seen enough of her legs to see those scars."

"I'm proud to say I haven't either," I retorted, giving a dry laugh and crossing my arms. Honestly, if I were talking to any other man in the world, I probably wouldn't be that proud.

"Point is," Emmit sighed, looking back at Delilah's swollen face. "This young lady has always learned things the hard way. When she wants something, she gets it, no matter how much it hurts her. I bet when she wakes up, she'll have some vital information for you on the man that attacked her."

It was refreshing to hear him say "when". Everyone else, including the doctors, had only said "if" she wakes up. And he was right; Delilah was a fighter. She was going to wake up and she was going to have something useful for us. I choked back something that felt a little bit like hope well up beside the already bulging lump in my throat.

We sat in silence after that, both content with being beside the woman we cared so much for.

It was a couple hours before anything disturbed the peace of the quiet room. Emmit had moved to the makeshift bed where family could sleep, and I had alternated between sitting in the chair beside Delilah's bed and walking around the room. I knew I wouldn't be able to sleep, so I had told Emmit to take the bed. He had knocked out within minutes of lying on the uncomfortable thing, proving I had made a good choice. It was around three in the morning when the doctor walked in with a clipboard.

I stood as he entered the room, walking to Emmit and nudging him awake. He would want to hear what they had to say, whether it was good or bad. He snorted a little as he stretched out his neck, going to stand again. The doctor held up a hand.

"No need to get up, gentlemen," he waved the clipboard. "I've only got a little bit of news. But it's good."

I looked hopefully at the middle-aged man; his lined face showed all the stress he must have seen during his years in a hospital.

"There is no ketamine in the system, which gives a substantially larger gambit for her to wake from this." His smile was so full of effort, like this wasn't really good news at all.

Emmit sighed, bowing his head in what looked like a silent prayer. But I wasn't going to celebrate yet. It was in my nature to be suspicious.

"What toxin was it, then, that you think entered her body?" I glanced over at Delilah. She would have looked completely lifeless if it weren't for her chest continuously expanding and detracting.

"Ah," the doctor rifled through some papers on the clipboard, avoiding eye contact. Emmit looked up again. "That has remained a mystery, actually."

"You don't know what she was poisoned with?" now Emmit stood, leveling the doctor with his eyes.

"Now, I wouldn't quite call it poison," the doctor stammered. This was why he had been so reluctant. "It was more of a drug–"

"Drugs are poison, sir," Emmit took a step forward, but I held his shoulder. He looked back at me incredulously. I nodded.

"We are surrounded by people that specialize in 'drugs'," I said, hoping to diffuse Emmit. I honestly wasn't happy with the doctor either, but this wasn't his fault. "Surely someone would be able to identify what it was?"

The doctor shrugged. "We have had many specialists look through her lab work. That's part of the reason for my late return with the results. It is unidentifiable, and almost untraceable. We were able to deduce how it had entered her body, however." He tried to look confident, as if this was an important piece of information.

"Well?" Emmit barked, plopping back down

on the bed with his hands on his knees.

"It was not injected or snuffed, which means it was in a gaseous state, having to be inhaled. However, her blood levels indicate that more of the drug entered her body then what the CT of her lungs had shown us," as the doctor continued, he grew more animated, like this was fascinating and not incredibly disturbing. "Which means it must have had some sort of osmosis factor that made it sink into and pass through her skin!"

He looked proud of himself this time. I tried to understand his point of view to stop myself from knocking his teeth out. This was something he'd studied his entire life, and never seen the likes of which before. I guess that could cause pride in a profession. I took a deep breath.

"Does that give you any clue what type of drug it was?"

His smile faded. "Well, no," he looked down. I almost felt bad for him. Almost. "It's nothing like we've ever seen. It must be homegrown, something never used, even in the streets. But it is part of the reason for her comatose state."

"Are you saying the drug knocked her out?" Emmit asked. I forgot I hadn't told him that she looked like she had been thrown against a wall when we found her.

"Partly, yes," the doctor looked down at Emmit, picking his words carefully. "She also had a traumatic head injury which we also see as a contributing factor. However, there is no obvious disturbance to her brain, meaning that the force used wasn't hard enough to keep her out too long. We believe the drug she absorbed somehow placed her body and mind into a dormant state, resulting in this," he motioned to her bed.

Emmit and I were silent for a moment. The news that Delilah had a better possibility of recovering from this was comforting, but the fact that even the professionals in this hospital were unable to identify the drug in her almost vanquished that hope immediately.

"Is that all you got for us, Doc?" Emmit leaned back, returning his gaze to Delilah.

"Oh, yes," the doctor said sheepishly before he backed out the door. "I'll just leave the lab results here in case someone wants to look over them."

"Thank you," I closed the door behind him, pulling the clipboard off the desk he had placed it on. "At least it's not ketamine." I muttered, flipping through the scribbled pages.

"I don't know what's worse," Emmit muttered, placing his white Stetson over his face as he leaned against the wall. "These so-called doctors not knowing what's inside my baby, or the fact that they are seeing her as a new science experiment."

I snorted. "At least we know it's something she'll wake up from." But how long will her consciousness last if whatever is in her kills her? I didn't voice my doubtful question, trying hard to hold on to the hope that she would be able to heal from this fully.

"So where was the drug when ya'll got there?" Emmit said sleepily. "If she had breathed it in and, what did that guy say? Absorbed it? Wouldn't it have been hangin' around in the air where you found her?"

I thought for a moment. That was a good question. And then it dawned on me. "The rain," I said, almost to myself. "The rain washed it out of the air before we got to her."

Emmit replied with a loud snore.

* * *

I was pouring coffee for what looked like an older version of Delilah when the song "Cold as Ice" came ringing through my head. I woke up suddenly, the glow from my alarm clock the only light in my bedroom. I reached up to switch off the alarm, then sat up and rubbed my face. My elbow ached in its cast as I got up.

It had been two weeks since I sat in Delilah's hospital room with her father. Emmit had left to catch his flight that next evening, departing with a prayer over her bed to help her wake up. A week after that the hospital matrons sent me home. I wasn't allowed to stay much longer given the fact that sleep and showers are essential parts of being a functioning member of society. Today marked her 16th day being completely inaccessible to the world, but she was still breathing. Ever since I was sent home, I had called the hospital every night for an update on her vitals. I would then call her dad to let him know as well.

Her heart rate had spiked near the middle of the two weeks, and then dropped to a dangerously low progression. As of right now it was still a bit on the slow side, but it had made the jump out of the danger zone three days ago.

I buckled my sling over my shoulder after I had gotten dressed. As annoying as it was, I could feel how it was helping. I grabbed my gym bag and made my way out the door.

I listened to the old rock station Delilah had turned my radio to on our first date on my way to work. On the phone last night, the doctor had not seemed optimistic about Delilah's state. I tried to forget his tone of voice; he'd sounded like she had already died.

Working out was harder than it ever had been these past couple of weeks, but I wasn't about to stop going to the gym. I couldn't do much with just one arm, but I still worked on my legs and core the best I could. It was a way for me to process and release any tension, which my body had been full of since the mission. I had been going earlier in the morning as well, to avoid talking with anyone.

My days were going by in a haze; one moment I was down in the gym, the next in a cubicle that I rarely ever visited before now, and the next back at home, calling the hospital for an update. Sometimes I'd think I had entered my own sort of coma, but would quickly admonish myself for comparing my now boring life to the devastating situation Delilah was in.

I had come to a conclusion during these two weeks where all I could think about was Delilah and how my life had become so monotone. I'm such an idiot. How could I have rejected the affection of literally the perfect woman? To save her? Yeah, we saw what good that did. Now she's comatose and I can't even say I'm her boyfriend when her nurses ask why I visit so often. It's embarrassing. And I had hurt her. The thing that depressed me the most, though, is that she may never wake up to give me the chance to make it right.

I was shuffling papers in shame at my desk when I realized someone was standing over me. I looked up to see Jameson leaning over my chair.

"Jace," his eyes looked excited. "Jordine needs you in her office, now."

I stood and followed him through the cubicles crowding our floor. "How's the desk job going?"

"Sucks," I muttered. Jameson hadn't been punished because it wasn't his idea to bring Delilah on the mission, even though he didn't object to it either. I silently wished he had now that I'd seen the outcome of having her along.

We entered Jordine's office just as she was setting down the phone. Grabbing her purse and jacket, she hastily spoke two words before running past us through the door we had just entered.

"She's awake."

CHAPTER 7

Delilah

My head throbbed as voices entered my previously silent room. I listened, trying to recognize any of them as the beeping indicating my heart rate set a monotonous tone. I felt warm and nauseated, like I had just exited a sauna after pushing a little too hard in a workout. I had opened my eyes once since I had woken up, but they've remained closed since because of how bright the hospital room lights were. It had given me an instant migraine.

I was alive. I still had my memory. I don't think I dreamt while I was unconscious, or if I did I don't recall what had happened in them. The last thing I remember is watching the man in the gas mask seemingly drift back as I flew into a wall. In the split second before I had made contact, I thought I was going to die. I was actually sure of it.

I had tried to sleep since I had woken up. I couldn't get comfortable, however, with a broken rib still in the process of healing. Being in a coma didn't feel like sleep. I can't really explain how it felt; all I know is that I still felt exhausted, as if I hadn't just been unconscious for the past however long. When the doctor had explained how much time had passed, I wanted to cry. I hadn't cried yet, though, and I was probably going to save any tears that may come till I got back to my apartment. They had tried explaining more to me about what had happened, but I had asked them to leave. I just wanted to sleep.

"How is she?" a familiar voice had entered the room. It was tight, strong and feminine. I could picture Jordine's pursed lips and lime-green eyes sweeping my hospital bed. I suddenly felt exposed; I was wearing absolutely nothing under the robe they had given me, after all.

I felt a hand on my shoulder. It was bigger than Jordine's, so I knew it wasn't her. The doctor who had tried to discuss test results with me was now speaking with her in hushed tones, still somewhere over by the door. I felt like I knew whose hand was on my shoulder, but I didn't want to get my hopes up.

"You up, Liles?" his voice was soft and cracked. I couldn't help it; I let a tear slide from my eye as I gave a slight nod, still not opening my eyes. He seemed to read my mind. "Can we turn the lights off, please? And less people in the room, if we could?" He called over towards the door. Jace's voice remained soft but loud enough for everyone in the room to hear.

I heard the voices near the door slowly

start to disperse, and the light beyond my eyelids dimmed to a single spot farther from my bed. I chanced squinting one eye open, the room considerably darker than when I had first woken up. Opening both eyes, only slightly because my head still gave a throb, I glanced over at Jace. His left arm was in a cast and sling, and his hair was disheveled like he had been tugging at it all day. I reached up to grab his hand on my shoulder, grimacing at the most effort I had put into any movement since waking up. He didn't say anything as he held my hand and sat down on the chair beside my bed.

"You okay, Rapunzel?" Jameson's deep voice came from my other side. I couldn't see him with my peripheral vision because I was still squinting to keep the light out. I turned slowly toward his voice, learning earlier that day not to move my head too quickly. When I could finally see him, I gave him a smile, even though it was weak. I hadn't felt like smiling all day, but seeing these two in my room, I had found a good enough reason.

He patted my shoulder. "You look horrible," he laughed, sitting down in the chair mirroring Jace's. "But you still look better than half the women back at the office," he quickly added.

Jameson's sense of humor was dry, which was why he didn't use it a lot. I think he was trying to overcompensate for the absence of the usual joker in their group, Lars. I chuckled, my voice dry and raspy. I tried to clear my throat but only ended up coughing.

Jace released my hand immediately and came back within seconds holding a paper cup. I turned back to him as he placed it in my hands. His eyes were glossy. I squinted, trying to convince myself it was just the reflection of the dim lights and not tears.

Taking a deep gulp of the water, I enjoyed the cool feeling stream through my scratchy throat. I smiled at Jace as he took the cup from my hands and went to fill it with more water.

"Jordine is in the other room, speaking with the nurses," I turned back to Jameson, my neck beginning to feel less tight. Maybe the trick was to continue turning, even if it was slowly. "She'll also be the one to call your family to let them know you've come to."

I nodded, unsure if I had a voice to hold an actual conversation with them. But I was content with their presence, especially Jace's. He didn't seem to have a voice either.

"How long have you been awake, Rapunzel?" Jameson seemed determined to get something out of me. He was beating around the bush. I tried not to think too hard about my responses.

"Couple hours, I guess," my voice was croaky and probably an octave lower than usual.

Jameson nodded. I turned back towards Jace, trying to reach my cup on the bedside table. That's when I noticed the flowers. And the balloons. Jace grabbed the water before I got to it and handed it to me again.

"Who sent those?" I gestured to the gifts adorning my bedside table after I had taken another long swig of water. Jameson and Jace looked at each other.

"We did," Jace's voice was tight. "And some were also sent from Edith and your parents."

I nodded. My dad was the only person in this world who knew how much I liked calla lilies, which would explain the small bouquet of vibrant white and yellow ones in the vase to the front of the bundle. I realized then that I had been knocked out before he had left New York.

"Did my dad –?" I couldn't think of what to say. Did he see me crippled on a hospital bed? Did he miss his flight home for me?

Jace took my hand again. "He came and saw you that same night. We stayed up for hours in here waiting for you to wake up," he stopped. I watched him as he stared at the floor.

"His plane left the next night," Jameson continued, "He stayed here till about two hours before it departed, then went back to your apartment to pack his things and feed your . . . cat?"

I nodded. Knowing my father, he probably cleaned my apartment and washed my jeep for me as well. I'm glad he caught his original flight; I wouldn't want him to miss work or whatever else he's got going in life because of me. Another tear came as I thought of him sleeping beside my bed. I wished I could tell him myself that I was awake, and okay.

"So how do you feel?" Jameson had left a respectful amount of silence before his next question.

"Exhausted," I tried to sit up a little more, but a throbbing pain came to the top of my spine and I grunted to a stop.

"We can raise your bed," Jace pulled a remote from next to the hospital bed's mattress. "Do you want it up more?"

"Yes, please," the bed moving under me felt weird, but the relief of the support on my back felt wonderful once it settled into place. "I feel like I just ran a marathon, even though I haven't moved for two weeks." A voice in the back of my head reminded me I haven't showered or brushed my hair or teeth in the past two weeks either. I tried not to get self-conscious as I avoided Jace's eyes.

"Fatigue is fairly normal for patients waking from a coma," a short man in maroon scrubs walked into the room, followed by Jordine and a couple of nurses. My gratuity for the company was starting to diminish as more people joined us.

"Delilah," Jordine came and placed a hand on the end of my bed. "I'm glad to see you are beginning to recover! Dr. Gubler, ladies, could you please excuse us for a moment?"

There was the confirmation that they were here for something. The man in the scrubs nodded as he ushered the nurses out of the room and closed the door behind them. Jace stood.

"Jordine, please," he stood in front of me protectively, as if she was about to pounce. "She just woke up. Why don't we give her some time to—"

"Time erodes memory, Jace," Jordine waved him off, stepping around him. "Delilah, I apologize if this causes any inconvenience, but we believe you may have retrieved some important information before your accident. If you could at least confirm this, we can leave the details for later."

Jace was right. I needed more time. I wasn't about to forget what happened, but I didn't exactly feel like sharing right now. Annoyed, I looked her straight in the eyes. "Where did those beliefs come from?"

"Well," Jordine hesitated, glancing at Jace.

"Your father said if you went down this hard, you must have at least learned something new."

Of course he did. "Well, I'm sorry to disappoint, but the only thing I think I learned before I got my head knocked from my shoulders was that McGregor knew what was coming."

It came out harsh. Jordine stood in silence, Jameson stared at the floor, and even Jace looked a little taken aback. "What do you mean?" Jordine's bright eyes seemed luminescent in the mellow light.

"I chased him into an alleyway, but he definitely wasn't the guy that threw me against a wall," I tried to remember what had happened. The effort hurt my head, so I closed my eyes and leaned back. "I was hot on his heels, but he took a hairpin turn and by the time I got back on track, he was gone." I remembered the fog and my eyes snapped open.

"I was drugged," I looked at Jace in a panic, "I ran into what I thought was fog and my strength left me within minutes, that's how the guy overpowered me. And he was wearing a gas mask . . ."

My voice faded away as I looked at each person in the room. No one looked surprised.

"The doctors tested for ketamine, along with about a hundred other drugs it could have been," Jameson sounded bitter. "They couldn't figure out what it was."

I stared around in disbelief. "Is it still in my system?"

"'It can barely be traced and therefore hardly plausible to remove'," Jace recited in a gruff voice. "But as far as we know it could have left your body the same night."

I closed my eyes again. At least it wasn't ketamine, right? *Right*, answered the voice in my head, *it's just some crackpot basement invention.* That's comforting. I reached up and rubbed my forehead.

"Are you sure—?"

"I think that's enough, Jordine, look at her," Jace cut Jordine off sharply. I tried not to pay attention to the disappointment in his voice. "She needs rest, not an interrogation."

Jordine sighed. "Alright. We will be needing a full report, when you are recovered, Delilah."

I nodded, keeping my eyes closed. I heard their footsteps as each person made their way out the door. At least I thought it was all of them till I felt strong fingers grip my hand. I opened my eyes and caught Jace inches from my face, sitting on the side of my bed. He leaned forward and kissed me lightly.

"Thank you for waking up," his fingers stroked my cheek as a tear rolled down his own. I had never seen him cry, and as I watched I hoped I never would again. "I'm sorry."

I shook my head. I felt tears well up in my eyes but did all I could to keep them back. I didn't think this would have had such a strong impact on him, seeing as how he said he didn't want to be in a relationship; but now he was sitting right there in front of me, tears rolling down his cheeks and his hand gripping mine tightly.

"It was my fault. . ." I said slowly.

"No, it wasn't," he bit his lip. There was sweat building between his palm and the back of my hand. "And while you were out. . . Liles, I think I made a mistake—"

"Ready to go Avery?" Jordine stood at the door, tapping her foot with her arms across her chest. Jace gave a weak smile before standing, squeezing my fingers again before letting my hand go and walking out of my hospital room.

* * *

I woke up with a start. I could still see the image of the gas mask in front of me, floating in the dark room above my head like a giant, flat-nosed mosquito. The machine monitoring my heart rate was beeping rapidly, and I tried to calm my breathing. That was the third time I had relived the memory of being mobbed in the alley in my sleep. I was starting to wish I could just stay awake all the time.

It had been four days since I had woken up and Jordine had made the house call. Or hospital call, I should say. Each day I had received something more of my strength back, along with nurses running in and out of my room performing tests and helping me use the bathroom.

Jace had visited me every day since I had woken up, and I found out from some of the nurses that he had visited frequently while I was in the coma as well. The women never ceased to remind me how lucky I was to have such a sincere hunk. He also advised me he had kept Dot fed with the key I had left for my dad, who had in turn handed it over to Jace. Don't get me wrong—I'm very grateful, but oh so confused. Last I checked we weren't in a relationship, but he sure was acting like a boyfriend. Thinking about it made my head pound more, however, so I decided to just see how things were about to unfold since he was the one taking me home from the hospital today.

The morning went by in a blur. The nurses were frantically but carefully taking their last blood samples and heart rates, scribbling results on clipboards and speedily disconnecting me from all the tubes and chords. I had received the regular motion back in my neck and was able to watch without any discomfort as the hospital staff made my final preparations to leave.

Jace came around eleven and helped me walk to the elevator and down to his car in the pickup parking lot. My head continued a slight throb near the tip of my neck, but it had diminished to a mere annoyance rather than the blunt pain it had been when I first woke up. I wore sunglasses in the car and the radio was turned off on our way to my apartment. Jace had recovered from the trauma he must have felt because he told me all the news of the office since I had been away as we drove, keeping his voice in a controlled, quiet tone.

We walked slowly up the steps of my complex, the impact bothering my head and my ribs probably a little more than it should have. Dot of course greeted us at my door, her excitement at finally seeing me again overwhelming her to the point she was tripping over herself to follow us back to my bedroom.

"Do you want to lie back down," Jace motioned toward my bed, "or would you like to shower first?" We had talked about showering on the way home, and how it would probably feel nice to get clean and not smell like the hospital anymore.

"I think I'll rest better if I'm clean," I used his shoulder for support as he led me to my bathroom.

"Need help with any of it?" he joked, winking at me before stepping out of the bathroom. I threw a lotion bottle at him before closing the door in his face.

"I'll just wait out here then," he laughed, and I heard him plop down on my sofa in the living room. I scrunched my eyebrows at my reflection as I remembered reading about people with the "sympathetic love" syndrome. Because that's exactly what I need right now, on top of all this.

The shower was pure bliss, but very hard. The warm water felt comforting as it ran down my back, but as my hair collected more and more my head became heavier. I slightly regretted turning down the offer for help, because every few minutes I had to crouch down and steady myself against the walls of the tub. I was already exhausted from just leaving the hospital, and the more weight my hair gained the harder it was to keep my head up. I tried to speed up the process so that I could go lay down faster, but the harder I tried the more I began to ache.

Finally finished, I turned the squeaky faucet down and stepped through the curtain into the steamy bathroom. As hard as it had been, the hot shower had helped the beating in the back of my head subside. Whipping my towel around me, I moved in front of the mirror and saw the distorted reflection of a gas mask staring back at me.

I stumbled backward into the wall, pain shooting down my back as I bumped into the towel rack.

"Is everything okay in there?" Jace's voice came from beyond the door as I gathered my senses.

Stepping forward, my hands shaking, I wiped the steam from the mirror to reveal my horrified face gaping back at me. I couldn't answer Jace as I continued to look at my reflection. There was a white line under my nose going down into my lip, and a light green bruise covering my cheekbone almost up to my eye.

I was not okay. I had almost died. I could still die, if that drug was still in me. And the man who had attacked me was everywhere I turned.

The realization of my situation hit, and I couldn't handle it. I shook my head, the pulsing aggravation returning as tears escaped my eyelids. The pain became so intense I began to fall to my knees. I tried to grab the counter to keep myself up but ended up grabbing the chord to the flat-iron that had been left on it. It clattered to the floor as my knees thudded down next to it, my head in my hands.

"I'm coming in," Jace had given the warning about two seconds before the lock clicked and the door to my bathroom opened.

I barely noticed him enter as I sobbed, the visions that haunted my dreams coming back to me as I knelt on the floor. I wondered aloud the question that had entered my mind the day I had woken from my coma.

"Why didn't they just kill me?"

I was angry that I had made the decision to follow McGregor into the fog, bitter that he had drugged me, and frustrated that it had left me so crippled. But most of all, I was scared I wouldn't be able to recover from the experience.

I felt Jace's hands on my bare shoulders, bringing me back to reality. I made sure my towel was secure around my body as he sat down on the floor behind me, grabbing my hairbrush from the counter on his way down.

"I always liked the feeling of someone playing with my hair," he said as he began brushing my hair. I sniffled, grabbing some toilet paper to wipe away the tear residue still fresh on my face. "I always found it a sort of relief."

I didn't say anything as he brushed through my hair, and as he finished he pulled me back against his chest, wrapping his arms across my shoulders. I appreciated that he kept his hands far from my blatantly exposed body, setting his elbows on top of my shoulders as his arms crossed my neck. I would have felt embarrassed if I hadn't felt completely helpless.

"I'll walk you to your room," Jace said softly in my ear. "Please just don't collapse while you're getting dressed."

I smiled weakly as he pulled my arm over his shoulders, helping me up and walking me back to my bedroom. He helped me sit on the edge of my bed and then walked back to my door.

"I'll be right out here," he pulled the door closed. "Holler when you've covered yourself up a bit more."

CHAPTER 8

Jace

Peeking around the corner of my cubicle to make sure the coast was clear, I dug into my McGregor file. It was technically off limits for me while in the probationary office, but I snuck it in along with some other essential cases that still required research. I wasn't about to sit here for five more months without any interesting work to do.

The day Delilah was attacked, I had resolved that once she was conscious again my first priority would be to find out what happened to her. I figured if I could find the man responsible behind the drug, I could get the information I needed to cure her. The only problem was, finding even a connection to McGregor had proven difficult the last time I tracked him, which had taken me nearly six months. I was worried I didn't have that much time.

My main goal was to shed some light on the drug that could still be in Delilah's system, aiming most of my research in the past couple of days on the recent meth lab busts around town. It was a homemade, seemingly gaseous bomb, from what

Delilah had relayed to me the day after she got home from the hospital. She still hadn't given a full report to the Board yet, but I felt like I had gotten all the information I needed from her. And it had given her a relief to tell someone about it. It was a win for both sides.

I rifled through the papers in the file, trying to find a link between the labs that had gotten shut down this week. Nothing seemed to connect, unless McGregor's shipments off the coast of Upper Bay Hudson were based out of Rochester, which seemed highly unlikely considering how many highways trucks would have to travel without being checked for illegal merchandise. It seemed that McGregor's shipments were mainly based off the coasts of Long Beach, which would make sense considering the drug market in Northern Africa. Unfortunately, all the drug labs that were overturned in the past two months were all more inland.

I started googling warehouses around the known ports of McGregor's merchandise, trying to narrow down where in the world the man could have enough room and people to invent something to make Delilah lose the use of her limbs. It almost sounded like a sedative, something that would make her go numb. But she distinctly remembered not even being able to move, and numbing would only make her unable to feel. I had researched types of anesthetics earlier in the week because it seemed like a plausible idea, but nothing added up to what Delilah described.

As I pulled the image and address of a suspicious edifice, I heard voices and footsteps nearing my corner. I quickly crammed the file in a cabinet with a lock, turning the key and stuffing it in my pocket as Jameson and Lars came into view.

"Avery would know," Lars came around my desk, glancing at my computer screen. "Are you house-hunting Avery?" he leaned forward, taking in the grotesque and seemingly abandoned factory on my screen. "Yeesh, you may want to let Hadley take that one. Your taste seems slightly, well, creepy."

Jameson laughed as I minimized the window, making sure to remember the main part of the address in case I lost the page. "Just looking stuff up," I spun my chair to look up at the two men, Jameson towering a head above Lars. "What can I do for you gentlemen?"

"First, we need you to settle a little, ah, debate we've been having," Jameson cleared his throat, looking from Lars to me and then back again.

"Jameson is sure that Jordine was widowed at a young age, her husband a fellow agent. However, given how intensely studious and prudent our superior is, along with her pure discontent with men, I begged to differ!" Lars shrugged as Jordine walked up behind the two of them. I tried not to smile. "Since you're the favorite, we both figured you would be able to settle the rumors?"

I looked down, my knuckles in my mouth as Jordine placed her hands on Jameson's and Lars' shoulders. I glanced up to see the pure horror in the grown men's faces, choking back my laughter.

"You boys really have nothing better to do than to spread rumors about my love life?" her tight voice was a mixture of amusement and annoyance. "I'll put them to rest right now; you're both wrong. You were right, however, in guessing that Jace would know the truth. Right Jace?"

Not expecting to be brought in to this, I stood and straightened my tie. "Jordine is still happily married to a lawyer, with two daughters and one son, all in their late teens or early twenties, if I am up to date?" I posed the question to Jordine, her average frame minute compared to the bulky men she was holding.

"Your knack for recalling unimportant details never ceases to impress, Avery," She smirked as she turned Jameson and Lars around. I stepped back, deciding to take her comment as a compliment. "In all seriousness, I do want to know why you two ventured out to this neck of the woods while we have a case that needs to be worked by your teams."

"Oh, we are progressing the case as we speak," Lars bounded into his explanation quickly, "We had just decided we could use Avery's intellect on the subjects we are researching. . ." his voice faltered under Jordine's gaze. Her pursed lips said it all.

"You boys know I strictly forbid anyone asking for his aid in their cases while in his probationary state. No offense, Jace," she shrugged apologetically in my direction. I nodded; I understood wanting your authority respected.

"And we have heeded that order, Jordine," Jameson stepped in, his silky voice making me think of how smooth chocolate milk is when you poor it. This was the tone he used when persuading others, and I had yet to see it fail. I smiled down at my shoes as he continued, "But since Avery specializes in criminal profiling, and we have been hitherto incapable of identifying the main subject's identity, we thought it beneficial to enlist him in the cause."

"Jameson, you use such grandiose vocabulary when you are trying to get what you want," the corners of Jordine's mouth twitched.

"We wouldn't be requesting his assistance if we hadn't been given a deadline," Jameson bowed his head. Thankfully Lars was smart enough not to interrupt when he was on a roll.

Jordine scowled at each of us in turn before turning her back to us. "He isn't allowed out in the field," She called over her shoulder. "All of his work must be done here in the office under supervision of someone on your team."

"It's like you broke a law or something," Lars muttered as Jordine turned the corner.

"Welcome back to the team," Jameson shook my hand, his bald head glossy under the effervescent bulbs. "It's been a long month without you."

I grinned, silently grateful as the two knuckleheads lead me to a part of the office where sitting in a chair meant you were on break.

* * *

I walked swiftly out of the building and onto the street, quickly hailing a cab and jumping in. I had exactly forty-five minutes to get home, and an hour after that to make sure the hot tub and dinner were ready for Delilah. That would give me the ten extra minutes of her undoubtedly being late to make sure I was presentable for our date.

Tonight would be her first time ever visiting my townhome, which was further out of the city then her apartment complex, meaning she couldn't take the subway. I hoped she wouldn't get lost as my cab pulled up to the sidewalk and I ran to get into the house. I had deep-cleaned it two days before to make sure that everything was pristine, after she had accepted the offer for a date night at my place. Our most recent get togethers were mostly based around her relaxing and getting the therapy she required during her recovery, and what could be more relaxing than a hot-tubbing dinner for two?

I started up the hot tub on my porch out back before running around my kitchen like a chicken with my head cut off. I had accepted that I have some form of obsessive-compulsive disorder, because everything in my house had its place and as I cooked, I would wash the utensils or cutting boards I wasn't using anymore and put them back, so they weren't out on my counters. My casted arm didn't make things any easier, and I stressed over the want of Delilah having a stress-free night, the thought of the paradox making me slow down. She probably wouldn't want me to stress either.

Finally getting the salmon in the oven, I went up to my bedroom and got ready for the night. I decided to get into board shorts right away, so it would be easier than having to change in the middle of the date; I also grabbed a plain white V-neck out of my closet that would match my neon orange bathing suit. I was excited to be with Delilah again, the feeling jolting through my body as I got her text saying she was on her way.

I was stirring up my asparagus in the frying pan as the knock came to the door. It was 6:10, precisely when I had expected her to arrive. I turned off the stove top and rushed to the door, realizing I still had my apron on at the last second. Embarrassed, I opened the door sheepishly. Delilah stood on my front porch, looking absolutely stunning in her sun-yellow swimsuit cover. Her face had healed back to its gorgeous self and she moved almost as normally as she used to, with only a slight limp catering her left side, where her rib had broken.

"'Kiss the chef'?" she laughed, glancing down at my apron. "Oh, the lips and hearts add a real manly touch," she smirked, holding up a pan of what looked like a giant square chocolate chip cookie.

"I meant to take this off before you got here," I said, leading her in and taking the still warm pan from her hands. "My mom gave it to me when she got fed up with my grease-stained shirts."

She flipped her straight hair behind her shoulder, looking around at the walls and furniture. "I think it's adorable," she followed me into the kitchen area, a look of pure amusement on her face.

"What?"

"It's just exactly what I expected," Delilah sat on the bar stool at the edge of my counter, now taking me in. "This place mirrors your personality almost perfectly."

"Almost?" I asked, stepping over to check on the salmon. "What's missing?"

"The equivalent to your messy hair," she giggled, reaching over the counter and messing my hair with her hand. She was flirting more than she had with me since she had woken up. I didn't mind.

"You haven't seen my bedroom," I said honestly, pulling the pan out of the oven. "What is this? I was expecting your box brownies again!" I motioned to her giant cookie.

Delilah laughed. "Nope, these are made from scratch, my mom's most notorious recipe."

"Notorious?" I raised my eyebrows.

"Notorious for being addicting," she corrected, and I sighed in relief. "I probably could have phrased that better."

"Probably," I gave her a sarcastic thumbs-up. "I'm excited to try them!"

She rolled her eyes but smiled shyly. I thought I almost saw worry run across her face, and I wondered if this was her first time baking anything from scratch. It wouldn't surprise me, based off all the boxed desserts I spotted in her pantry.

"Well, tonight I have prepared for you," I whisked off my apron and took her hand, leading her to my tiny kitchen table, "A baked black salmon with asparagus and lemon zest. I also have wine in my garage, but if you don't feel like getting frisky to-night I have got apple juice or beer in the fridge."

Delilah laughed as she sat down, keeping hold of my hand. "I don't drink alcohol, but I would love some juice."

I brought the *V8* bottle to the table, pouring the golden liquid into each of our glasses. "The only reason I have that wine is for when my parents visit, anyway," sitting down across from her, I shrugged, "I should make not drinking my New Year's Resolu-tion. It would make cost of living a lot cheaper."

She laughed as I dished up our plates and we began eating. The conversation remained on my parents as she asked a lot of questions about my family. I felt a twinge of deja vu as I gave the same an-swers I had on our first date. That's okay; I mean, the woman just woke up from a coma. She was polite as she ate, and I again admired her grace and ability at conversation. But then she frowned.

"What's wrong?" I set down my fork.

She looked up at me, her blue eyes dilated slightly. "Jace, be honest. What are we?"

"What do you mean?"

"You're acting like you want to date me again. But I thought you had decided. . ." she looked out-side, her hands on the table.

I realized I had never gotten to tell her how seeing her in the hospital made me realize what an idiot I had been. About to answer, I choked on my words as Delilah's hand began to twitch. It was a spidery motion, as if she were stroking piano keys, but in a jerky manner. I had never noticed it before, and I felt like I had been pretty vigilant about her body language lately.

"You okay?" I asked, nodding to her spasmodic fingers. She gaped.

"I'm not doing that," she sounded worried, as if this was the first time she had seen it as well. I reached across the table and held her hand in mine, feeling the fingers jerk a little more before settling down. "I'm sorry, I don't know why my fingers would do that, I've never had a twitch like that in my life."

"Don't be sorry," I felt bad for pointing it out, because the possibility of the drug still being in her system just grew a little bigger. "You've had a lot going on lately; maybe it's just a side effect from the meds they've got you on."

"Maybe," she said, glancing back out the window sadly. I squeezed her hand.

"Liles I was an idiot to tell you we shouldn't date."

She scoffed. "This isn't just one of those 'you had a traumatic experience and I feel guilty so now I'm in love' kind of things, is it?"

My jaw dropped at her bluntness as I let go of her hand, unsure of how I could convince her that it was definitely not that.

"Jace, I like you. But before this happened," she motioned to her head, "you didn't want to date me. Now your kissing me and inviting me for fancy dinners. . ."

"I wanted to date you," I defended. "But look what happened. Feelings for coworkers in this field ends dangerously, almost always."

She looked down. "So now that it already has turned dangerous –"

"I realized in the hospital, while I was praying for you to wake up," I said hastily, "that I missed you. Just talking to you, I missed you more than I've ever missed anyone in my life."

She shook her head slowly. "I like our friendship, Jace. But after what happened between us, and then to me. . . I need time to think about this. And it's hurting my head too much now."

I nodded. I could respect that—I guess I figured we could pick back up where we left off on our last date. It was obvious how that wouldn't work now that she pointed it out, though. Wanting to change the subject after a sufficiently awkward pause, I asked; "How is your dad?" I didn't want tonight to be a pity party for the accident; Delilah had already had a week's worth of those since she wasn't back at the office yet.

"Oh, he's fine," she looked back at me, gratefully picking up on the turn in the conversation. "He's been talking more with my mom, which could either be really good for both of them or just really bad for him."

We finished the meal swapping stories of bad relationships, and how we've seen some go from the worst to the best in a matter of months. She talked hopefully about her parents, as if deep down she wanted them to get back together, even though hearing her side made the situation sound less than ideal.

The sun was just about to set outside as I got up to place the dishes in the dishwasher. Delilah got up as well, refusing to let me turn down her help. We loaded the washer together, and then made our way out onto the porch with her pan of cookies. I tried not to stare as she took off the swimsuit cover, revealing a simple light pink one piece that made her skin glow even more in the setting sun. And there were the scars her father had mentioned; about halfway up her thighs were patches of skin that looked almost shriveled up, a pale pink tone showing where the cells were destroyed by the fire that licked her legs. Even with the scars, she looked like she could be on the cover of a swimsuit magazine. Averting my eyes and pulling off my shirt, I stepped into the bubbly water and held out my hand to help her in.

Goosebumps erupted on my skin as a soft breeze picked up around us, the slight chill contrasting against the steamy water we sat in. Delilah sunk in up to her chin, resting her head on the edge, contentment spreading across her face. I let silence overcome us as I watched her relax. Her skin was smooth and tight across her muscles, like even it couldn't contain her height.

I reached behind me to where we had put the pan of her giant cookie, careful to keep my cast above the water. Cutting a square out with the knife she had brought, I glanced at her still closed eyes. If I didn't like it, I could throw it behind me and act like I could only eat one. I took a bite into the gooey dessert, instantly being reminded of the Pillsbury commercials where the chocolate pulls apart just right to show its meltiness. It was like a brownie and a chocolate chip cookie put together, and I couldn't help but scarf down the rest as if it were the last one on earth. I dished myself up another, quietly wondering if she had put some sort of drug in it as I felt like I could eat the whole pan.

"You like them?" she asked, her eyes still closed.

I quickly swallowed my mouthful. "They're amazing," I stood, shivering against the breeze as I reached over her to turn on the lights around my porch. "Don't you want any?"

"I might wait," Delilah opened her eyes and patted her flat stomach. "I'm still super full of your salmon. I'm glad you like them though."

"I'm going to need to get your recipe," I dished up another square, trying to savor this one but still finishing it before a full minute had passed.

"Oh, I don't give it out," she smiled, moving through the water towards me. "It's mama's secret recipe, and only stays with the females in the family."

I laughed, and she elbowed me softly, the water absorbing most of the blow.

She put her hand on my leg, and I felt her fingers twitching again. I decided not to bring it up this time, however, as I enjoyed the fact that she was already back to being comfortable enough to at least touch me.

"How long are we going to keep doing this?"

"Doing what?"

"Being off and on. You can't keep kissing me and then telling me we can't be together."

I sighed. I had hoped we had moved on from this, at least for now. "I'm not going to do that again. Now I'm just waiting on you."

Her chuckle had a slight hint of bitterness that made me tense up with guilt "But I can't just trust the first guy to show interest in me in New York; especially a guy that looks like he stepped out of a *Sports Illustrated* magazine."

I felt my cheeks grow warm. "Maybe for boxing," I pointed at my chipped tooth. "That's the only thing to explain this in a manly way."

"I think it adds to your character," Delilah shrugged, making me feel less self-conscious about it. "How did that happen, by the way?"

I regarded her wide eyes. They looked like sapphires in the sunset. "It's actually really stupid, and I won't tell you if you can't keep it a secret."

Delilah smiled. "Oh, I can keep anything a secret."

I looked to one side, and then to the other to make sure there wasn't anyone else maybe hot-tubbing on my porch. "Truth is," I said, looking down, "My brother and I were using couch cushions for a pillow fight, once, and he hit me so hard I fell forward onto my parents' stone fireplace."

Delilah clapped her hand to her mouth. "That's horrible!"

"Yeah, blood everywhere," I got a bit more animated, encouraged by her reaction, "Long story short, the tooth went through my lip and broke off on the stone. That's why I have this scar too," I touched where I knew the small white line in my bottom lip was.

Delilah's body jerked suddenly, and her hand went straight for my arm, gripping it tightly. When her nails started digging into my skin and her body didn't stop, I wrapped my arms around her, my cast over her shoulders, holding her tight to steady her rapid breathing. After about two minutes her body relaxed again, and she pulled away, tears in her eyes.

"I don't know what they did to me," she said quietly, pushing the water between us to move away. She didn't seem as surprised this time, like her body had done this before. I didn't let her move back though and, pulling her closer to me through the water, I put my chin on top of her head.

"I'll figure it out," I promised, holding her trembling body and feeling even more determined in my goal.

* * *

I walked down the puddled sidewalk toward the docks. The street lights flickered, making the pavement shine for brief moments before becoming dull and gray again. There was no moon to be seen in the sky tonight due to the dense clouds covering New York. I was a little disappointed the rain had stopped before I left my apartment, because it would have been a perfect cover for an investigation.

I had visited the first warehouse I had come across earlier in the week, along with the second, third, and fourth where additional drug labs were suspected but not yet infiltrated. It had been to no avail, however, as I discovered each of them as abandoned on the inside as they looked on the outside. It was finally the weekend, but I wasn't going to take a break; I had to know what was surely still in Delilah's system.

The drug analyst at work, Marco, analyzed her symptoms for me. I relayed how it entered her body and what was happening to her now. He couldn't come up with anything that would cause her unusual symptoms, so he told me unless the attacker had mixed multiple narcotics and sedatives into one, he couldn't identify what it was. He also said even that was a doubtful suspicion because of how lethal combining drugs could be.

Sticking my hands in the pockets of my

jacket, I felt relief at not having a cast to hold me back anymore. The doctor had taken it off earlier that day, telling me the rest of the healing could be done without. My elbow still felt achy, but usable as I walked toward the gentle sound of waves crashing against the shoreline. Frustration mounted with each step, however.

I felt like I was hitting a brick wall at every turn I took; I couldn't find a possible source of the drug, and the drug itself remained unknown. And from snippets of conversations I gathered eavesdropping on Jameson and my team, they had no new leads on McGregor. I wasn't going to give up, though, and the drive to help Delilah is what led me to Hudson Bay in the middle of a Friday night.

The wind picked up around me as I remained close to the main road, the chill making me pull my baseball cap low and my hood up over it.

Harry Guzman, captain of *The Trickshot*, was Jameson's contact when we invaded McGregor's ketamine operation. I requested the information from Jameson so I could question the man myself, and he offered to help me do some negotiating. I refused his offer, mainly because I don't think the man would be very welcoming to him again since we let McGregor go last time. He had answered the phone when I called, however, and that told me he was at least still alive. I hadn't told him I was from the FBI, or exactly what I wanted, just that I knew he was a guy to get information from concerning some trades within the port. I set up the meeting and suspected from his ready compliance that I was walking into a trap. I didn't care, though, because I needed to get closer to McGregor anyway.

I turned down an alley between the last two buildings on the street before the docks, approaching the three smoking men ahead of me. None of them fit the description of Guzman Jameson had given me, but I took out my cell regardless. We had discussed over the phone that Guzman could identify me by my *Giants* ball cap and my smartphone in front of me. If any of these were the man I was looking for, they would know it was me; if not they would just think I was another loner heading to the bar on the other side of this alley. The front of the bar was where Guzman and I were to meet.

"Goin' for a drink, my frien'?" one of the men asked, blowing the scent of tobacco into my face as I passed.

I looked up from my phone nonchalantly, feeling the presence of the other two men on either side of me. They were all watching me as I stopped in front of the shortest, the one who posed the question.

"One of those days," I shrugged, looking at the other two, "You guys care to join me?"

I sized them up; the one I faced stood favoring his left side, indicating some sort of current or past injury to his right knee or ankle. Out of the corners of my eyes I recognized the biggest to my right, hunched in the back to show a shoulder injury of some sort. The one to my left was a couple inches shorter than me, and by far the skinniest; if these men were about to jump me, he would be the easiest to take out first.

"Girlfriend," the big one grunted, stepping forward and placing a heavy hand on my shoulder. "Or work?"

"I guess you could say both," I started inching towards the bar again, but the hand on my shoulder held firm.

"Tha's a nice phone you got," the short one said again, taking a step towards me. He smelled like fish and smoke. He smiled at me, revealing a missing canine. "Where does a guy work to get somin' like tha'?"

"A law firm, unfortunately," I said convincingly, sliding the phone into my pocket and spreading my hands wide. "Another reason a guy likes to get wasted on the weekends."

"Makes sense," the short one nodded, and I saw him glance up over my right shoulder before swinging a meaty fist toward my jaw.

I reached up and stopped his fist with my hand, grabbing it and using the momentum to sidestep the guy behind me, who had been reaching for my shoulders, and fling the short one into him. They tripped over one another as the skinny boy wrapped his arms through mine from behind and with surprising strength flipped me onto the ground. My breath caught as I hit the pavement, but I swung my leg around, making contact with his and bringing him tumbling to my level. I stood quickly and held up my fists, trying to keep the gun concealed at my side as a last resort.

The other two men had recovered and were advancing toward me as the thin one coughed and sputtered on the ground. They launched themselves at me a second later, the tall one going for my upper back while the short one went for my gut. I had played rugby in high school and knew how to get out of this illegal tackle, but I let them take me down. If these men worked for McGregor, I wanted a word with them. If not, I could get out of whatever they might think would keep me at bay.

My body flipped, my feet flying backwards over my head as my chest hit the pavement. I used my forearms to soften the blow, feeling pain shoot up my elbow and having a hard time catching my breath as the big one picked me up. My feet were almost off the ground as he shoved me against the wall to my right and let go. The man with the missing canine came uncomfortably close to my face.

"Now wha' would a lawyer wan' with ol' Harry Guzman?" his breath was putrid and warm against the chilly night air.

I smiled; these men were working for McGregor. He punched me in the stomach as the skinny one stood up again. I evaluated the situation, making my decision as I stepped forward, grabbing the short man's shoulder and jumping up. With my downward motion I angled my foot to land directly against his right shin. He yelped in pain and fell backward as the big man grabbed me from behind. I twisted and turned, interlocking my arms with his until I heard a snap and a groan, and then flipped him over my back and onto his own on the ground.

I looked up to see the scrawny man standing between me and the bar, a gun pointed directly at my chest. He looked pleased with himself as his comrades lay incapacitated behind me.

"You may want to answer his question," he nodded to the whimpering man holding his leg. "Because we know you ain't no lawyer."

I stepped forward, my hands up. "You're right," I continued moving forward, and the man kept his gun trailed on me. Apparently, they hadn't been given permission to kill, or he would have already taken the shot. "I'm no lawyer. But Guzman has information concerning a friend of mine."

I was almost within reaching distance of the gun. I tried to take a step closer but the man whipped the gun back and cocked it, pointing it at my head this time. "You know, some powerful people don't like little people like us asking questions," he sounded like his IQ was below 50, but he was also the one with the loaded gun in his hand, so I stopped moving.

"You work for McGregor." I wasn't asking. I kept an eye on the gun in his steady hand, but I also saw the surprised look on the man's face. Taking advantage of his moment of hesitation, I dove forward and grabbed the gun out of his hands. Grabbing his arm and pulling him closer, I twisted it behind his back and held the gun to his head.

"What do you know of McGregor's drug?" I said quietly as the other two men on the ground stopped groaning. I had to speed this up.

"What, ketamine?" this guy was weak; I could tell by his scared voice he valued his life more than his loyalty to McGregor. It was really a gamble either way, but I wasn't about to point that out. "I know its nasty stuff, man."

"Not ketamine," I pushed him into one of the surrounding walls. "Something new, even to the streets."

"He doesn't know anything," came the gravelly voice of the giant trying to stand up further down the alley. "He just barely started."

I used the butt of the gun to knock out the kid, turning and aiming the barrel at the man now standing up and holding his shoulder.

"Where were you the afternoon of the 25th last month?" I didn't like the stupid smile spreading across this guy's face. His light brown skin glistened with sweat.

"A bit odd holding an interrogation here, of all places," he took a step forward. "You must be working off the books."

I stepped toward him as well, my gun aimed to kill. "You know, then," he stopped advancing, grimacing and holding his arm. And then realization dawned on his face.

"She was your partner," he chuckled softly with a look of pity. "That leggy agent was your partner. Boy you got yourself a steal, I'm guessing she's your girlfriend trouble as well?"

My finger twitched toward the trigger. "How do you know about her?" I tried to keep my voice steady.

The man continued to laugh as he took another step toward me. I swung forward and punched him in the jaw, letting the gun drop to my side. Was he the actual person that attacked Delilah that night?

"McGregor originally wanted her killed, once her little chase had started," the man continued to smile as blood pooled at his lips. I had to have knocked out some teeth with that punch. I swung again, this time higher up on his face, hearing his nose crack. My anger was taking over.

"But then he called me," My foot launched into his stomach, backing him into yet another wall as he doubled over.

"Why didn't he kill her?" I kicked again, then reached out and yanked his collar up so he could look in my eyes. "What did you use to drug her?"

The man's smile was eerily disconnected, as if he were slipping out of consciousness. "He always liked his experiments to be pretty." I struck at his temple before I could stop myself, making his head whip back and hit the bricks.

His body slumped from my grasp and onto the ground. I should have left him conscious enough to answer more questions, but his smile had infuriated me. He was proud of what he did to Delilah.

I dragged the men together, cuffing them to each other and then emptying the action of the gun in front of them. Dialing 911 on my phone, I left an anonymous tip for the cops about some mobsters at this address. Jordine would be furious if she found out I was the one that busted these guys while off duty, let alone the reason I did it.

As I walked away from the alleyway and into the bar on the other side, the man's last words echoed in my head.

Delilah was an experiment.

CHAPTER 9

Delilah

Dot lay curled on top of the blankets of the bed in between my legs, making it impossible to get into a comfortable position. I had woken up thirty minutes before my alarm was supposed to go off, and I didn't really feel like getting up till I actually had to. Today was going to be the first day back to work since my accident, and while I looked forward to it, I felt nervous at the same time.

I was going to have to relive what had been haunting my dreams for the past week and a half in front of a board of advisors today. The only person I had told basically anything to since it had happened was Jace, and even he hadn't heard the entire story. I had called my parents to let them know that I was alright, but thankfully neither of them pressed much for details; my mom was just glad I was okay and I'm pretty sure my dad knew I didn't want to talk about it. I had tried to prepare my report the night before, but even writing it down didn't do justice to how I felt that night. I just hoped I could portray my recovery well enough to the Board today that they would let me back into the swing of things in the office; even though I was still trying to convince myself of it as well.

I felt guilty that Jace had been blamed and punished for what happened to me. He had tried to stop me, and my feelings for him made me ignore his warnings. I couldn't help but wonder sometimes what would have happened if I had just stayed behind with him. McGregor had gotten away regardless; now I just looked like the over-eager rookie who couldn't listen to instructions.

Glancing over at my phone, which doubled as my alarm clock most mornings, I saw that it was nearing the time to actually start getting ready for the day. I switched on the lamp on my bedside table, accidentally knocking my favorite classic, "The Strange Case of Dr. Jekyll and Mr. Hyde" onto the floor. I had been reading it last night to help calm my nerves enough to sleep, but really all it had done was bring grotesque images of the gas mask man transforming into Jace and back again into my dreams.

I rose from my bed, dressed and tied my hair in a ponytail high on my head. I had gone for a jog or two here and there throughout the week of my recovery, but today I was determined to get back to the gym. It was 5:30 in the morning, which thankfully meant very few if any people would be there the same time as me. Packing a yogurt cup and some granola into a brown paper bag for my breakfast, I put food in Dot's bowl quickly before grabbing my gym bag and making my way out of the dark apartment and down the street to the subway.

The underground of New York remained alive even this early in the morning, with people rushing up and down the stairs and crowding the entrance to the train. I started to feel motion sick as the subway accelerated, and I sat down quickly to avoid vomiting. I wondered if my perception of speed had just slowed down as a result of being in a coma for two weeks. I also felt that the brakes didn't work as well as they used to, (which wasn't that great in the first place), but every stop felt like we crashed into a boulder.

As I walked through the parking garage to the elevators that would take me down to the basement gym, two men in deep blue suits were exiting a stairwell. I didn't recognize either of them, but one gave me a crooked smile as they passed, and I felt the unmistakable sensation of them turning around and watching me walk further. I decided not to look back; I know I looked ridiculous in my sweatpants and sweatshirt, and they probably thought I didn't belong in a business complex like this.

My expectations, (and hopes), were correct as I entered the desolate gym. I flipped up the giant power switch on the wall, illuminating the court, wrestling mats, track, punching bags and dummies scattered throughout the huge basement. The A/C had been turned off, but I didn't turn it back on. That way, I would just feel the temperature of my body, which was important when coming back from almost a month of laziness. I knew I had to take it easy today considering my inactivity lately; the jogs I had tried out during the past week weren't too bad but running outside always made me feel winded.

I began with a few laps around the track, warming my body up enough to take my sweat-shirt off and start running. The feeling of actually moving felt heavenly on my stiff limbs. I did a few stretches and yoga poses before starting into simple exercises like sit-ups and push-ups. My breath was short and rapid the harder I went, but I didn't feel any strains in my muscles. Maybe I hadn't completely fallen out of shape.

As I made my way over to the pull-up bars, Jace and Lars walked onto the court, Jace finally out of his sling. I waved but didn't say anything as I tried to catch my breath.

"Good morning Hadley," Lars returned the wave as he set down his bag and pulled out a jump rope. "I'm surprised you're here this early on your first day back!"

"I was hoping to beat the crowd," I said as I jumped up and grabbed the bar with both hands. Jace walked over to me.

"Are you sure you're feeling well enough to be working this hard, Liles?" he had a hand on my back. I kicked out at him as I started pulling myself up and down.

"I actually feel really good today, thanks doc,"

I lowered my voice, "And my body hasn't sporadically twitched since Friday, so I am taking that as a good sign."

Jace smiled, nodding and patting my leg before walking back to a jogging-in-place Lars. He looked good even in gym shorts and an Under Armour T, and I watched him for a minute before continuing to pull my chin up above the bar and then lower myself again. I shook my head, reminding myself that I was frustrated with him. Unconsciously counting each pull-up, I realized as I reached 35 that I was doing more than I could even before my accident. I still felt fine though; my muscles didn't ache or quake, and my breathing remained rapid but steady.

After 50 I dropped, wondering why I could do so many when I had never been that great at pull-ups. I turned around to see Jace and Lars watching me.

"What?"

Lars laughed, "I don't think I've ever seen a woman do so many pull-ups in one try."

I shrugged, "I told you, I feel good today."

Jace had this strange look in his eye, a worried kind of pity. I raised my eyebrow at him, and he seemed to realize what he was doing. He nodded again and walked over to the bench press, standing by the edge as Lars began putting weights on each end of the bar. He was strangely quiet this morning, even if Lars was here with us. Maybe he was just surprised to see me there.

"She's nuts," I heard the whisper as I was making my way to the punching bags. I glanced over my shoulder to see Jace spotting Lars with one hand.

"Excuse me?" I asked as Lars started pressing. Both looked over at me.

"We...didn't say anything," Lars said in that I'm-trying-to-hold-250-pounds-stable voice.

"Sure," I said, turning my back on them and starting to attack the sandbag.

I wasn't annoyed. Of course they'd think I was nuts; if I had just watched someone do that many pull-ups their first day back from an accident like mine, I'd think the same thing. But I wasn't worried about it; it was actually really exciting. My confidence swelled as I began punching the bag and it swung further than it had for a while. I felt invigorated by the fact I wasn't already dead on the floor; this workout was surpassing what I could do before the accident, and I was improving on a level I hadn't expected from myself.

I attacked the bag with different combinations and sparring techniques before deciding to bring in my legs. After my first few kicks, I brought my right leg up for a roundhouse as I felt a tremor race down my left leg. It kicked out from under me, and because my other leg was still connecting with the bag, I fell hard on my back. I gasped, trying to regain the air that had been knocked from me, and I felt the tingling sensation of a limb waking up from being asleep spread through my left leg. I glanced down as I heard Jace and Lars rushing over to me and watched as my left leg jerked back and forth on the floor.

"Are you okay?" Lars was standing over my head with his hands on his hips. Jace had come and knelt by my trembling leg, putting a heavy hand on my thigh.

I felt the warmth of his palm seep through my sweats as my leg continued to twitch, however the tremors had subsided considerably from the first. I felt my cheeks get warm as I realized how stupid that must have looked.

"Maybe you should keep the workout to this for now," Jace said quietly, watching my leg as the jerking stopped completely. He and Lars helped me to my feet, by now my left leg feeling quite numb.

Lars offered to be my human crutch after I tried to walk over to my bag and almost fell again. I declined, massaging feeling back into my leg for a moment before continuing. I limped over to my bag and pulled it towards the girls' locker room, aware of the two men following close behind in case I took another spill.

"I'm fine, guys, really," I smiled as I reached the locker room doors, starting to feel more embarrassed than worried about what had just happened. "I probably just pushed a little harder than I should have this morning."

Lars nodded and walked back to the benches, but Jace stayed where he was. He gave me a look that said, "Huh, I totally told you so," before stepping forward and grabbing my hand. "I thought you said the twitching stopped?"

"It had," I squeezed his hand. "I really think I just went a little harder than my body was ready for, I bet it just triggered it again. Momentarily of course, I feel fine now." I tried to sound convincing as I struggled to convince myself.

"Just be careful, okay?" He had that look in his eye again, and I felt like there was something he wasn't telling me.

"I always am, Jace," I stepped forward, letting go of his hand. "What happened? Are you okay?" I noticed a small cut over his eyebrow. I reached up to touch it.

He shrugged away from me. "Nothing, I'm just worried about you," he smiled. "I'm glad you're feeling better today, though."

I watched him walk back to Lars before entering the locker room. As I showered and dressed in my business-casual attire, my thoughts were consumed with the way Jace had looked at me. Was it because I told him I had to think about our relationship? Sure, now he gets to play the victim. I missed our friendship. I thought about what I could do to make him not feel awkward around me as I brushed through my long hair, flipping it to the front of my shoulders so that I could reach it better.

I finished my mascara just as the clock over the mirror struck 7:30, marking a half hour before I had to go relive my nightmare. I looked at my reflection in the mirror, my low ponytail and rose earrings standing out the most. I just had to remember that this was protocol, and completely normal; no one knew how much it had affected me but Jace, and to remain being seen as professional, I was going to keep it that way.

Jace and Lars waved to me as I made my way back to the elevators and up to my desk. It looked like they had left the weights and were now sparring on the mats. I wondered where Edith was, since I hadn't seen her since the day I woke up from my coma, when she came to visit. She was still on crutches then, but thankfully the surgeons had dug every last bit of those pellets out of her leg. I was excited to see her, but when I got to our desks she wasn't there. There was a card standing in front of my keyboard however, and judging by the rainbow and "Welcome Home" unicorn on the front, I figured it was from her. It had a stick figure picture on the inside of what I assumed was Edith laying upside down on her desk with crosses over her eyes, and a caption reading "Me, the whole time you were gone!" As well as a short note welcoming me back to work and stating how much she missed me.

I laughed to myself, setting down the card next to the framed picture of my dad and his horse, Donnie. I had no pictures of my mom on my desk, but that was only because the desktop picture on my computer was her and I at Disneyland in front of Cinderella's castle. It was a good memory, and before she had become a successful business woman, so I preferred it over any other pictures I had of her.

I slowly made my way through the office as

more and more people started arriving. I had received an email earlier from Jordine telling me where we were to meet for the debriefing. I reluctantly walked between cubicles and around people holding their precious cappuccinos, breathing in the strong smell of coffee beans and cream. It had always been one of my favorite scents, either in the mornings at home or at local bookstores connected to coffee shops. It helped calm my nerves as my watch ticked closer to 8:00.

I walked to a side of the floor I had only visited twice in my time at the office, where the cubicles were further spaced apart and there was a big glass office on one side, the view into which was blocked by drawn blinds. I walked past a group of men and women speaking in hushed tones around a larger cubicle.

"She must be crazy," I heard one of them say as I passed. I looked back, shocked that someone would be so forthright when I had never even spoken with them before. None of the people acknowledged me, however, as if they hadn't even said anything. They probably thought I didn't hear it.

I rolled me eyes and continued on. Maybe they heard about my accident and were surprised I was back already. I smiled at the ground as I neared the glass wall, thinking of how resilient and hardworking this must make me look. The truth was I just get bored out of my mind when I sit home with only my books, my piano, and Dot for company.

I rapped on the closed wood door with my knuckles, hearing the scraping of chairs and movement on the other side. As I waited, Jameson sidled up next to me with a file and briefcase in his hands.

"Hey Rapunzel," he said quietly, smoothing his tie under his suit coat.

"Hey Jameson," I watched as he fidgeted with his briefcase. He had dark bags under his eyes and a crease on his forehead. "You okay?"

"Just a long night," he smiled weakly. "And I was invited to this meeting last minute, literally, like two minutes ago. I guess because I was the head of the mission they expect me to testify with you."

"Testify?"

"Give an account. I already had my debriefing but apparently they needed someone other than Jace to sit in on this one."

I was about to ask why not Jace when the door finally opened, revealing Jordine and a group of men and women I had never seen before.

The meeting was long and consequently quite boring. Apparently, this board of people was the head of the catastrophic department, or in other words when things can go wrong or do go wrong they are the ones to deal with the mess. None of them looked the least bit surprised at McGregor getting away, however after I gave my account, standing in the front of the room like a schoolgirl giving an oral report, a few took interest in the fact that I was there at all. They asked many questions concerning how the drug felt entering my system, and if I've noticed any side effects since. I decided that I had to be honest considering I was reporting with the FBI, so I explained the nightmares, the sleepless nights, and the twitching muscles.

People were taking notes all around me as I spoke, making me feel like I was an inspected lab rat. I didn't like the feeling, so I spoke quickly and loudly, ensuring the fact that I didn't have to repeat myself and was able to sit down faster. Jameson gave a quick account on what happened on his side of the loading crates, and how Jace, the other team lead, had been incapacitated. He stressed the fact that the accident wasn't my fault, I was just a victim of the circumstance. I appreciated that.

Eventually Jordine dismissed Jameson and I, signaling our time to leave as the men and women in the room began comparing notes and discussing the situation. I stood up gratefully and Jameson followed me out of the room.

"I had no idea," he said quietly, looking at me as if I was a different person then who he had walked into the room with an hour and a half earlier.

"I'm fine now," I said, patting his shoulder. "That's all that matters."

"I guess that's true, I just didn't know the extent of your accident, or how the drug affected you and is still apparently affecting you."

I flinched. Jameson needed to think before he talked, because I was still very sensitive to the fact the drug was even still in me. "I know. Hey," I tried to turn the conversation. I was done feeling like an experiment gone wrong. "Why couldn't Jace have come into that one with us?"

"He's on probation," Jameson picked up on the hint. He started making his way back through the large cubicles. I followed. "The Board chose to put him there and didn't feel it was his right to share an account since they already heard his side."

"It wasn't even his fault," I muttered as we passed Jordine's office back on our side of the floor. "It was solely my choice."

"Don't burden yourself with the guilt, Rapunzel, and don't worry," Jameson clapped me on the back as we began parting ways. "He is still in on one of our cases, and if you would have been pinned for this one, you wouldn't be able to help us with it either."

He smiled, walking back to where his cubicle sat in the corner near the window. I didn't know if that was supposed to be comforting or not. I guess I was relieved they were inviting me in on another case so soon, but at the same time I was worried I would mess this one up as well.

* * *

Dot scoured the floor as I put my honey mustard chicken in the oven. I had made two pieces; just enough for a filling dinner tonight and a good lunch at work tomorrow. It had been a long day, and I looked forward to just sitting and relaxing. I set the timer on the microwave, then walked into my living room and glanced at the mirror hanging on the wall. My low ponytail hung in tangles down my back and my eyes had bags almost as large as Jameson's under them. I didn't notice I looked so tired till now and wondered if this appearance found me after I had faced the Board today.

I turned away from the mirror, not wanting to look into it again till I could get more sleep tonight. Jace had asked if I wanted to go on another date, but I had declined. And then, feeling bad about turning him down, I invited him over for a quiet night in. I was too tired from my first day back to do much else.

My head swam as I thought about our conversation earlier that day. He said he had tried to find more information about what drug had entered my system, but that he didn't get anything useful. He told me his source said it was an experimental drug, which did not make me feel any better about the situation. When Jace had given me the news, his eyes were sad, and his body language made me think that he was disappointed at having such little information. I was just moved that he even tried to find anything out when even the doctors couldn't detect it. Was this still just because of his guilt?

Sitting down at my piano, I started to play some simple melodies, trying to express my feelings through the keys. It was harder than I remembered though; my fingers continued to twitch toward the wrong notes, and I was hitting with more force than usual, making the loud clanking echo through my apartment. As I grew more frustrated with the sudden difficulty of playing, my thoughts turned to the gas mask man again, and how there was virtually no mercy when he attacked.

My emotions took over as my frustration turned to pure anger. This feeling had come over me a lot lately, mainly when I couldn't sleep because of the nightmares or when my body would convulse. I pounded out a made-up tune on the piano, deciding that playing songs I'd had memorized for years wasn't helping with anything.

As I played, I noticed my G key sounded off. Still thinking about McGregor and his ambush with the drug, I played a couple of scales to identify if it was just the one key that was out of tune. I hated it when my piano got out of tune; it made it unbearable to play. Thankfully, I had taken a piano tuning class a couple of summers after my senior year in high school.

I wrenched the top of the standing grand up, experiencing an involuntary flashback to the gas mask man picking my limp body off the ground before chucking me against a wall. I shook my head, trying to release my anger and focus on the thousands of strings connecting the keys to the backboard of the piano, all with tiny knobs to twist and turn to make it sound right.

I didn't have the equipment, but I felt confident I could do it by ear. I struck the G key again, listening to the dissonant sound only an out of tune key could make. I identified which strings were attached to it and reached in to twist the coinciding knobs.

The timer on my microwave went off, making me jump while I fingered the strings. I involuntarily jerked back, and with an ugly *clunk,* ten strings ripped up and out of the piano in my hand. Jerking again, I punched the strings back into it, dislocating several more in the process and leaving a gaping hole in the back of the piano.

Letting go of the strings and backing away, I looked at my hand where angry red lines and slivers were forming. I knew pianos were delicate, and needed to be treated with care, but I shouldn't have been able to pull out ten strings at once. I walked forward, stroking some of the keys. No sound came from the first four, but the fifth I hit was even more dissonant then the G that had started this whole mess.

Tears spilled over my cheeks as I placed the top back onto the piano. This was beyond repair, and I was in no financial state to buy a new one. I walked angrily to my microwave and punched the "Timer Off" button, my finger going completely through it and a spark jumping out at me. I stared at the hole I had just made in my microwave keypad, confused and frustrated. Everything was breaking.

The smell of burning mustard reached my nose and I put my head in my hands. I counted to ten to calm my breathing, then opened the oven gently and put on a mitt. Pulling out the smoldering chicken, I set down the pan and sat in a chair, looking around.

I had just broken my piano and my microwave in the space of two minutes. For the first time that day, my whole body felt rigid, tired. I lost my appetite as I looked at the chicken and ran to the bathroom to spit up the bile that had risen in my throat.

What was happening to me?

A knock came to my door. I stumbled towards it, feeling clumsy and exhausted. I thought about what happened earlier, and as softly as I could I pulled the door open. It swung in normally, revealing Jace on the other side with some flowers.

I smiled, relieved to see him. And then I collapsed onto the floor.

CHAPTER 10

Jace

My drive home was lonely. Radiohead played softly through my speakers as I waited in the traffic, my mind still slightly scrambled by what had happened. I had hoped to surprise Delilah with flowers and a movie, so that I could maybe get a chance to hold her, but she had passed out right as she opened the door. After carrying her to her bed, I put a damp towel on her head in hopes of reviving her, but she didn't wake for two hours. While I waited, I fell asleep next to her. I woke up to her poking my cheek and asking why I was in her bed.

After I explained that she had passed out, and asked if she had maybe gotten dehydrated, neither of us could figure out what happened. The pain in her eyes made me think there was a little more going on than she was telling me, however, so now in the busy midnight streets of New York my head spun with questions. Why didn't she trust me enough to tell me the full story? Why did she pass out right when I got to her door? I was silently grateful it had happened when I had arrived, however, and not when she was alone in her apartment. In the end, neither of us felt much like a movie, and while she did let me cuddle her as a comfort, our night was cut short.

I pulled up to a red light, right in between an empty taxi and a Coca-Cola semi, as my phone starting buzzing in my pocket. I pulled it out to see Jameson's name flashing across my screen. I tapped the answer button as the light turned green.

"Hello?" I asked, pulling forward.

"Jace, I need you at my place," his voice was panicked, "right now."

I merged lanes to better set a course for Jameson's apartment complex. "Is everything okay man?"

"You just—I just," there were pots clanking in the background. "I need your help."

"On my way," I ran a yellow. "Don't do anything stupid, man."

"I'll explain when you get here," *Click*. He was gone.

Reginald Jameson had always been a good friend of mine, and quite a sane person, but lately he had looked wearier and more exhausted than I had ever seen him. I secretly wondered if he had started using drugs or drinking more because the man hadn't looked well since we had gotten back from the McGregor mission. I was there when he gave his report, and I know some of the guilt of what happened to Delilah was resting on his shoulders as well. I often wondered if he felt the same way I did about it: that it was our fault.

It was a good thing no policemen were prowling the side alleys or streets as I flew down the road, trying to get to his complex as quickly as possible. That kind of guilt caused by this profession can result in serious trauma or depression and can lead people to make rash decisions. The more I thought about it, however, the more I realized that Jameson has dealt with a lot worse than an agent getting drugged. I ruled out the possibility that was clawing at the back of my mind; he wouldn't take his own life over this.

Pulling into the parking lot and jumping out of my car, I began to wonder if it was a hostage situation. Who would be after Jameson? Scenarios of what I could do to help ran through my mind as I skipped up the steps two at a time and came to a halt at the top of the hall. I listened; the door to my left revealed someone watching *Friends* behind it, and the door to my right was completely silent. I crept quietly down the hallway to 4B, Jameson's door, waiting to hear some sort of signal or indication the something wasn't right inside.

Nothing came. I heard the repeated creak in a floorboard behind his door, like someone pacing inside. Confused, I knocked.

The door opened right away, revealing a very haggard-looking Jameson. His tie was loose and crooked, his button-up untucked and only one sock on his foot. I would have thought he had been beaten up if I hadn't spotted the hickey he was trying to hide on his neck. Whoever she was, I hoped she wasn't still there.

"Thanks for coming, man," he ushered me inside, keeping one hand over the almost black mark on his already dark neck.

"What's going on?" I looked around. His front room was a mess; old newspapers and magazines scattered the coffee table, along with multiple plastic cups and plates with half eaten burritos on them. That was my confirmation that there were no women in the vicinity.

"Let me explain," he muttered, sitting on the edge of his couch and ringing his hands. "So, I never told you this, but I am in a relationship. Have been in one since, well, for almost two years."

"Two years?" I had never had the slightest inclination that Jameson had been in a relationship for longer than two months. "How'd you keep that from the whole office?"

"I'm in an interesting position with work. You know," he looked up. Seeing his eyes straight on for the first time tonight, I noticed the excitement in them. "I don't want any undesirable people finding out anything that could jeopardize my partner."

"I get it," I thought about Delilah. I wished I could just whisk her away so that I could hide her from the cruel criminal world. But I would never take her from doing what she loved, and that was what landed us in the predicament our relationship is in.

"Well, we were getting really serious, but

after the McGregor infiltration, with the close call I had with that one gangster and Delilah being attacked, she lost it." The memory made his face fall. "She said she couldn't handle the trauma of dating a secret agent, being kept a secret, and not knowing if I'll come home."

I nodded. I'd seen this many times. No wonder he had been looking so sick; he's going through a breakup.

"Jace you don't understand," he seemed to have read my mind. "Bridget's the best thing that has ever happened to me. She became my everything over the years; she's the reason I work so hard, the reason I continue to try and improve rather than be content where I'm at."

The reason behind Jameson's success was a girl. As cheesy as that sounded, I could kind of relate to the feeling.

"After she had her breakdown, she wanted to take a break. I couldn't handle it."

His voice wasn't bitter but determined. I felt like I was watching a soap opera.

"I decided to show her everything I could offer her, how good I was at not getting killed, and how I can protect those I care about. Jace, I wanted her to know that I would always protect her."

"Is this why you asked me over, Jameson? To confess? It's okay, we all go through bad breakups at some point in our lives."

Jameson's head snapped up, his face almost angry. But then it relaxed into a grin. "Break up?

Dude, we didn't break up!"

"Oh," I raised my eyebrows. Jameson was not the best storyteller, but this by far had to be his worst. "So, what happened, I guess?"

"After I proved to her what I could and would do for her, Bridget began to believe in our relationship again. We started going out almost every night again, and tonight. . ." his voice trailed off as he looked into space. "Tonight, she said she would marry me if she could."

He took a deep breath. I waited for him to go on, but that seemed to be it.

"So," I watched him to make sure I wasn't about to earn myself a knuckle sandwich. "Are you going to propose?"

He nodded slowly, unable to form the words with his mouth. He looked like he was going to vomit as I clapped him on the back and laughed out loud. This was way better than what I was expecting to find in this apartment, even if it was totally a conversation we could have had over the phone.

"Good on you, dude!" I stood, pulling Jameson up with me and guiding him to his refrigerator in the kitchen. Due to the depressing no-alcohol-on-weekdays policy, I pulled out two cans of Dr. Pepper. "Congratulations! When do I get to meet the lucky girl?"

"You don't think I'm crazy?" he held his soda limply. I took my celebration down a notch.

"I can tell you're crazy about her," I patted him on the back encouragingly, "Plus, girls drop subtle hints when they kind of want something. Blatantly saying that she would marry you? Come on, that's like waving the answers to your test right in your face."

Jameson smiled before downing his pop, crushing the can with one hand and walking to his bedroom. "One second," he said, leaving me standing alone in his messy kitchen.

He swaggered back out with more confidence than I had seen him with all week. He thrust a framed picture into my hand.

"Isn't she gorgeous?" the admiration in his voice made me smile. I could relate to being completely head-over-heels for someone. I pushed the fact that she may not feel the same out of my mind.

Glancing down at the picture, I saw Jameson with his arm around a skinny and tall red-head with a prosthetic leg. They were on a beach that I assumed was in California, judging this was from his summer trip last year. She had short cropped hair and millions of freckles splaying across her bare shoulders and one leg. Her smile was perfectly straight, and her dark eyes were bright with a look that could only be explained as love.

"Beautiful," I agreed. I kind of had more of a thing for darker girls, but as I looked at the picture of the two of them together, Jameson's smile made it apparent he had his whole world in his arm.

* * *

My phone buzzed loudly beside my pillow, waking me from a dreamless sleep. Squinting against the bright flashing screen, I saw Delilah's name shining next to the time. It was 4:57, earlier than even she should be waking up, especially because of what happened last night. Unplugging the charger cord, I sat up in the darkness and put the phone to my head.

"Hello?" I asked groggily, wiping sleep from my eyes.

There was sobbing on the other end. "Jace," Delilah's voice was panicked, "Jace, I need you to come over right now. I'm sorry."

Feeling more awake, I pushed off my bed sheet and walked to my door, turning on my lights. What are the chances of getting two urgent calls requesting my presence in the same 24 hours? "What happened? Are you okay?"

"I don't know," she didn't sound in pain, but she definitely sounded scared. "I woke up because I felt something wet against my face, so I turned on my lamp and...and..." she started crying again.

"What is it, Liles?" I had her on speaker now as I pulled on some basketball shorts and a hoodie.

"Jace, there's blood covering half my pillow," she said it softly, as if someone else was listening to our conversation that she didn't want to hear it. "I think...I mean, it's got to be mine."

My stomach dropped as I grabbed my keys and ran out the door. "I'll be there in a minute. Stay lying down if you can, not on that pillow though."

"I'm sorry," she said again, and I heard the creak of her bed. At least she hadn't tried to get up.

"Don't be, I'm already heading over," I jumped in my car and pulled out of my garage. "Stay where you are, I'll be there soon."

I raced through the streets of New York as the city was just beginning to wake up. People were already running to the underground station and calling taxis in the streets. I swerved around people as quickly as I could, avoiding the already growing lines of traffic and taking side streets with no lights. This was taking too long.

Finally, I pulled into Delilah's apartment parking lot, barely staying in the lines as I parked my car and jumped out. Taking the steps two at a time for the second time that night, I ran up to her floor and down the hall to her door. Trying the knob, I found that it was locked. I took a breath; I couldn't show my panic because I knew she probably felt enough already.

I knocked softly, wishing I didn't have to get her out of bed but not seeing an alternative short of breaking down her door. I waited patiently, but it didn't take long for her to come and open it up. As the door swung inward, I stared at Delilah. Her eyes were bloodshot, and her face was pale. Her right cheek and ear were tainted red where I assume the blood had collected under her head. I walked in, closing the door behind me before wrapping her robed body in my arms. I felt her go slightly limp, putting the effort of holding herself onto me for, again, the second time that night.

"I don't know what it's from," she said quietly as we shuffled slowly back to her bedroom. Turning on the light as we walked in, she pointed at her pillow without a word. She looked utterly disgusted.

I did my best to keep a straight face. I had to keep my composure for the both of us to avoid freaking her out more, but it was definitely a struggle once I saw her pillow. She was right; half of it was dominated by a pool of blood, slowly starting to dry onto her pillow case. It was dripping off the edge of the case onto her sheets, meaning there was enough there to explain why she was so pale.

Delilah stayed by the door. I turned back to her. "Are you feeling okay? Did you look for where it came from?"

I led her back to her bed, the side opposite the blood, and sat her down, picking through her hair to see if there was a cut on her head.

"I don't deal well with blood, Jace," she sounded woozy, and I could feel her shoulders sagging. "And I don't feel hurt at all. I have no idea where it would have come from."

Her scalp seemed intact, and apart from the little bit of dried blood above her ear, there wasn't much evidence pointing to a head injury. I knelt in front of her and held her face to look into mine. There was blood on her ear and the side of her face she would have been laying on. As I looked closer I saw a deeper and more fresh red in the corner of her mouth on the same side.

"Do you taste it?" I reached up and wiped the blood from her lips.

"Well yeah, but I woke up in a pool of it," she looked like she was going to throw up. I helped her up and led her to the bathroom.

"Stay here," she dropped to the floor and I propped her up against the toilet in case she did vomit, then walked out to her kitchen and got a glass of water. Coming back in, I handed it to her. "Swish a little bit of this around in your mouth, Liles."

"Okay," she tentatively sipped from the cup, swishing the liquid around with her cheeks.

"Now spit it out, don't swallow," I watched as she spit a stream of watery blood into the toilet. She looked up at me, horrified.

"At least now we know where it's coming from," I knelt and put her arm around my shoulder, helping her back up off the bathroom floor. "Let's get you to the doctor. If anything, they can at least pump the blood you're losing back into your system."

She nodded slowly. I walked her to the bedroom, too worried about how pale she was to investigate her mouth further. The physician could patch up whatever was bleeding as well, so my priority was to get her to the hospital. Delilah pulled on her sweatpants under her robe, then asked me to leave so she could put on an actual shirt. I waited outside her bedroom door, listening carefully for any sign of her falling over. Thankfully she didn't, and she opened the door to reveal what looked like a very comfy set of pajamas.

Dot had been curled up at the bottom of Delilah's bed through this whole thing and didn't seem too interested in us leaving either. Apparently, it was too early in the morning even for the cat. We grabbed Delilah's keys and purse as well as my keys before walking out of the apartment. I picked Delilah up at the top of the stairs to make sure she didn't fall down them and carried her to my car. After we were all situated, and she was lying back in the passenger seat, I drove like a madman once again through the streets of the city.

I wished Delilah lived closer to the hospital. It was ridiculous how busy the streets of New York can be even at five in the morning. The ride was silent, and it took longer than I liked to finally pull into the parking lot of the Emergency Care. I got out of the car and walked around to Delilah's side, opening her door and scooping her into my arms. She wrapped her arms around my neck and rested her non-bloody cheek on my chest as I walked up to the sliding doors.

I basically ran through the waiting area to the front desk. There was an older couple sitting in the corner, looking worried. They whispered something, and Delilah shot them a nasty look, but I hadn't heard what they said. The worker at the desk looked as tired as I felt, but she gave us her attention as soon as we stood in front of her.

"She's lost a lot of blood," I said before the

lady could even ask, and she thankfully shot into action straightaway, typing on her computer with spidery fingers. “She woke up in a pool of it this morning. She’s not in pain, and doesn’t know where it’s coming from, but I think it’s from her mouth. Her name is Delilah Hadley.”

The woman nodded as she finished typing. “Please sit in that front block to you’re right, a nurse will be out in about 3 minutes to get her. I will need her insurance information before the end of the visit. You’re fine to bring it out once she’s stabilized.”

As I set Delilah down in one of the chairs and let her head lean against my stomach, two men in deep blue suits and sunglasses swaggered in through the front doors. I wondered what business these men in suits had in a hospital, but didn’t have much time to dwell on it because not a minute later a nurse came out calling Delilah’s name. They had brought a stretcher as well, so I helped perch her on it before they wheeled her away.

I followed them down the hall and tried to walk into the room with them, but one of the nurses stopped me. “We will stabilize her and start pumping blood into her system. Then we will find the problem and see if it is something we can fix without surgery. Please wait out here until we are finished.”

I nodded, watching over the short man’s head as two doctors and a couple nurses surrounded Delilah’s bed. I sat down hard on one of the chairs they had lined up on the back wall of the hall, my head in my hands. Delilah was worth it. I didn't have to tell myself this, I already knew. I knew because the way Jameson talked about his soon to be fiancé last night; that was how I felt about Delilah. I just wished I could fix it for her, take away all the side effects of what had happened to her. But I couldn't, so the next best thing was to be there for all of them.

The reality of only getting three hours of sleep hit me like a bag of potatoes, and my head drooped from side to side as I waited for someone to come and tell me everything was going to be alright. Many people in scrubs walked in and out of Delilah's room, some carrying bags of blood, others carrying samples in bags of who knows what. I tried to stay awake as I waited, listening carefully to see if I could get any insights on her condition.

Just as I had given up, placing my chin in my hands and letting my eyelids flutter, a Hispanic nurse placed her hand on my shoulder. "You are good to go into the room with her, *carino*," she smiled kindly. "She is stable and awake. A doctor will be in to give you what we found."

I walked into the small room, Delilah smiling up at me weakly from her bed. Her eyes looked heavy, like it was hard for her to keep them open. I knew how she felt; to an extent anyway. As soon as I sat down beside her, she stuck out her tongue. A huge patch of white gauze was taped around it.

"Grosh, huh?" she laughed bitterly as she drew it back in, the gauze causing her words to slur and adding an extra "sh" to the end of everything.

"How do you feel?" I put my hand over hers, relief washing over me to see her at least joking about it.

"Weak, but okay," she flipped her hand over so that our fingers could intertwine, excluding the one that had the clamp thing on it to measure her heartbeat. But then she let go. My shoulders sagged. "Apparently I ground off the side of my tongue with my teeth." She made a gagging noise.

"Yeah that is kind of gross. Wouldn't that hurt, like, a lot?"

"You would think," she shrugged as a tall, potbellied man walked into the room.

"How are we doing Miss Hadley?" he asked Delilah as he started checking all of the machines she was hooked up to. I had a horribly vivid flashback to the last time we were in a hospital room together and Delilah wasn't even conscious. I said a silent prayer of thanks that that wasn't the case this time.

"I'm alright," she looked at me with her big blue eyes before turning back to the doctor. "Do you know what happened?"

"As far as we can tell," the doctor started, making me feel less confident in him already. I learned last time that they don't always know exactly what is going on. "You grind your teeth when you sleep, and your tongue got caught in the crossfire last night. What we can't figure out," he tapped his clipboard. "Is why it didn't hurt and wake you up right away."

"That's what we were just wondering," I nodded, "Have you guys heard of anything like this?"

The doctor nodded, and Delilah gave a relieved sigh. "You see, when people take intense pain killers, it numbs the nerves. Makes it so you can't feel. While we couldn't trace any such drug in Miss Hadley's system, we have seen people come in before with similar injuries because they couldn't feel the pain of what they were unconsciously doing."

"So, you're saying my nerves are shot?" Delilah asked quietly.

"The symptoms are pointing to that as the solution. However, the effects of such drugs wear off after about 48 hours. Have you recently felt less aching in your limbs, maybe as you lift heavier objects or do things you haven't done in a while?"

I looked over at her. She was able to do more pull-ups than before the other day. She had related to me how her muscles hadn't felt sore after.

"Have you been taking any drugs that may result in these kinds of extreme numbing effects?"

Delilah turned slowly to me, and the realization hit me the same time I saw the fright flash through her eyes.

"Not willingly," she replied as a tear slipped down her pale cheek.

CHAPTER 11

Delilah

Wind howled through the buildings as rain pounded the pavement. I walked swiftly toward the tall brick building looming over an abandoned park, glancing over my shoulder as I went. I felt like I was being followed, but I couldn't see anyone behind me. Facing forward once more, I picked up my pace, but I didn't seem to be gaining any ground toward the building. I peeked down the alleyway that was passing by and saw a giant man in a gas mask running full speed toward me.

My legs jerked as I tried to run, waking me from the nightmare. I glanced over at my alarm clock, the red light shining an early 4:07 into the room. I sat up and clicked on my bedside lamp, checking my pillow for any more blood. Thankfully the case was as green as it was when I had gone to bed. I rubbed my hands down my face, apologizing for kicking the now meowing Dot at my feet.

I doubted I would sleep anymore, so I got up and dressed. I found out a few days ago that I had virtually no noticeable physical limitations and, deciding I should see exactly what I could do, I figured it would be a good time to experiment. No one, not even Jace, would be at the gym this early in the morning.

I decided to take my car since it was so early —there was no chance of me being late. It was raining lightly and with each pitter-patter on the roof of my jeep I would think vividly of the nightmare I had just had. When would these dreams stop? Would I be stuck with them forever? As I parked and made my way through the garage, I noticed the same two men in suits who I had seen earlier last week sitting outside the door to the gym. Neither of them spoke a word as I passed, but one gave a curt nod before lighting a cigarette. I thought it was odd they would be here this early, but last time I saw them they were leaving a little later in the morning, so maybe they just worked a night shift in the same building. The thought didn't diminish the uncomfortable feeling of them watching me walk through the doors, however.

Again, I was relieved to find the gym empty and dark. Switching on the lights, I didn't know what I wanted to do first. If I had no limits, did I even have to warm up? I decided to take a jog around the track just in case, feeling the familiar sensation of being watched. There were no windows throughout the entire gym, and as far as I could see it was completely empty. I figured it must have just been aftershock from the nightmare, so I pushed the feeling out.

I worked tirelessly, moving from push-ups to pull-ups, from sit-ups to the weights, and back to running around the track a couple of times. I did burpees and jumping jacks and medicine ball exercises, all without feeling the slightest bit of weakness in my muscles as I went. Deciding to take a break and walking over to my bag for a water bottle, a thought struck me: I had poked a hole in my microwave. I had punched and broken my piano. While not feeling any limit to my exercises was one thing, I had never been strong enough to do something like that before.

Sitting down, I tried to think what might have happened. As I had done my weights earlier, while I could do more reps than before, I didn't feel like I could handle more weight. I drank my water, trying to think what would cause a bout of seemingly extra ordinary strength. Was I doing anything different at the time those things happened than I normally do?

A feeling of breathlessness overcame me that had nothing to do with the workout I had just done. A possibility occurred to me, but I had no idea how to test it. Standing and walking over to the punching bag hanging from the ceiling, I inspected it. This was a fairly new sandbag, one the maintenance had put in just a month or two ago, because it wasn't here before my accident. I stood back, thinking.

I was angry when I had pulled out the strings of my piano, angry when I made sparks fly from the microwave pin pad. Placing a well-aimed punch to the midsection of the bag, my mind began to race as I tried to think of things that would make me angry.

My mom was one. She left my dad to "be free". He was now alone in the house he had worked so hard to build for a family he thought would live there forever. I kicked the bag with all my might. Now his would-be lifelong companion was off gallivanting with so-called businessmen in Nashville and his only daughter had been attacked and left. . .crippled.

Crippled. I elbowed and kneed. I was crippled, not only physically but emotionally as well. They left me with no nerves. I performed a combo on the bag that made it swing dangerously. They left me with these nightmares. I could feel something surging through me as I swung my fist out powerfully, connecting with the bag and hearing a simultaneous tear and *thwomp.*

I stepped back, breathing hard. The bottom of the swinging bag had burst, and the sand that used to be encased now covered the perimeter of the floor below it. I swayed as I stared, beginning to feel slightly lightheaded. I staggered to my bag, dragging it behind me as I made my way to the locker room. I heard the now empty punching bag fall off the hook and hit the ground as I closed my eyes, my head spinning as I felt my way into the bathroom.

Collapsing in front of a toilet, I wretched and gagged till water and bile surged from my throat. A ringing in my ear left spots in my vision as I continued to lose whatever liquid had entered my body in the last few hours. I slumped against the wall of the stall, closing my eyes and willing the incessant throbbing to stop reverberating through my brain.

My experiment had been successful; now I just had to deal with the results.

* * *

I had spent more time in the locker room than I originally planned and clocked in a little later than I would have liked upstairs. My body felt exhausted; not in a sore way however, but in an "I-just-threw-up-my-entire-stomach" way. By the time I made my way up to mine and Edith's office, the whole floor was buzzing with people already busy with assignments. When I first arrived, my little corner was empty, but as I sat down and turned on my computer Edith sauntered in with a cup of coffee.

"No crutches!" she said excitedly, shaking her legs at me. And then her eyes narrowed, "Are you okay?"

"I'm fine," I said truthfully; after spending an hour or so recovering in the locker room, I felt mostly back to normal. "Why?"

She watched me suspiciously as she sat down in the desk beside mine. "You look as pale as, well, not a ghost because you're too dark for that, but close."

I took a sip of my water. "I threw up this morning," I figured I could give her some honest answers concerning what happened that morning, if not everything. "I must have eaten something bad last night."

Edith leaned forward and felt my forehead with the back of her hand. Reflexively, I jerked back, feeling a rush of mistrust for her. She drew her hand back, her eyebrows raised.

"Sorry," I said, leaning forward so her hand could rest on my skin again. I didn't know what my problem was; the motion wasn't even threatening.

"Well, you don't have a fever," she said slowly, still watching me out of the corner of her eye. "I'm sorry you threw up!"

"Oh, it's alright," I tried to play the whole thing off. I don't know why I felt so suspicious of her checking my temperature. I felt shaken by a motherly act, and I had no reason to be. "I feel fine now. Congrats on not being gimpy anymore, by the way."

The rest of the morning went by without incident; by the time noon rolled around it was as if my little episode hadn't even happened, and apparently the color had come back to my face. Edith had offered me oatmeal and bananas, saying I should get something in my stomach, and, after finally giving in, she chatted the hours away like normal, satisfied that I was healthy again.

I made my way to the break room alone to grab my lunch, slightly disappointed that I hadn't seen Jace all morning, but also slightly grateful. I had been battling with myself, debating whether to tell him what happened in my workout. I didn't know where our relationship was going, or what I could trust him with anymore.

"She's completely out of her mind," came a voice from behind a cubicle wall. It was a soft whisper, and I couldn't help but feel the speaker was regarding me. I peeked over the wall and saw a chubby man with a big mustache.

"Hadley!" Gordo glanced up at me, a wide smile ruffling his impressive mustache. "I didn't know you were back in the office already!"

The voice I heard had not sounded like Gordo's thick German timbre; however, I noticed another man in a dark blue suit that looked like he was walking away from the cubicle. I wondered if they had just been discussing rumors about me.

"Hey Gordo," I smiled, reaching over the wall and shaking his hand, "I've been back for a week or so! I didn't know you worked on this side of the floor."

The big man stood up, putting his hands on his hips and stretching his back, making his round belly flop over his belt. "Oh, it's just a temporary office for now; my cubicle is on the next floor up, actually! They have decided to do some renovating up there, so I was relocated down here last Friday."

"Renovating? I haven't heard any sounds from that..." My stomach started to rumble greedily, but I wanted to ask who the man was that Gordo was just talking to, so I continued the conversation.

He stroked his furry lip, glancing up at the ceiling. "You sure about that? I hear them drilling from the time I get in to the time I leave. . .maybe they're only working right over my head though."

"Yeah, maybe," I looked in the direction the man had walked away. "Hey, who was that man you were just speaking with?"

Gordo suddenly looked uncomfortable, confirming my suspicions. "What man?" He scrunched his bushy eyebrows at me.

I resisted the urge to roll my eyes. "I swear I just a saw a man in a blue suit jacket walking away from your desk," I pointed in the direction I saw him go. "Plus, I overheard voices in your cubicle before I stopped in."

Gordo's acting improved slightly as he began to look confused. He glanced back in the direction I pointed and absently reached up to straighten his tie. "Hadley, I think you're seeing things, I haven't seen any blue suits around here since the 80's."

I was about to argue when I realized I had seen the man before. He was one of the men smoking outside of the gym that morning. Maybe he was talking to someone else in the vicinity, as there were two other people sitting in cubicles connected to Gordo's. How Gordo didn't manage to see him, I had no idea, but I decided to let it go.

"You're right, I'm probably just hallucinating." I waved before continuing toward to the breakroom.

As I pulled out my Tupperware full of leftover stir fry, Jace came rushing into the room. He looked anxious and annoyed, but as soon as he saw me his eyes brightened.

"Liles," he walked over quickly, reaching out as if to grab my arm but rethinking last minute and reaching up to comb through his hair with his fingers. "How are you? I'm sorry I haven't been in contact, it's been. . . busy."

Feeling comforted that he felt some remorse for not visiting, I led him over to a microwave and popped my food in. "I'm alright! I got a little sick this morning, but I'm fine now," I wondered what had him so worked up, and almost felt jealous toward it till I realized there was no relationship for me to be jealous for. My head throbbed slightly at the prospect of the mess of a friendship we had.

He looked behind his shoulder at the groups of people throughout the room. "I'm sorry you were sick," he looked upset. "I would have come to your office earlier, but Jameson has me running around like a chicken with my head cut off," he leaned in, keeping his voice quiet, "He thinks he may have found another lead on McGregor's whereabouts."

My heart skipped a beat as I dropped the fork I was pulling out of my lunch bag. "Another lead?" I asked, trying to sound casual as a nervous lump formed in my throat.

Jace picked up the fork and went to hand it back to me. I had to fight the instinct to back away like I did with Edith, again questioning what was wrong with me.

"We may even be debriefing Jordine on it this afternoon, if we can get all our ducks in a row," he sounded optimistic, but there was an edge to his voice. His eyes grew concerned. "Jameson wants to include you in all of it as well, but if you're not ready —"

"I'm ready," I said resolutely. An overwhelming desire for revenge flooded my gut at the prospect of finding McGregor again. "I can handle it, and I would love to help you guys out."

Jace didn't look convinced, but he smiled nonetheless. "I'll let Jameson know to include you in the email, then," he shrugged and looked around again, as if scared we were being overheard. "I would do it myself, but I'm not technically supposed to be working on anything like that."

The microwave beeped, making me flinch. Thankfully, he didn't notice as he tugged absent-mindedly at his tie.

"How's your elbow?" I nodded to his bruised arm as I started shoveling broccoli and carrots into my mouth.

"Could be better," he checked his watch. "I think the doctor took the cast off prematurely, but I've got most of my motion back, so I'll be okay. Listen, I've got to get back to Jameson so that we can finish up this mess."

I nodded, setting down my food and following him out into the hallway. As we passed a table, I heard multiple whispers and caught the word "insane", but I told myself the world doesn't revolve around me and the chance of a bunch of strangers talking about me was slim.

It was obvious that Jace was in a hurry, but all I really wanted to do was talk to him about everything going on. I grabbed his arm before he turned the corner.

"Could we do something tonight?"

"I can't tonight," he glanced away awkwardly. I raised an eyebrow suspiciously. "Oh, nothing like that," he said quickly, putting up both hands in defense, "My mom called and told me she may be stopping by tonight, and I would rather be at my home with her than have her there alone."

I smiled. "I could come meet her," maybe I wouldn't tell him tonight, if his mother was present. "It's only fair; you've already met my father."

Jace chuckled softly. He ran his hand through his hair again and I bit my lip, trying to resist kissing him. I was feeling oddly impulsive today. "I don't know if she could handle meeting my girlfriend—I mean, a girl friend tonight, Liles," when he looked up, his eyes were sad. "My grandpa, her dad, just passed away."

I tried to ignore the awkward correction and pulled him into a hug, wrapping my arms around his neck. "I'm sorry," I said softly. I meant it. "I understand. If she goes to bed early, give me a call, okay?"

He nodded, sniffing slightly as he pulled out of the hug and told me he'd catch me later. I watched him go before heading in to finish my lunch, plotting which dessert would best express my condolences, and affection.

* * *

The conference room was crowded, with few chairs to sit in, leaving the space standing room only. Agents from Jameson's team who had last investigated McGregor lined the walls, while Jordine and some of her consorts sat in the back talking quietly. I stood next to Jace, who was trying to blend in as much as possible to avoid being asked to leave.

Jameson stood up in front of the room and cleared his throat. The room quieted down, however many people continued to mutter conversations from the corners of their mouths. Feeling bugged, I rolled my eyes before facing the front.

"Thanks for meeting here everyone, and on such short notice," He looked around, his shiny bald head glinting under the fluorescent lights. "We think we may have had another breakthrough in the McGregor case."

Silence swept through the room, making me afraid everyone would hear my pounding heart.

"I'm just going to get straight to the point," Jameson hesitated for a split second, looking uncomfortable. He wasn't as confident this time as he was before our last mission, and his voice seemed more tired and strained then I'd ever heard it. "Since we were so close to getting him the last time we investigated, my team and I figured we were headed in the right direction. Conducting reconnaissance and investigations throughout a trail of rumors followed from the shipment dock we first infiltrated, we have zeroed in on two possible hideouts for McGregor and the heads of his gangs."

A girl in the corner whispered something in her partner's ear. I heard other's exchange thoughts as Jameson let the sentiment settle in. I tried to catch Jace's eye, but he continued to look forward.

"He's acting weird," Jordine's voice whispered from behind me. It was odd to hear her say something like that, so I glanced back to see her sitting quietly and watching Jameson with pursed lips. I agreed, of course, but if that was loud enough for me to hear it was definitely something Jameson would have heard as well.

Jameson raised his hand to quiet everyone, then continued, "We have identified a tunnel leading off the underground in west Manchester to the basement of an old hotel that is not in the schematics of the building; this is where we think his main contacts for operations are held."

"And the second place?" a tall man with a deep voice asked from the corner. He had wide ears and a skinny nose; I had never seen him before, not even in the last mission.

Jameson glanced quickly in my direction. "The second is an abandoned pharmacy just west of Jackie Robinson Parkway, which is where we think he is manufacturing a new homemade drug."

I took a deep breath. McGregor was making the drug he poisoned me with right under our noses.

And now we knew where he was. The anger that had boiled inside me earlier surged through my body again, surprising me. I tried to push it down as Birdy moved next to Jameson, holding up a file folder.

"We have received information that McGregor has been in town since Sunday and is planning to stay for the next week or so, at one of these two locations," her voice was melodious and deep; it was the first time I had heard her talk in person. "We will want to move quickly if we want any chance to apprehend him. Jameson and I have already strategized a course of response, now we just need to assemble teams and choose a date of action. I personally think tonight or tomorrow would be best."

Many people started talking at this point, not bothering to keep their voices down. I saw the fiery red hair of Paula Gray in the corner, her mouth speeding off as she conversed with a very tan and chiseled man in a gray shirt. Checking over my shoulder, I saw Jordine in a deep and quiet discussion with the woman sitting next to her, a hand covering her mouth as she spoke. Again, I looked to Jace for any sign of a reaction, but he continued to watch Jameson with such an intense gaze it made me uncomfortable. What was he watching for?

Following Jace's eyes, I watched as Jameson was shuffling through the papers in front of him, shaking his head slightly. His demeanor made it seem like he was having some sort of internal struggle, but not till he cleared his throat and raised his hand in front of the crowd once more did I notice his watery, bloodshot eyes.

"No," he said, looking from Birdy to the rest of the people in the room in turn. His eyes lingered on Jace slightly longer than anyone else. "No, we cannot and will not send a response team so quickly."

Birdy's face flashed surprise before nodding quickly and stepping aside again. Apparently, Jameson was the superior in their partnership. People shared quick glances, but the room remained quiet as Jameson sighed, running a handkerchief over his dark, glistening forehead.

"I apologize, but the lack of additional substantial evidence and the feeling in my gut are telling me that this is premature," Jameson nodded as if trying to convince himself that he was right. "I feel like we need a bit more to go off than what we've got. I'm sorry."

He hung his head as people began conversing again, some complaining loud enough for the whole room to hear. Birdy came to her partner's aid, slamming her file folder on the table to get the room's attention.

"We will continue investigations till we feel satisfied enough to act," she stood boldly in front of the restless room. Apparently, I wasn't the only one waiting to get my hands on McGregor. "We will assemble again at that point. Thank you."

Taking the dismissal, people slowly started filing out. Jace excused himself and went up to Jameson quietly. Frustration and disappointment washed over me, but I willed myself not to be angry with Jameson. He was just being cautious, right? Never mind the fact that the man responsible for everything that has happened to me is so close and so vulnerable.

My hands jerked and twitched as I scooted into the line of people exiting the room. I clasped them together, trying to hold them steady as I heard Jordine whisper behind me, ". . . It's suspicious, for sure," her voice turned toward me. "You should keep an eye on him."

I turned around, seeing Jordine a step or two behind me. She made eye contact with me and then nodded before looking back to the same woman she had conversed with earlier.

It wasn't often Jordine was so indirect, but I took the order in stride as I supposed she was trying to be discreet. She was right, of course, that Jameson was acting suspicious. As I got back to my desk, I figured I could keep tabs on him for the rest of the time we were at work, just to see if we were maybe missing something important.

I made my way over near Jameson's cubicle anytime I could, ignoring the printer closest to my desk and crossing the entire floor to use the one to the right of his. I decided now would be a good time to print all the documents on my computer that needed signatures. Jameson sat at his desk whenever I passed, typing on his computer or shoving things in his filing cabinets. Noticing the McGregor file being among the papers stuffed in a cabinet as I walked past, I finally let my frustration take over. Why wasn't Jameson working on it harder? We could finally put this lunatic in a high voltage prison, and Jameson wasn't even trying.

I saw Jace once or twice throughout the rest of the day, however he seemed as distracted as Jameson each time. I had to keep telling myself that he had just lost a relative so that my anger wouldn't get directed toward him in any way. I didn't want all of this overflowing to Jace and ruining any chance we had together. His actions were perfectly normal, whereas Jameson's were completely unacceptable in my mind.

Five o'clock came around quickly and, giving up on the monotony of checking on Jameson's boring endeavors, I decided to clock out just a couple of minutes early. Slinging my purse over my shoulder, I said goodbye to Edith and made my way to the office doors, taking out my phone to send a text to Jace. Looking up as I reached the connecting hallway to the staircase, I saw Jameson standing with his head down in front of the elevators. I hesitated as I watched the numbers ticking past floors as the lift reached them; I usually took the stairs to at least the tenth floor, but this would be a good chance to watch Jameson one last time. I felt anxious about entering an enclosed space with someone I had been so upset with all day, though, which made the choice a bit harder.

Making a last-minute decision as the elevator doors began to close, I tripped past them, running into Jameson's broad chest. He caught my arms, gave me a weak smile, and steadied me as he pressed the button for the 17th floor, the floor above ours. I tried to not look surprised.

"Hey Rapunzel," he said, his voice contrastingly scratchy to his usual smooth tone. "Aren't you going down?"

Why was he going to the floor where there was construction? I guess this is what Jordine meant. "Actually, I have an appointment up on the 20th," I said, watching him punch the button for me before stepping to the side. "Are you okay today?"

"Oh, I'm good, just a little tired," he replied, keeping his eyes to the floor. "Got a lot going on. I'm sorry if I got your hopes up about the McGregor case."

I tried to act nonchalant as a weight dropped in my stomach. "It's no big deal, I trust your gut." The lie came quietly as my hands began to quiver. I shoved them into the pockets of my jacket as the elevator doors rang open on the next floor up.

"See you later, then," he said, before stepping onto the demolished wasteland of a floor. I glimpsed at least four broken pillars and construction tape surrounding the perimeter before the doors clanged shut again.

Promptly pushing the next floor up, the elevator came to a rattling stop and let me out in an unfamiliar office. Hoping no one there noticed how ridiculous I must have looked, I rounded out of the elevator and towards the stairs. Skipping down them two at a time, I quietly opened the door to the 17th floor, hearing someone speaking as I entered. I picked my way around the wreckage of the remodeling, trying to identify where Jameson's voice was coming from. As I continued forward I began to better understand what he was saying.

"...in the time that we have," he said exasperatedly. He was somewhere over to my left. "She has no idea what's going to happen, but I think she's beginning to catch on."

Inching forward as quietly as I could over the broken pieces of drywall, I peeked around a fallen beam and caught sight of him. Jameson was standing in front of a window that overlooked a good part of downtown, fiddling with something on the only desk still standing on the debris-covered floor. The light from outside made his silhouette too dark and hard to look at, so I focused on the floor as he continued.

"I know it isn't going to work right now, that's why I'm pushing it back," he sounded annoyed. Was he talking about the McGregor infiltration? "We have to have the element of surprise on our side, and if it works the way I want she'll never see it coming."

She? From what I'd seen McGregor was definitely a man.

Jameson paused, evidently listening to the person on the other end. I stayed quiet, crouching mostly hidden by the beam in between us, but if he turned towards me any more he would be sure to see me. Taking the moment of silence, I bent lower and looked around. I wondered why I hadn't heard any of the tools that would cause so much destruction right above me.

"She knows some kind of change is happening," Jameson said slowly, knocking something off the desk where he fiddled. As he bent down to pick it up, I used the distraction to move my position to where his back was facing me completely. "But she doesn't really connect that it's because of my choice. I just don't know how she'll handle the changes once they all come to light."

My breath caught as a thought struck me. Was he talking about me? Jameson knew something was happening to me, he must be the reason I felt like I was always being watched. But could he be the cause of it?

"... Still beautiful, yes," his voice was starting to relax, he sounded less frustrated. "She still feels some pain from the accident but for the most part everything is falling back into place. I just know the Boss is happy she's even still alive."

Rage surged through me. Some pain? That accident has caused so much more than just some pain. Who was this "boss" he was talking about? Was it McGregor? I felt my leg quiver slightly, putting me in danger of falling forward into the beam covering me. I shifted my weight to my other leg as I squinted against the light of the window, trying to see what Jameson was messing with on the desk.

"I'm just waiting for his permission to proceed, that's all," Jameson started to turn, making me duck down lower so that he wouldn't spot me. More silence followed as he surveyed the desolate floor.

"No, I'm just on the 17th collecting some things I left up here before the demolition is completed."

As I stayed low behind the beam, looking out through a little hole level with my eyes, I finally saw what he was fiddling with on the desk. I felt like the wind had been knocked out of me as I recognized the straps of a gas mask in his fingers, the rest of it facing down on the desk. There was also a map with different pins splayed across the desktop along with two or three testing vials.

My mind reeled as I connected Jameson's height and girth with that of the man who attacked me, as well as how none of the man's skin was showing to reveal his ethnicity in the alley. With my stomach churning and my breathing rapid, I flashed back to how Jameson's health and overall demeanor had changed since the accident. That's how McGregor got away so easily, how Jameson wasn't there for any of the action on our end and allowed Jace to get injured.

He was working for McGregor.

I stood, pure fury surging through my limbs as they quaked. Jameson gave me a surprised look before setting down the mask he was fiddling with.

"Hey, I've got to go," he said quietly, setting down the phone. "Were you listening to my private conversation, Rapunzel?" As he came nearer a concerned look came over his face, taking in my defensive stance. "Are you okay?"

I wanted to scream at him, tear him apart. He was double-crossing everyone, not only Jace and I. He was betraying all of us and acting like I was the one that needed help. "It was you." I accused, stepping around the beam that separated us.

Jameson stopped his advance toward me, looking confused. "What was me?"

"How long have you been working for him, Jameson? Or is Reginald Jameson just an alias you live under?" My voice trembled as much as my body.

He held up both his hands. "Delilah, what are you talking about? Work for who?"

"Stop lying!" I said loudly, frustrated that he was still trying to keep up the nice guy act.

"I haven't even said anything," His bloodshot eyes swept over me as he took a step away. "Calm down, Delilah."

"Calm down?" I felt hysterical, tears spilling from my eyes. "How can I calm down?"

Feeling the same strength break through me as I had this morning, I picked up the dense concrete beam I had hid behind and broke it over my knee, barely aware of the debris ripping my pants. "Look what you did to me!"

Fright flitted over Jameson's face as he watched the broken beam fall to the ground. I continued advancing as he backed into the wall behind him.

"I didn't do anything to you," his voice

quivered slightly as he kept his eyes locked on mine. "Delilah, I think you're misunderstanding—"

I screamed and lunged myself at him. I was in pure shock at his double-crossing, and I felt determined to get a confession out of him. He stepped forward to catch me but I ducked out of his reach, twisting and aiming for his side.

Jameson dodged away just before my fist connected with his rib cage, continuing to face me and turning his back on the rest of the floor. My frustration and rage tunneled into attack mode as I chased after him, not wanting to hear any more of his lies. I swung and kicked sporadically, trying to catch an arm or a leg, just to cause enough pain for him to give in, to feel what I felt. But he danced further away, heading towards the exit.

He could not get away. I was not going to make that mistake again. Taking advantage of a second-long glance over his shoulder to the elevators, I jumped forward and threw my fist into his chest. A disgusting crack reverberated up my arm as he flew ten feet back, slamming into a wall and collapsing another beam over the top of him.

My breath caught. Tears flowed freely as I ran across the floor, lifting the beam off of Jameson's limp body. My hands were covered in dust as I reached to prop him up, his ebony head shiny with blood. Lifting my fingers to his neck, I searched relentlessly for a pulse.

There was none.

I screamed again, devastation washing over

me. I felt the adrenaline quickly leaving my body, and not wanting to be found standing over a dead body, I raced back to the elevators and pounded the parking button. The button stayed in instead of popping back out as I became briefly aware of the nausea overcoming me. Miraculously, no one joined me for the ride down. I staggered forward as the elevator doors opened, barely making it to my car before vomiting all over the cement in front of my parking space. After I was sure I didn't have anything left in me to throw up, I lay in the back of my jeep, waiting for the pulsing in my head to alleviate before attempting to drive.

It seemed impossible to stop the pounding, however, because my mind was still reeling at the fact that Jameson was dead. I couldn't let anyone know what happened, not even Jace. I had to prove Jameson was a traitor before anyone found out how he died.

CHAPTER 12

Jace

I really wasn't planning on lying to Delilah. I've always prided myself in being an honest gentleman and tried to find comfort in the fact that my lie wasn't fully untrue. My grandpa had just passed away; I had received the news this morning. However, he lived in Washington, and that was where the funeral would be this weekend, meaning my mother would be nowhere near New York anytime soon.

Guilt washed over me as I drove down the pot-holed road. The setting sun glowed on the squat, yellowish penitentiary ahead of me, its tall barbed wire fences stretching as far around the building as I could see. I shook off the feeling of regret as I pulled to the checkpoint before the fence, rolling down my window and flashing my badge to the security cameras. No words were exchanged through the intercom as the fence began sliding apart. I watched, convincing myself it was better to keep this idea to myself for now. I doubted Delilah was quite ready to meet her attacker.

As I pulled my car into a faded parking space, two armed guards walked forward from the only entry I could see on this side of the building. I got out of the car to meet them, holding up my badge and opening my suit to show my gun.

"Mr. Avery," one guard read aloud as they approached. He shrugged. "I'm sure you know the protocols of entering a prison." He nodded to the gun at my side.

"I'd feel more comfortable leaving it in the care of one of your guards then in my car," I replied in a business-like manner. I had to show that I wasn't here out of personal interests. "Can I drop it off at the front desk with my keys?"

Both men nodded, leading the way into the old building. We passed through several badge-activated doors just to get to the lobby, where a man and woman sat with multiple computer screens in front of them. The one window behind them did not relieve the overall suffocated feeling in the room. The pair both looked up from their monitors as we entered.

"Jace Avery?" the woman asked in a monotone alto. She looked middle-aged and hard, like she could break the desk in front of her in half if she wanted. "Identification please."

I pulled out my badge once more, along with my passport and my wallet with my license in it. Laying them on the desk in front of the woman, I watched as she went through each form, typing things into her computer with pudgy fingers.

"Please remove any weapons from your person," she said, placing my things back on the edge of the desk. "You will also have to go through a screening before entering the facility."

Unstrapping the holster from my belt, I placed the gun in front of the woman, as well as the switchblade from a pocket and my other pistol from an ankle strap. "Do you mind watching over these, as well as my wallet and keys, while I'm in?"

Without looking up, the woman grunted and elbowed the silent man next to her. He coughed and stood, collecting my things from the desktop. "I'll put them in my lock box here," he gestured to a cabinet near his feet, one I hadn't noticed until he opened it and set my personal items within. "When you're all done, I will return them to you."

"Thank you," I said, making sure I saw his key turn in the lock before allowing myself to be led from the area. I had called ahead to make this appointment, giving the excuse of investigating a previous case for information on a new one, which was sort of true. They hadn't questioned, thankfully, when I made sure they knew who I was there to see.

For the past two weeks, I had been researching the men I had apprehended in the alleyway. I was able to find names and previous felony records once I had located which prison they had been carted off to. It helped that, given my position at work, I had access to any information I wanted.

The man I was visiting today was whom Delilah had labeled "The Gas Mask Man", the one that had attacked her, and the one I had knocked out that night in the alley. He was a scientist named Elliot Rodolpho who had been fired from the pharmaceutical community for using stolen steroids to enhance his physical strength. He had several other misdemeanors after that, but a couple of years ago simply fell off the grid, from what I could tell. I would guess that was McGregor's doing once he had employed him.

We walked through several more electric doors, through hallways with iron doors closing off cells and artificial light making everything a bit too bright for the circumstance. We passed a large window where I could see several men in bright orange jumpsuits sitting around a dirty courtyard, some together visiting in groups or playing basketball, while others walked around by themselves, picking up rocks and throwing them against the building's concrete walls.

I wondered what it would be like to live a life of crime. I was the polar opposite and had never found myself in a position to be tempted into it. As I watched the men lounging in the courtyard, I felt pity mixed with curiosity, wondering if some of them were even content with the incarcerated lives they lived.

Finally, we reached a white door next to a square window looking into a very plain room. There was one desk in the middle of the floor, with one chair on the right and two chairs on the opposite side, all facing each other. The one on the right was occupied by a big man whose hands were cuffed to the table. One arm was still in a sling and he had a sealed up cut above his eye. He stared straight ahead, his short-cropped hair and big nose reminding me of my old G. I. Joe action figure.

"Whatever you say in the room will be recorded, for your and the inmate's security," one guard said as he stood on one side of the door. "If you would like, you can take the recording with you when you leave, but it will be reviewed first."

The other guy moved silently to the far side of the door. I waited before entering. "This can't be reviewed," I said sternly, once again holding up the one item I had brought with me: my badge. "I am under strict confidence with the bureau in an elite investigation, and what happens in this room could make or break us." The two men looked startled. "I will have my superior review the recording in the office tomorrow, however if word gets out of what we're doing, it'll be on this fine establishment's head."

They nodded their understanding, the one radioing something undoubtedly to the front desk about my demands. I waited for the cue to enter and then let myself into the claustrophobic room.

"You again," Rodolpho's gravelly voice didn't sound surprised to see me.

"Me again," I repeated, taking a seat across from the giant. I leaned back to stay away from the cuffed hands on the table. "How do you like it here?"

He smiled, showing straight, wide teeth.

Chuckling to himself, he shook his head. "You know, as far as the big house goes, this isn't the worst."

I didn't smile. I still felt the fury I had on the night I had met him. He was the reason Delilah was in so much pain and stress, and I was going to find out exactly what he did to her.

"That's unfortunate," I said quietly, not breaking eye contact with the massive man. His face was rugged and his eyes beady. "I was hoping you'd feel at least the slightest bit of remorse once you'd been locked up."

As if it were possible, his smile widened to show even more teeth. "I don't feel much of anything anymore," Rodolpho looked me up and down. "You're definitely still angry about it, though, I can tell that much."

I struggled to keep my composure. I glanced at the mirror where I knew the guards were watching from the other side. I couldn't let my anger show, so I bit my lip and looked down, begging my emotions to stay professional.

"I need information," I said through clenched teeth, wringing my hands together underneath the table.

"Figured as much," the man looked over to the mirror as well, ignoring his reflection as he tried to look beyond the illusion. "But they record everything that goes on in here. I can't go giving away our secrets."

"I've secured the recording," I said, hoping this sentiment wouldn't give the oaf any ideas. "The information you give will reach no one other than you and I."

Rodolpho leaned forward, placing his chin on his fists awkwardly seeing as he could only lift them a couple inches above the table. "You see, there is another dilemma," he looked innocently up at me, the act making it harder not to knock out those wide teeth. "I'll be out of here soon enough, and how would my boss repay me if he found out I was spilling all his beans?"

"You're planning to make a jailbreak?" I asked incredulously, rethinking my idea to keep the recording to myself.

"Me? No, not particularly," he smiled smugly, leaning away from the tabletop once more. "But I am one of boss man's favorites, and he's done me several similar favors before now."

I wasn't shocked by the news. It wasn't unheard of, McGregor's henchmen getting busted out of prison soon after they'd been locked up. But Rodolpho was right about the dilemma; he wasn't going to give any information with the hope of getting out of here on the line.

I took a deep breath. "Look, Rodolpho," I was hoping not to have to bribe or make any promises I couldn't keep, considering I was here unauthorized. "All I want to know is what poison you used on that agent. You don't need to tell me how or where it was made, or anything that would lead me to McGregor."

He chuckled again, the sound like pea gravel

getting crunched underfoot. “Poison? That ain’t no poison, what she’s got in her body,” his face grew serious. “What’s happening to her?”

“What do you mean?” I hesitated, not wanting to show my curiosity at his curiosity. “Do you not know what you put in her?”

Rodolpho’s face finally broke, and a slight bit of anger twisted his features before he regained his composure. “Of course I know what’s in her. I made it!” he leaned forward to scratch his head, and then added nonchalantly, “But I also know it has different effects on different people. I was curious to see what would happen to her specifically. Never had such a pretty specimen.”

Anger flared inside as I resisted the urge to flip the table at him. He spoke about Delilah as if she was his experiment. His *model* experiment. I closed my eyes and fought to remain calm. I focused on the other parts of Rodolpho’s answer.

“Different people?” I asked, opening my eyes to see a faint smile on his face. Pushing back the urge to close my eyes again, I leaned forward. “You’ve done this to others?”

“All resulting in different effects,” he replied proudly. “McGregor of course keeps an eye on all of them, but since you landed me in here I haven’t been able to hear how it has affected the ‘Amazon Woman’ from the alleyway.”

“She is not an ‘Amazon Woman’,” I said with disgust before I could stop myself. Rodolpho laughed aloud this time.

"You're right, she's too pretty for that one," he watched me with amusement. "I need a different name for her, like I've got for all my test subjects."

"McGregor keeps an eye on them?" I mumbled, using everything I had not to lunge across the table at this insane man. "So, he's spying on Delilah?"

"Delilah," he repeated, sighing and looking off as if in a daydream. Rodolpho's smug grin returned. "That's her name? It is fitting, she looked like a Delilah. Oh, but I've said too much already."

My mind raced as I tried to remember if I'd seen anything or anyone suspicious around Delilah recently, and then I realized I haven't been around her much lately anyway. She's been slightly more unavailable as of late, but I hadn't realized till now because of how busy I'd been trying to track down the creep sitting in front of me.

"Why do you keep calling them experiments or test subjects?" I asked suddenly, "You seem so confident in your drug, why would you need tests?"

The grin slipped from Rodolpho's face as his beady eyes stared hard into mine. "It has side-effects we had not accounted for," he seemed hesitant. "Just like the results of the drug, these inescapable symptoms differ with each person."

"What have you seen so far?" I asked breathlessly. I already knew Delilah's loss of feeling had to be one of these side-effects, but I wanted to know what else may happen.

"Ah, I see you are a man of knowledge," Rodolpho smiled at me knowingly, and I struggled once more to keep a straight, uninterested face. "You are curious and fascinated by my beautiful creation. We have seen but a few. Loss of sleep, uncontrollable tremors, the occasional seizure. Like I said, the results vary with the person."

"How many people have you infected?"

"Infected?" Rodolpho leaned forward to put a hand over his chest in a hurt way. "This is not an infection but a fulfillment! An uncovering of one's true potential. And that information, my friend, is classified."

I wanted to yell in frustration. He was giving me some new information but nothing that would help me in my goal. "Is there a cure?" I asked, grinding my teeth.

"A cure?" this time Rodolpho looked truly confused. "This is the cure, man, for the incompetence of mankind."

I sat in silence. I realized Rodolpho was convinced what he was doing, while maybe not right, was beneficial, just like any scientist. He was of course the man who had invented the drug, but did that mean he knew all the ins and outs of McGregor's game? Or was there more than just "uncovering one's true potential"?

"But is there something to reverse it?"

"Classified information once more, friend, you're overstepping your boundaries."

I pushed my chair back and stood. He was done giving information, and I was in no state to sit any longer in the same room as him. I walked to the door, not looking back as Rodolpho spoke softly in my direction.

"I hope we meet again, sir," his gruff voice was even scratchier in a whisper. "I would like to know what has happened to the sweet lady."

As I walked out and down the hall, the guards on either side of me remained silent until the last set of doors. The one on my left spoke up before swiping his badge to admit us to the front office.

"Did you find what you needed, sir?"

"I found that that man belongs in an asylum," I said as I entered the office and waited at the front desk for my things.

* * *

I had called Delilah twice in the past three hours, and still sat alone in my house. She had picked up the second time but couldn't come over for one reason or the other and apologized profusely as she thought we weren't going to be getting together tonight. I had decided I needed to talk to her and get any information I could concerning any effects of the drug, and maybe tell her about what I had found out, but I didn't want to do it over the phone. We set up an actual date for tomorrow night, and I tried to prepare myself for how much this subject would ruin it.

I sat in my kitchen with my third bowl of *Reese's Puffs* in front of me, the oven clock showing that it was almost midnight. I had the cereal locked away in one of my cabinets because it was my guilty pleasure and was only eaten in emergencies. I figured with all that had happened these past couple weeks, and today especially, I needed to binge.

As I scooped the last spoonful of peanut butter-chocolaty goodness into my mouth, my phone began to buzz on the countertop. Picking it up, I saw an unknown phone number flashing across the screen.

"Hello?" I answered, wondering who would be calling me this late at night.

"Is this Jace Avery?" Emmit's deep voice came over the speaker loudly.

I pulled the phone away from my face. "Hey Emmit," I said, happy to hear a familiar voice and not some robot pretending to be the IRS. "How'd you get my number?"

"Liles gave it to me in case of emergencies," he definitely sounded like an old man who didn't know how to use a cell phone.

"Is there an emergency, sir?" I asked, feeling alert. Usually Delilah was the one to call me, but I felt confident in the fact that her father would call me as well. Or that she even considered me as an emergency contact.

"Not entirely," his southern accent sounded sheepish. But then his tone turned threatening, "I was just wondering; did you break up with my daughter?"

I raised my eyebrows. "Sir, we weren't really

dating in the first place. . .but she has been. . .distant lately."

"Sure you weren't, you were just making out in her hallway," he said exasperatedly. "But if you're saying that, it definitely explains the way she's been acting lately."

"The way she's been acting?"

"Not answering my phone calls, replying to my texts with one-word answers," he sounded solemn. "That is not how my Delilah deals with things normally, and since you're her first boyfriend, I figured it must be relationship trouble."

"Well she's the one that told me she needed to think about the whole. . .us thing," I said defensively. "I would never hurt your daughter, sir."

"You bet your bottom dollar you won't," Emmit snapped. "I just wanted to make sure I didn't need to fly up there and whoop you."

"Right, like I said," feeling slightly alarmed, I wished Delilah was here now to cool off her dad. "Just waiting for her to decide if she wants me or not. Definitely no reason to come beat me up."

"Yet," he corrected, and then he chuckled. "Anyhow, you notice her acting strange lately?"

I felt awkward. If Delilah hadn't been telling her dad what was going on, it sure wasn't my place to. I decided that being vague was the best way to avoid the father's future anger. If there was a future with her.

"I have noticed her being slightly less herself," I said slowly, choosing my words carefully. "But I really think it's just because of her accident, you know? Anyone would be traumatized after something like that."

There was silence on the other end, and I wondered if Emmit had accidentally hung up on me. "That does make sense," he finally replied. "I just hope it doesn't last. I miss my daughter."

I stayed silent, unsure how to respond. I missed the real Delilah as well, but considering what she'd been through, I couldn't let it sway my feelings for her.

"Well, I'll stop keeping you up," Emmit said finally. I didn't realize we had been sitting in silence until he broke it. "Keep an eye on Liles for me, would ya? And keep me updated, 'cause she sure as hell ain't."

"You got it, sir," I said, thankful that the conversation was ending as quickly as it had begun. "Have a good night."

"You too." The phone beeped, and the line went dead.

* * *

My dream was once again interrupted with the bright light of my phone shining into my room, the buzzing making the mattress rumble beneath my head. I sat bolt upright, fully awake and worried it was Delilah with another bloody mess on her pillow. But when I picked the phone up, I saw that it was Lars, and that it was already 6:30 in the morning.

I silently wondered why my alarm hadn't gone off already as I swiped the green button.

"Hello?" I answered blearily, wiping sleep from my eyes.

"Where are you, Avery?" his voice sounded urgent and clogged, as if he'd been crying.

"I'm in bed, my alarm didn't go off," I reached over and clicked on my lamp. "Why, what's going on? Did I miss a meeting?"

"You're still home?" he sounded immensely sad, which was not Lars at all. "You don't know?"

"Don't know what?" I asked, feeling impatient.

"You know how the 17th floor is under construction?"

"Sure, what about it?"

Lars took a deep breath on the other end. "When the worker's arrived this morning, they found a body in the rubble."

I groaned, positive this was literally the worst wakeup call of my life.

"Jace, it was...it was Jameson."

I dropped the phone.

CHAPTER 13

Delilah

I wrote vigorously, the marker smudging on the side of my hand as I went back to scribble out my previous statement. My living room mirror sat discarded in front of my useless piano, reflecting the string diagram now plaguing the wall it previously hung on. I had realized earlier after frantically searching the apartment that I was fresh out of paper, but my mind was racing, and I had to get my ideas on something. I eventually decided to use my nonpermanent markers on the space of wall where I hung my mirror; that way it would be easy to hide and eventually easy to wipe off.

Scolding myself for not at least keeping a notebook handy, I continued to jot down the connections I kept thinking of. I had written in the top left corner where I was the night the accident had happened, (obviously the scene of the crime); in the top right, I wrote where Jameson wasn't, (Jace was left alone until after I was already unconscious, according to their story). I wrote the approximate height and weight of my attacker beneath that, as well as what I assumed was Jameson's. As more and more things began to connect in my head, I ran out of space to write neatly and ended up having to use some black thread from my sewing kit and the pushpins from my empty mail corkboard to keep an order to my thoughts.

Reflecting on Jameson's actions after the accident seemed the most plausible way of proving he was guilty. He became sickly and exhausted, which was something I had never seen in him before. I pulled a thread from that idea to a big red "*GUILT*" written in the middle of the square of wall I was using. That had to be the only explanation; what would cause a man to grow so feeble all of a sudden? The guilt of what he had done. Or maybe McGregor was coming down on him for leaving me alive. I jotted that idea just below my "guilt" center.

I leaned against the back of my sofa, my chin in my hand as I examined my visible train of thought. Everything led to the last bit of proof I could think of in the bottom left corner that read "Gas Mask". Jameson had been handling a gas mask identical to the one my attacker had worn when I apprehended him. It was on a desk filled with more of his possessions, including suspicious vials and a randomly marked map. I scowled. I had tried visiting the same place early this morning before any workers got to the 17th floor, but someone had already cleared it up. Which also could mean that it was one of McGregor's other men that had come and cleaned up all the proof! I moved forward to write that idea above the gas mask marking.

Something still nagged at the back of my mind. Jameson had always seemed so loyal to the mission of the bureau. What would cause him to turn into one of McGregor's stooges? The thought made my eyes moist as I let myself fall backwards over the sofa, landing with my back on the seat and my legs in the air. My hands trembled slightly as I put the lid on my marker, staring up at my blank ceiling and willing myself not to feel upset. This was the man that was responsible for all the pain that I felt and am no longer able to feel. It was an accident, but until someone proved he was innocent I refused to let myself feel remorse for what I did.

Dot came streaking in from the hallway, slowing down as she reached my free-falling hair and swishing her tail in my face. I threw my hands over my head, beckoning her to come up with me, and she jumped on my stomach, making me jolt upright.

"Oh kitty," I said, stroking her ebony fur with the tips of my fingers. She purred quietly, the vibrations of it tickling my hand.

"I know," I replied, glancing back at the marked wall. "I've made a mess. But for a good reason."

Dot meowed loudly as I tugged her tail. I laughed, pulling her into my arms and squishing her against my face. It was always a feeling I loved, her fur on my cheek, even though I knew it was not her favorite.

"Now, why did he do it?" I sighed, letting go of the struggling cat. She bounded away from me, turning back to give me an almost humanoid-look of "never-do-that-again".

I giggled to myself. That cat had always been one of my best friends, and even though she couldn't speak, I always had the inclination that she could understand what I was saying. With a whisk of her tail, Dot slipped into the kitchen where I could hear her chomping on some of the treats I had left out.

Turning my attention back to the diagram, I searched desperately for a reason. I knew the how, when, and where; the puzzle remained incomplete, however, as I contemplated why Jameson would work for the drug lord.

Then my mind flashed back to a couple of weeks before my first mission with Lars. Edith and I had been sitting in the breakroom eating donuts when Jameson had walked in hastily. He declined our offer to join and left without saying so much as a "see you later". At the time, both Edith and I had found it odd but nothing to really worry about because the FBI is of course an environment of stress and pressure most of the time. But now that I thought about it, the behavior didn't stop with that day. The anxious and stressed Jameson became more apparent and frequent than the laid back and happy Jameson.

I stood, walking back to my almost illegible square of wall. Uncapping my pen, in between the space of the crime and the absence of Jameson, I began to write all I could remember about my encounters with him leading up to the accident. The more I wrote, the more I saw how melancholy he had become in the workplace, and I realized that maybe he wasn't doing it of his own free will.

I took out a green highlighter and wrote the words as they popped into my head: blackmail, threats, promises. I pinned a thread above the list and led it around the other statements to where I had asked the question "WHY?" in the same green marker.

Stepping back, I finally felt at peace with the mess of fragmented sentences and strings. I knew I had to prove that Jameson was the one that attacked me before they finished an autopsy on his body, or they would eventually trace his death back to me. My stomach clenched as I thought about what I had done.

I had never meant to kill. I just wanted him to confess, maybe feel enough pain for me to get through to him. The worst I felt about the whole situation, however, was when Jace called me this morning.

His voice had been thick like he had been holding back snot and tears all night. He remained composed on the phone, but I could tell he was surprised and grieving. I put my head in my hands as I remembered the anger I felt, wanting to yell at him and tell him that Jameson was a traitor, not a friend. But I couldn't. I silently listened as he told me, acting surprised and appalled at the disaster that had happened. When I saw Jace at work later in the day, I didn't have to pretend to show my distress over the situation.

We didn't talk much throughout the day, mainly because we didn't see much of each other, but he did hug me slowly after my shift ended. He told me he would call me tonight and squeezed my arm before walking back towards his cubicle. I felt sick to my stomach lying to Jace and keeping so much from him, but it would be too soon after what I'd done to bring it up now. My desire to prove Jameson's guilt surmounted as I thought of how mine and Jace's relationship may actually have a chance at blossoming into something real once I got this whole thing cleared up. Jace had been really kind and respectful through my whole ordeal, and I was beginning to realize that I didn't much like going a day without him either.

My thoughts were interrupted by my phone buzzing in the pocket of my jeans.

"Hello?" I answered, walking around and sitting on my sofa with my back to the diagram.

"Hey," Jace replied. He sounded slightly happier than he had earlier, but not much. "You got anything tonight?"

"Just waiting for this call," I said, trying to sound comforting. "What did you have in mind?"

"I need you right now, Liles," he coughed away from the phone. "Instead of going out, can I just come over?"

"Sure." My shoulders sagged as I silently fought the urge to breakdown and tell him everything I had done in the last 48 hours.

"I'll be over soon," he already sounded like he was getting in his car. "Thanks, it means a lot."

"Of course," I said, dragging my nails down my arm in an effort to stay put together. "Drive safe."

As the conversation ended I rose, heaving my mirror back over to the wall and hanging it on the designated nails. Stepping back, I was relieved to find no trace of my thoughts visible behind my reflection.

* * *

Jace sat at my table with a bottle of Coke in one hand and a cell phone in the other. I sat across from him, watching anxiously as he read the text he had just received from Jordine. I stretched my leg under the table so that it bumped up against his. We had been sitting there since Jace had arrived at my apartment, mainly discussing the events of the day. I had been biting my tongue for hours, trying to keep my composure as we discussed Jameson's "accident".

"It looks like they'll begin the autopsy tomorrow morning," Jace sighed, pocketing his phone and looking up at me. His eyes were puffy and sad. "All indications imply an accident, but they still want to clear the field of any foul play."

I calmed my breathing. I had less than 48

hours to prove he was guilty. "Don't know how much they'll find," I said slowly, breaking eye contact and nodding toward the living room. "Want to go in there?"

Standing, Jace reached out for my hand. I took his, letting him lead me over to the couch. "According to the report this morning the whole 17th floor was a hazardous area." I said, plopping down and letting him put his arm around me after he threw his phone on the coffee table. I couldn't tell if he was doing it out of the need for empathy or the need to be with me. It frustrated me. "What was Jameson even doing there?"

"He had a desk on that floor as well," Jace's arm fell limply to his side as we both stared at the blank TV. "I guess he needed to gather the rest of his things before they demolished the entire area?"

That's what he wants us to think, I thought, swallowing the bitter taste in my mouth as I felt my leg jerk. Why had he moved his arm?

Jace sat back. "I thought you said the tremors had stopped?" He looked worried.

Pushing my feelings down, I met his gaze. "I've noticed them coming back when I feel strong emotions," Feeling comfortable with the truthfulness of the explanation, I continued, "They've been pretty regular since I heard about Jameson."

Jace wrapped his arms around me, shifting on the sofa as we hugged so his face was in my hair. I took a deep breath. "It sucks, doesn't it?" His voice was gentle but scratchy.

"Yeah, he had so much more to live for," I let go of the breath, rolling my eyes behind his back.

Jace pulled away, his hands on my shoulders. "Well, yeah, that sucks too," he ducked his head to catch my eyes because they had wandered down to my hands clasped in my lap. "I was talking about your situation, though."

I looked up, surprised. He had seemed so immersed in Jameson's death that I'd thought he had forgotten about all the pain I was going through. I shuddered in relief, some of the anger that had built up throughout the day finally exiting my body in the tears that slid down my face. He still felt bad for me. Jace pulled me into another tight hug, this time stroking my hair with his hand.

"I'm glad they're doing the autopsy," he whispered in my ear, and I felt his body tense against mine. "First your accident and now this, I just can't help but feel it's all... connected."

I closed my eyes, trying to keep my body from trembling again, this time out of anxiety. We pulled apart and I felt the distance left between us was too wide.

"Why do you think that?" I asked tentatively, again avoiding eye contact and staring at his fingers now toying with a string connected to his pants. I wished he would hold me again.

"I don't know," I could see through the corner of my eye that Jace wasn't looking at me either. "He was acting weird in the briefing yesterday, and then tried to back out of a major find on McGregor," his fingers stopped, and he rubbed his hands down his thighs. "And I've. . . uh. . . had the feeling that we're all being watched ever since the incident at the docks. I can't help but think McGregor found out how close we were getting to him and decided to take Jameson out."

His voice died with the last word. I watched as his face grew slightly pink; he was holding his breath and blinking fast to keep tears from escaping. I felt angry that Jameson had betrayed us and brought so much hurt to one of his best friends, but that anger didn't diminish the depression that overwhelmed me at the thought of someone seemingly so good turning out to be so evil. Mainly, however, I was distressed by what Jace thought he had lost. It motivated me to prove Jameson's guilt faster than ever, so that Jace could stop mourning. I kept trying to convince myself that once Jameson's faults came to light, everyone would be grateful he was gone.

Jace reached over and squeezed my arm. "Not to turn this around on me or anything," he lifted my chin up. Our eyes drew level and I watched the deep, swirling brown as his pupils contracted in the light. "But I feel like McGregor is doing this on purpose."

"Doing what?"

"Targeting the ones closest to me," he stroked my cheek, then drew back abruptly. I exhaled quietly in frustration. "Which is a stupid thought considering I'm a no-name FBI agent."

"You have a name, Jace," it was my turn to

hold his chin up. "And that is a horrifying thought, but it doesn't change my mind about. . .getting closer to you."

Jace looked up in surprise. "You've. . . you've made your decision, then?"

"I've had time to think about it," goosebumps erupted on my arms as I thought about what I was about to say. "And I was just realizing how well things were going. . ."

"I agree," he said enthusiastically, raising his eyebrows. This was the happiest I'd seen him all day, and it made me happy too. I smiled as he leaned forward, reaching his arms around me once more.

Dot jumped in between us. She meowed loudly and snuggled up under Jace's arm. "Looks like I've got some competition." I said, feeling a spontaneous urge to shove Dot off the couch and cuddle up into Jace's arm as well before realizing how absurdly ridiculous and desperate that would look.

Jace rolled his eyes before stroking Dot gently. I laughed, trying to shrug off the feeling.

"You know," Jace reached his other arm around Dot and grabbed my hand, "I am completely devastated about Jameson," his voice grew soggy. "But I am even more grateful that it wasn't you."

I felt a surge of guilt and love drown my heart as he sat there, looking at me with his big puppy-dog eyes. What in the world was I supposed to say to that? Yes, it *is* great that Jameson died instead of me? I willed myself to keep eye contact, allowing tears to brim my eyes again to show what that meant to me. He squeezed my hand with a pained smile on his face before returning his gaze to Dot.

We sat in silence for a minute, Dot making sure her butt and head were in contact with each of us the whole time. I let my thoughts drift to when I could finally relax around Jace again, when all this was over. I hoped he would still feel the same, by then.

"Do you want to watch a show?" I asked after a while, driving myself crazy thinking of how much time I was wasting when I could be researching more of Jameson's plight, but at the same time loving having Jace close again. "Take our minds off things?"

"Sure," Jace answered, not looking up at me.

Grabbing the remote, I realized this was the first time the two of us had decided to just sit and watch something together. Most of our get togethers, (before now I had refused to call them dates), were made up of card games and surprise movies he had brought. As we flipped through channels, I realized how much we didn't have in common on what we liked to watch television-wise. I was also quite distracted at the fact that Jace was slowly but obviously moving his hand closer to mine the whole time. I thought about just reaching out and grabbing his but decided to let him make the move for himself.

The coffee table started vibrating loudly as Jace's phone lit up on the top of it. We both groaned as Jace reached across me and picked it up.

"Hello?" he asked. I pulled Dot onto my lap as I sat cross-legged, watching Jace expectantly.

His face grew serious as he nodded slowly. I waved at him then raised an eyebrow questioningly. "Do you mind if I put you on speaker?" he said quickly. "I have another agent here who will probably want to hear this as well."

I watched silently as Jace pressed a button on the phone and set it on the table.

"Okay, Derek, we now have Agent Hadley listening in as well," Jace turned to me, "Liles, Derek O'Reilly is who we are speaking with, Jameson's girlfriend's brother."

I swallowed the lump in my throat. Jameson had a girlfriend?

"Hello, Agent Hadley," a nasally voice answered. "I was just telling Agent Avery that I may have some information to help in the investigation of Reggie's passing."

I pursed my lips tightly. Did Jameson have a girlfriend, or was this another one of McGregor's henchmen?

"Go on, Derek," Jace was at full attention, and his swift change in demeanor annoyed me. I felt my hand twitch slightly.

"Well, I just think you ought to know, I spoke with Jameson just yesterday," the voice sounded exhausted. "We had been talking about his plans to propose to my sister, Bridget."

My stomach seemed to drop to the bottom floor of my apartment complex as I inhaled sharply.

I tried to convince myself this was part of the trick.

"Reggie was concerned about his plans for the big engagement because the Boss—er, excuse me, my father, if you couldn't tell by his title, is a very particular and powerful man. Plus, my sister had an accident that cost her her leg not long ago, and he didn't want to push too many things on her at once."

I stood quickly, motioning to Jace that I was going to still be listening but needed a drink. He nodded, solely concentrated on his phone as I walked into the kitchen.

"He had this big elaborate surprise, but the timing didn't work out because of a procedure she was having done, and he just wanted her to be comfortable with it all."

My knuckles turned white as I braced myself against the countertop, breathing heavily as I tried to drown the voice out. It continued to echo through my apartment however, and I had no choice but to sit there and listen to it.

"Anyway, the important thing is, because of this conversation, I know that Jameson wouldn't go and do something reckless. I mean, I've never seen a man so smitten by Bridget."

I felt a crack beneath my fingers as the edge of the counter I was holding began to shudder.

"That makes sense," Jace spoke for the first time. "He had told me just the other night that he had made the decision to propose."

"Exactly," the voice sounded worried. "I hadn't seen my sister in a year or so, but I know their love was still going strong. She won't even talk to anyone right now."

Tears flowed freely down my cheeks as the edge of the counter broke off, crumbling to the floor. Thankfully, Derek started talking again just then, so I doubted Jace heard it.

"Also, I think you ought to know that Reg ended our conversation really fast. He was explaining how he had to pick up some things from the construction zone in your building, because we were to meet last night to finalize plans, when he hastily said he needed to go." This time the voice sounded quite hurt. "He didn't even give me time to say goodbye before he hung up."

I brushed my hands off, picking up the big pieces and throwing them in the garbage. Wiping my moist face on my sleeve, I grabbed a bottle of water from the fridge and walked back into the living room, struggling to compose myself. Jace was still staring intently at the phone.

"Now that is interesting," he looked up at me as I sat down, his eyes immediately flashing concern. I kept my eyes to the floor. "We will keep that in mind, Derek. Thanks for all your help."

"Hey, Reg was like family," the man's voice caught. When it came back on, it sounded even more congested. "I'll do anything to clear this up, and I almost pray it was only a thoughtless accident."

We said our goodbyes before Jace picked up his phone again and pushed the red button. Scooting over to me, he swiped through some pictures before pulling one up of Jameson standing next to a tall redhead with an explosion of freckles covering her body and a prosthetic leg. They both looked like they had just won the lottery.

"I didn't know till a couple days ago," he said quietly, holding my shaking shoulders as I stared at the picture. "But I know it makes it all worse. Sorry to spring it on you like this."

* * *

I sunk to the floor of my entryway, folding into the fetal position as I listened to Jace's footsteps fade down the hallway. I let out a muffled squeal into my arms, clawing my shoulders and rocking back and forth.

What had I done? Jameson was planning a proposal, he wasn't the thug that had poisoned me! My head pounded as I thumped into the wall and Dot approached me cautiously. I had killed my friend.

I was a murderer.

I had to stop the autopsy from happening. It was the only way to keep myself out of prison. It was under false pretenses, I was suspicious, and he had a gas mask for heaven's sake! Why wouldn't the horrible thing trigger the attack sensors in my brain? They were bound to find some piece of my DNA on him, even though I only touched him once. Then they would ask questions. How had I killed him? Nobody knew about what this drug had done to me, not the full extent. What if they experiment on me, drag me in like a lab rat? My hair engulfed my crunched body like a blanket and I pulled on it frantically.

Concerns for myself fled as another wave of grief passed through my body for Jameson. He was gone. His girlfriend, whom he had planned to marry and spend the rest of his life with, was now alone. What would I do if someone killed Jace? I bit my bicep and screamed, squeezing my eyes shut and tugging at my hair.

I couldn't handle this. I had to get away from Jameson before I could hide what I did, or my grief and guilt would overcome me. Walking numbly through the apartment, I grabbed a pair of kitchen shears before running to the bathroom. My ears rang as I looked at my reflection. My face was bright red and shiny from all the tears. My eyes were blood-shot and puffy, and my arms had claw marks down them.

Pulling my hair into a high ponytail on top of my head, I leveled the kitchen shears with it. I had no time to make an appointment, no time to do this right. Jameson's favorite nickname for me was Rap-unzel, of course because of my hair.

Closing the sharp edges one time was not enough. I hacked and cut the multiple strands of hair until I finally felt the weight of it leave my head. Looking down at the ground covered in my dark locks, I felt grief inching its way back in. I pushed it down.

No one could call me Rapunzel anymore.

CHAPTER 14

Jace

Throwing my keys on the counter, I went to my cupboard and pulled the box of *Reese's Puffs* from the top shelf. After the call from Derek, Delilah had seemed eager for me to leave, which was something I hadn't expected would happen after she finally decided she would date me. In all honesty it worried me, but I was also sure she was the type to mourn alone.

I was definitely not, however, so as I sat eating my cereal in my dimly lit kitchen, I felt a single tear slide down my face.

I have only cried three times in my life, or at least those are the only times I can remember. Each time was caused by the death of someone I was close too, or Delilah's accident, and today was no different. I had felt numb all day, trying to go about the office as usual with this weight on my shoulders. I was hoping to speak with Delilah more about it, sure she would be able to help relieve some of the pain I'd been feeling since that morning. She had cheered me up, of course, but the reality of the circumstance was still weighing heavily on my body.

I chomped the round corn puffs in my mouth, unable to really taste as I poured more into my bowl. Jameson was dead; gone forever. One of my favorite partners at the bureau, and a good agent. Delilah as the exception, I had probably grown closest to him out of anyone I had ever worked with. We even went far enough to have pool nights at the club once a month, and I rarely did anything outside of work with my associates. I tried to stop my shoulders from shaking as I thought about his girlfriend, Bridget. I had never met her, but I knew Jameson wasn't the type of man to settle. She must have been something real special for him to want to marry her, and now neither of them would ever get the chance. I wiped my face pathetically on my sleeve.

Something nagged at the back of my mind as I hunched over the counter, shoveling endless spoonfuls into my mouth. It had been bugging me ever since I left Delilah's, and only now, in my pitiful state, did I allow myself to think of it.

Being the observant and suspicious man I was trained to be, I felt something off as soon as I had walked into her apartment. At first, I thought it was just because of the situation, and the grief that hung in the air; the more I paid attention however, the stranger the look of her apartment seemed. I felt I had been there enough to notice any changes, and only today did I realize how much had changed. She had covered her microwave with a dish towel and her piano had collected dust. There were marker prints on her hands and clothes and fingerprints on her mirror. The thing about the apartment that bugged me the most, though, was that her mirror reflecting the piano was crooked, and had a little black string dangling from behind it. That was something that wasn't there before, or else that I had never noticed.

The atmosphere of the apartment had changed as well. The rooms were stuffy like she hadn't turned on her air conditioning yet, in the middle of August, and the air felt thicker than usual. Delilah seemed on edge almost the entire night, even before we got the call. I felt like I was walking on pins and needles while we talked at her kitchen table and she watched me with a blank expression on her face.

Putting my head in my hands, I stared into the murky milk swirling in my bowl. I thought back to my conversation with Emmit a couple nights ago, about Delilah acting strange. I saw it now but wondered if it was just because of Jameson's untimely death, or if it had been building for a while now and I had simply failed to notice. There was a lot going on with trying to figure out what McGregor had done to her, as well as where to find him. It almost made me wonder if she even meant what she said about us —or if she was just trying to make me feel better.

I put the empty cereal box in the trash can and placed my bowl in the sink. Resolving to talk with Delilah about what had happened at work tomorrow, I allowed myself to sink into my bed and slip into a thankfully dreamless sleep.

* * *

"She isn't usually this late."

"She hasn't called in yet either; I checked the schedule in case I had to pick up her workload for the day."

I sat on the edge of Edith's desk, watching the door anxiously. It was already nine in the morning and Delilah had yet to make an appearance in the office. I had texted her that morning but had received no reply. Edith sat in front of her computer, looking frantically from the empty hallway to the schedule pulled up on her monitor.

"Liles was devastated to hear about Jameson," Edith thought aloud, "Maybe she took a personal day?"

"Maybe," I scrunched up my face, fingering the string hanging from the seam on the side of my slacks.

We sat in silence for a few more minutes, both watching the clock and the door eagerly. Finally, I stood, not wanting to waste more of my workday with Edith.

"Let me know if she calls in," I said before heading out the door.

As I rounded the corner into the hallway, I collided head on with a woman coming full speed from the breakroom. She dropped the purse and hand mirror she was holding.

"I'm sorry," I said, bending down to pick up the items. As I straightened up to hand them back to their owner, my breath caught in my throat and I choked. "Delilah?" I sputtered out.

Her hair was gone. I stared as she ran her hand through a choppy pixie cut just shy of the bottom of her ears, with pieces sticking out unevenly. She had dark circles under her eyes and a cut on her chapped lips. Her striking beauty was intimidated by the extremity of her hair.

"Hey Jace," Delilah said breathlessly, taking her purse from my hand and stuffing the hand mirror inside.

Suddenly aware that my mouth was hanging open, I closed it quickly.

"Hey," I walked with her back to her desk. Edith looked up and let out a horrified squeal.

"Liles!" She said sharply, jumping up and walking around her desk. "What on earth happened to your hair?"

It always amazed me how straightforward one woman could be with another. If I had asked that as abruptly as Edith I probably would have been slapped across the face.

"Oh, yeah," Delilah set her things on her desk before nervously running her hand through the explosion on top of her head again. "I was making a card for Jameson's family last night and got glue in my hair."

"So, you chopped it all off?" Edith cried incredulously, reaching up to her own hair protectively.

"Well, of course I tried washing it first, but it was hot glue. And you know how long my hair is," Delilah stepped behind her desk defensively. She was beginning to look less shy and more dangerous. "It was getting on everything, and I didn't have time to make an appointment with a professional. I called one this morning though, so this is only temporary."

She smiled and motioned to her hair with both hands, acknowledging that it was a mess. Sitting behind her monitor, Delilah looked up at me with big, glistening eyes.

"I know how it looks."

"It's not that bad," I grabbed the hand that was currently on her mouse. "And you have the perfect face shape for a. . . uh. . . what kind of haircut is it?"

"Pixie," Edith said airily, staring at Delilah like she had never seen her before. I began to feel defensive for her until I saw Delilah's eyes flash.

"Edith, seriously, I'll get it fixed," she snapped, not looking up from her computer again. "I'm not in the zoo, so quit staring."

The harsh statement brought Edith out of her reverie and she retreated to her desk looking hurt. Delilah showed no sign of regret and continued to keep her eyes down.

"Well," I said awkwardly, backing towards the door. "Liles, I'll see you at lunch?"

"Sure," she still didn't look up from her computer. I saw a tear roll down her cheek.

I walked back to my desk slowly. How much glue did Delilah get in her hair to cut it all off? Why was she using hot glue to make a card in the first place? I didn't really peg her as the overachieving craftsman. I waved to Lars as I passed his desk, then doubled back to warn him.

"Okay, Delilah chopped her hair," I began, wanting to be tactful about my new girlfriend's serious bad hair day.

"Hey, short hair's more fun," Lars winked, "Gets in your face less."

"No, dude, I mean like boy short," I said, struggling to keep from punching him. I raised my hands to stop the inevitable laugh that was about to burst out of him. "And I wouldn't say anything because it was the result of an accident and she is really self-conscious about it."

The smile faded from Lars' face. "She did have pretty hair, I doubt she would have cut it just for fun. That sucks man."

"I'm serious, Lars," I leaned forward, not breaking eye contact. "If I hear word that you're giving her a hard time—"

"I won't man," there was no twinkle in his eye, no edge to his voice. Lars was serious for once. "Everyone's going through a hard time with what happened to Jameson. I won't say a thing."

I nodded, not trusting myself to speak about my depressed girlfriend and my dead best friend in the same conversation. Getting back to my desk, I unlocked my computer and tried to remember what it was that I was supposed to be doing that day. As I distractedly pulled up a file on McGregor I had made unauthorized, an IM popped up on my screen from Edith. Surprised, I clicked on the flashing box.

Something's wrong.

Good observation Sherlock. I backspaced, using self-restraint on my reflexive sarcasm. *I know. What's happening?*

She's covering up her computer. And she hasn't talked to me since you left.

Do you guys normally talk a lot?

An emoji with a tongue sticking out of the mouth and the eyes squinted came in reply.

We aren't men, Jace, we socialize throughout the entire workday.

Touché. You think she's hiding something?

The bags under her eyes, the marker on her hands. Is she on something?

My mouth felt dry. Was Delilah on something? I didn't smell anything funky in her apartment last night. Or was that why the whole thing felt off? Another message popped from Edith.

Now she's crying. Trying to be quiet but failing.

Okay. I'm going to investigate. Let me know if she leaves.

I didn't wait for a response before locking my computer and standing up. Walking quickly to Jordine's office, I nodded to Mori Stevens before knocking and letting myself in. Jordine had mountains of paperwork splayed across her desktop, but she disregarded it as she stood in front of her window.

"What do you need, Jace?" she turned slightly before resuming her glare across the city's skyline.

"A personal day," I stood behind the chairs facing her desk, wanting to make this quick.

Jordine quickly turned around, shock replacing the grief that had been clouding her eyes. I hadn't asked for a personal day since I started. She watched me silently for a moment, trying to dissect me with those lime green eyes. I let my grief show, slumping my shoulders and plunging my hands into my pockets. I knew she was feeling the loss of Jameson maybe more than anyone else in the office, other than me.

After a few more scrutinizing moments, she looked back out the window. "I wish I could take one too. Go for it—but be back tomorrow."

"Will do," I mumbled as I walked quickly out of the office. I took my phone off vibrate as I wound my way through the cubicles and to the elevator, keeping an eye on the time.

The drive to Delilah's apartment was short, mainly because my mind was running about a hundred times faster than my car. Had she gotten addicted to any of the medication prescribed to her after her accident? Or had she been hiding an addiction from long before that? The possibility was quickly shut down as I remembered in the hospital, when the doctor told us they had found no trace of an active drug in her system.

Searching her apartment seemed to be the

most sensible place to start; if there were any drugs or anything else to serve as evidence of her strange actions there, it would be at least something. As I took the steps up to the 3rd floor two at a time, I tried to remain calm and not look anxious. If anything, I could just play the suspicious boyfriend card, searching his woman's apartment because he thought she was cheating. I had a key so technically the only thing I was missing was permission.

At the top of the steps my phone vibrated in my pocket. Reminding myself to put my message tone on a ring in case I needed to hear it later, I pulled it out and saw a message from Delilah asking where I had gone. Thumbs flying across the keyboard, I replied that I had gone out for lunch and a phone call with my mom. Hoping she wouldn't get offended that I hadn't invited her, I walked to her apartment door and turned the key in the lock. Her reply came fast and only said three words:

Ok. have fun.

No emojis. Feeling guilty that I was about to search my could-be girlfriend's apartment without her permission, I walked sheepishly into the entryway. Dot looked around the corner curiously, probably unsure who would be here at this time of day. Seeing it was me, she bounded down the hall, sliding into the little side table before making it to me and clawing at my pant leg. Not wanting any sign that I had been there, I quickly squatted down and calmed the cat, wiping her shed off my leg before continuing into the apartment. Not knowing quite where to start, I went to her bedroom. Sniffing as I walked through the hallway and feeling slightly like a search dog, I didn't smell anything suspicious within the apartment, not even faint cigarette smoke, which is literally everywhere in New York.

Her bedroom was tidy, the bed made with no clothes on the floor. Delilah's dresser had pictures of her and her parents at different theme parks, and nothing seemed to be out of place. Feeling intrusive, I decided I didn't need to be in her bedroom unless I couldn't find anything anywhere else.

Dot padded at my heels as I walked into the kitchen, again taking a deep breath to try and detect any noxious fumes. Still finding the air clean, I immediately noticed the edge of the counter below the sink was broken off. I walked over to it, feeling the edges of the jagged granite and hearing a light hissing noise coming from the cupboard below. I bent down to look under the sink and found a leak where a crack ran from the broken counter to the middle of the sink and down the pipe. I wondered what Delilah would have dropped on the counter to cause such damage, and then I remembered the towel on the microwave.

Making a mental note to help Delilah fix her sink, I turned my back on it and went to the blue shaggy hand towel covering the front of the microwave. I felt like it was a fire hazard to have something flammable on top of the electric appliance, and as I pulled it off I checked for burn marks. My eyes wandered to the microwave as I ensured there were no scorches, and I found a nickel-sized hole in the keypad. Leaning in closer, I discovered several wires behind the pad hanging loosely like they had been broken. Had she stuck a dowel in her microwave? Maybe that's what she dropped on the counter, and the faucet made the hole? That seemed like a stretch.

Why was she covering it up, though, if that's what happened? I would just buy a new microwave. Maybe I'll get her one for her birthday. Dot meowed loudly, pawing at my shoe and making me remember why I had come to Delilah's apartment in the first place. I bent down to stroke her softly before putting the towel back over the microwave. Resolving that if I had enough time, I would grab Delilah a new microwave and have it here for her before she got home today, I made my way into the living room.

Unable to restrain myself, I made for the piano. I am no musician, but I loved to play around on any instrument when I got the chance. Flipping up the fall board to uncover the ivory keys, I stroked the ones closest to me, spreading my fingers wide in what I thought would be a comprehensible chord. The sound that was emitted reminded me of shrieking violins, the dissonance and shrillness making me pull my hands back and cringe. It hadn't sounded that bad when I'd heard Delilah playing it a month or so ago, and I knew I wasn't horrible enough to make the keys themselves sound out of tune. Bracing myself, I played one note at a time down the keyboard, flinching at the ugly tones. When I got down to the middle of the piano the sound cut out abruptly, the keys clunking with an echoing silence.

I stopped. I don't know much about pianos, but I knew enough to see that this one was not in good shape. Lifting the back panel, I discovered several of the strings disconnected and dangling pathetically in the void, and a small hole in the wood of the backside. I fingered the broken strings and traced the hole, careful not to get splinters. Replacing the panel, I pulled the bench out and sat on it. What was Delilah doing to make such a mess of her place? I couldn't replace everything in here, especially not the piano.

My puzzled face stared back at me from the opposite wall, and I remembered the main reason I had been suspicious of the change in Delilah's apartment. Walking over to the mirror, I noticed the string I had seen before was no longer hanging down from behind it. Running my hands around the edge of the frame, my fingers brushed against multiple protuberances and fuzzy things that I assumed were more strings. Either Delilah had a textured wall she was covering up with this mirror, or she was trying to hide whatever artwork she did behind it. As I felt along the side of the mirror to check for similarities, my text tone rang out from my pocket, a faint jingle of bells.

I pulled out my phone to discover a text

from Delilah, immediately followed by a text from Edith. I checked Delilah's first:

I'm taking an early day. I'd love it if you came over tonight.

My palms grew sweaty as I switched screens to Edith's text:

She just left, better wrap things up.

Deciding my time to investigate was more important than responding to either text at this point, I reached up and, as gently but quickly as I could, pulled the mirror from the wall. It was an extremely thick mirror, making it much heavier than it looked. Balancing it carefully, I grew disoriented as I watched the reflection of everything in the room shift with every step I took. I leaned it against Delilah's couch, and then turned to face the uncovered wall. My jaw dropped.

What should have a been a blank square of wall was covered in sloppy marker, different colored strings, and push pins. Some of the writing was so tiny that I couldn't make it out, while other pieces of paragraphs were almost completely covered up by the web of strings crisscrossing the diagram. Three words, all written in capital letters, stood out the most from the jumbled mess: *JAMESON*, *MCGREGOR*, and *GUILT*. I stepped back, trying to make sense of what was before me as questions rambled in my head. First of all, why in the world did she write on her wall? What did this diagram even mean? I tugged at different strings, trying to see what else she had written.

Dot meowed loudly, and I remembered that I was running out of time. I stepped back once more, thinking if I could maybe get one last look at the big picture it would make sense. Receiving no divine intervention, I lugged the mirror back over to the wall.

* * *

I reclined on the squishy sofa, Dot snuggled up under one arm and Delilah leaning on the other. I had put on some quality acting, flipping on the TV and telling Delilah I would meet her at her apartment because my lunch call was over anyway. As she walked through the door, I couldn't help but imagine what it would be like to live with her and see her right after work every day. But then my mind instantly went to all the weird stuff going on, and it made me worry.

"Do you know what time they'll be done with the autopsy?" Delilah whispered, making me jump because I thought she had fallen asleep.

"My estimation is tomorrow morning, but I spoke with one of the Forensic Pathologists in the department, Dr. Meyer, and he said they may wait longer to see if any newer injury or disease shows itself in the meantime; that's all up to their director though," I felt detached; we were talking about my best friend. "Which means at the latest it will be completed tomorrow evening."

Delilah sighed, and I felt her anxiety release

into the air around us, like she was leaking the emotion. I tried not to absorb it.

"What?" I asked softly, not needing to try to sound worried.

"I just wonder if," her words were low and slow, as if she was thinking hard about them. Or maybe she was just falling asleep. "if it was because of McGregor. Something he did."

I felt as though a lightbulb had alighted atop my head. The diagram behind the mirror—Delilah was investigating Jameson's death! Did she think it was murder?

"I've been feeling the same way," I squeezed her shoulder, pushing down the impulse to kiss the top of her head. I still didn't know where I stood with her or what she would be comfortable with at this point. "I'm hoping not, but if the autopsy does come back as homicide, I'm going to make McGregor pay."

Delilah's entire body flinched in my arms. She sobbed out a single reply:

"Me too."

CHAPTER 15

Delilah

I tossed and turned in my bed, Dot's irritated meow materializing in the black room. Jace had left an hour or two ago because I had told him I needed to go to bed. I couldn't sleep at all as images continued filling my head, images of the Forensic Pathologist and several police officers approaching me with my DNA sample. It was only a matter of time; autopsies don't usually take longer than one day, let alone two.

I thought about making a run for it. I could escape in the night, grab some essentials and hop on a plane. But to where? California, I guess. I could leave Dot to Jace and start a new life. My eyes welled up with tears as I thought about leaving either of them. Dot was family and Jace was slowly becoming that. My heart flopped as I thought about how we were just starting our relationship when my life turned upside down. Maybe he was bad luck, but that didn't make me want to leave him. I figured what I felt for him must be love.

Driving myself crazy by lying in the dark, I

threw off my covers and flipped on my lamp. I let my eyes adjust before looking around, knowing they'd play tricks on me with the shadows the light cast. Dot jumped off the bed, giving me a reproachful look.

"Oh, you can sleep anywhere, Dot, go find somewhere else for tonight," I shooed her away, annoyed by her sass.

Sitting up didn't make me feel any better. I felt warm and fidgety, itching to do something to stop my fate from coming in the morning, but I had no idea what. Once they found my DNA on his suit coat, or tie, or whatever I hit, I was done for. My foot trembled slightly as I put my head in my hands. The only conclusion to save myself and those around me was to run for it.

I sobbed, thinking of how hurt Jace would be. The last thing I wanted to do was hurt him. Of course, that was the last thing I wanted to do to Jameson, but I lost control; who knows if next time it will be Jace? The thought made my tears come full force, and I bit down on my knuckles. I couldn't let that happen to him. I had to leave.

Kneeling to the floor, I dragged my suitcase out from under my bed. I just needed some clothes, toiletries; really anything to get me through the trip. I would stop at an ATM before leaving town to take out as much cash as I could; I know how tracking credit cards worked, I did it for a living. I resolved to call my dad at a halfway mark pay phone, also making it harder for them to track me, but hopefully making the blow to him easier. Despite the depression brought on by the thought of leaving, I smiled. I had learned enough about hunting criminals that I knew exactly how to avoid being tracked.

As I began pulling some of my most comfortable and plain clothes out of my closet, my phone buzzed on the nightstand. Glancing at my alarm clock, I wondered who in the world would be calling at 1:30 in the morning. I expected Jace's name to be on the lit-up screen; he was the only one that would want to talk to me this early. When I saw that it was an unknown number, I ignored it. Probably just a sales call from overseas.

But then it rang again. Not two minutes after it had stopped, with the same number flashing across the screen. I picked it up. No voicemail had been left from the last call. I answered.

"Hello?"

"What are you doing?" the voice was male, not particularly deep, but not high-pitched either.

"Who is this?"

"I asked first," he sounded irritated, like I had insulted him already. "Why are you packing?"

I gasped, automatically looking to my window. The shutters were completely closed; I couldn't even see into the street, let alone someone see in.

"Who is this?" I repeated, moving silently to the door. "How would you know if I was packing?" I put my ear to the door, waiting to hear a man's voice either in the hall or elsewhere in the apartment.

"That's none of your concern," the only place I heard the voice was through the speaker on my phone.

"I'm pretty sure it is if you're watching me," I crossed to my lamp in two long strides and switched it off, plunging the room into darkness once more.

"It's for your own safety, but if it makes you feel any better I can't see anything now that you've turned you're light out."

My heart beat fast as my eyes quickly adjusted to the dark. I glanced around, looking for the glint of an unseen camera.

"My safety?" I felt around the walls, stepping quietly. "Who are you, how did you get my number? Why are you watching me?"

"Slow down, woman," the voice snapped, "I am the one in control here. Obviously."

The smugness in his voice made me want to slap him through the phone.

"What do you want?"

"I always keep an eye on my experiments," he said menacingly, "And if you were to leave it would make it much less convenient for us to watch over you."

"Experiment?" I stopped dead beside my dresser. "What do you mean 'experiment'?"

"What, you haven't experienced the change since my man attacked you?"

I choked. "McGregor?"

"Let's get on a first name basis, shall we, Delilah?"

A sour taste filled my mouth as he continued to speak.

"I have many names, but the first name you can call me is Owen."

I put my back against the wall and slid down, hugging my knees. "What have you done to me?"

"I personally didn't do anything, unless you mean that by targeting and sending the order to attack you, that I am the reason you're this way," he took a deep, aggravatingly impatient sigh, "Then yes, it is I who has done this to you."

My hands trembled as tears that never really went away began to cloud my eyes once more. "Why?"

"Why else?" McGregor chuckled on the other side, "The lust for knowledge! The love for science, the desire to defy it!"

I couldn't keep my thoughts to myself. "Science?" I spat, "What does a notorious drug lord do with science?"

There was a pause on the other end. "There is more to me than just my industry, Delilah Hadley," by the tone of his voice, I had struck a nerve. "You will find out soon enough."

I shook my head, my elbow jerking back and ripping a hole into my wall. I tried to stay calm.

"Ah," McGregor's tone was smug once more. "So. You have extraordinary strength, have you not? This is what my sources tell me, though I have yet to witness it myself. I believe that noise, however, was maybe a piece of it, eh?"

I didn't say anything but tried to take deep breaths.

"I will ask one more time," his voice became business-like. "Why are you packing?"

I didn't know how much he knew, and I didn't want to give him more than what he already had, so I began vaguely, "I have to leave."

"Why?" there was some whispering in the background. "Oh, because of the man you killed."

He stated it in a matter-of-fact kind of tone, and while he was completely right, the shock of the situation still hit me like a train. I sobbed, trying to cover up the receiver.

"Oh, you poor thing," McGregor didn't sound sorry for me at all. On the contrary, he sounded like he was smiling. My leg trembled at the thought of this sick man. "Yes, that was a surprise, no doubt. I had no idea you had it in you."

"I don't!" I said sharply, wanting to chuck my phone at the wall, but curious as to what else McGregor would say.

"Sure," I could almost see him shrugging, "Whatever you say kid. The first time is the hardest, but it gets easier after this, I promise."

"I'm not planning on doing it again."

"Of course not," the sarcasm leaked through the phone. There was another pause, and then, "You don't have to leave, you know."

His voice had softened, as if he *was* concerned. I took a deep breath, recalling studying these types of sociopaths. If the spider shows enough compassion, the fly ends up trapped.

"And why wouldn't I?" I threw caution to the wind, "I killed a man; not any man, a colleague. And what's worse? I work for the damn place that's going to put me behind bars. And I have no control over what I can do, so who knows who I'll hurt next."

"You're worried you'll injure Avery," his voice was quiet. I felt bile rise in my throat.

"Anyone, really," I managed.

"But him specifically, of course," McGregor sounded like he was thinking, then said almost to himself, "We could easily get rid of him but the only good that would do is damage the FBI, plus the psychological effects on the subject could prove—"

"Don't you dare touch him," I growled into the phone. I set it down and turned on the speaker for fear of breaking it in half, I was holding it so tightly.

"Are you threatening me Delilah?" McGregor sounded like a parent scolding a child. I pulled my hair.

"You said you haven't seen what I can do yet," I grumbled. "Why don't you tell me where you are and I'll come show you?"

"Tempting, yes," he sounded amused. I squeezed my eyes shut and grinded my teeth. "But you see, you only get to meet me once we deem you a protected asset."

"Once you trust me, you mean?" I wanted to

throw up. "I'm afraid to say you'll never be able to trust me because I don't work for you. And I never will."

"Never say never, my dear," he replied, "We'll see about that."

I counted to ten as I remembered the main reason he called. "Why wouldn't I have to leave?"

"Oh yes, back to the task at hand!" I heard a clap in the background. Was I on speaker too? "We've taken care of everything for you, Delilah. Ties in well actually; step number one to trusting me."

I wanted to pick up the phone again, feeling violated with his sly voice hanging in my room like he was actually there, but I didn't feel calm enough to not break it as soon as I touched it.

"I won't trust you," I said stoutly. "What's been taken care of?"

"The elevator, Delilah, the elevator!" he sounded exasperated. "Do you not remember what happened in the elevator?"

"What are you talking abou—" and it hit me; I ran into Jameson as I got into the elevator with him. My DNA was on him from the start. My breathing calmed slightly.

"We can make sure the footage of the elevator is seen as soon as they find any trace of you on him," McGregor breathed, "We've already destroyed footage of the actual murder from that desolate floor, disguising it as a construction accident. We have also cleared any evidence that he had any reason to be on the floor in the first place."

The image of the empty desk from the previous morning unfolded in my head as McGregor continued:

"You were never with him after the elevator ride that day, and he was in a restricted and dangerous area. All signs point to an industrial accident."

I couldn't help but feel relieved. But suspicion also crept in. "Why are you helping me?"

"Delilah, I really must keep our chat short," it sounded as though he were walking swiftly, a faint whooshing reaching me from his side. "But really, use common sense; how do you test an experiment if it is behind bars?"

Click. He was gone.

I crawled over and flipped on my lamp once more, still not trusting myself to pick up my phone yet. I was off the hook, but at what price? I just had the city's biggest criminal help me escape a murder trial I was definitely guilty of. My body trembled as I realized what I had become. I had to come clean, I had to tell someone. I was not about to help that evil man with whatever plan he had for me. Jail would be worth it.

Or would it? He's giving me a golden ticket, a get-out-of-jail free card—literally. Am I just not supposed to use that? My moral compass struggled inside me as I continued to stay on the floor, just in case McGregor was still watching. He had also threatened Jace. The temperature rose within me as I let my imagination run wild with all the different outcomes of this situation. Maybe, if I stayed a good little puppet and played along, he would leave Jace alone. But we're talking about a ruthless man here, so would he really? Or would he use him as leverage to eventually get me to work for him? I bit my knuckles again, trying to see a way out of what my life had become.

I couldn't take it any longer. Standing, I walked quickly to the kitchen, turning on a light and grabbing a glass from the cupboard. It broke to pieces in my hands, cutting deep into my fingers as I let it fall to the ground with a crash. I winced as I held my bloody hand under the faucet, turning the nozzle gingerly with two fingers.

I cried aloud, reaching up to flip my nonexistent hair over my shoulder as I leaned over the sink. The empty air my hand swept through made my sobs even more pronounced. I had been avoiding my reflection all day. The weight was off my head, but I still had phantom feelings of my hair on my arm or trying to comb my fingers through it. Looking up at the window above the sink, I saw the street lights shining onto an empty street. How had he been watching me? Did McGregor plant cameras in my apartment?

Anger flooded my body at the aspect of losing my privacy. How long had the cameras been here? No wonder they knew about Jace, he had been over practically every day since my accident. Apparently, they were also keeping an eye on the cameras at work as well. How were they doing this? Were there spies in the FBI that were working for McGregor? He hadn't seemed that resourceful, though he had plenty of gangsters at his command.

My legs trembled as depression and fury raged through my blood. I wanted to hit something, I wanted to break something and hear the crash. But I couldn't make anything crash, not this early in the morning on the third floor of an apartment.

I reached up, dragging my hands down my face as uncontrollable shaking engulfed my body. I ran to the living room and grabbed a pillow, holding it to my face and screaming into it. I screamed so long my head began to pound, and I unconsciously ripped the pillow in half as I pulled away to take a breath, fluff and material raining down to the coffee table.

I glared at the table. I didn't want to find out what damage this energy would do to my body if I kept it in. Kneeling down, I grabbed a leg of the table and ripped it off, the wood splintering but not loud enough to wake any neighbors. I caught the edge of the table before it could hit the ground and moved to the next leg. One by one I ripped the legs off, and as I pulled at the last one Dot came bounding up to me, jumping around as if we were playing a game.

"Not now, Dot," I mumbled, trying to push her out from under the only upright corner of the table.

She nipped at me playfully, but I was not in the mood. I shoved her out of the way and swiftly tore off the last leg, feeling the quake of my body being replaced by nausea and exhaustion.

Dot came back up, clearly offended as I tried to rid myself of the nausea. Wondering if staying occupied would keep the feeling at bay, I continued to splinter off pieces of the broken legs. Dot swatted at my hands, begging for my attention as it slowly became harder for me to break the wood.

"Quit it, cat!" I took a swipe at her, and her open mouth bit down on my wrist.

I jerked my hand back, feeling the pulsing from the puncture tingle up my arm. She had small teeth, but growing up on the streets, this cat had learned how to use her jaw properly. I looked down at my wrist and saw four holes beginning to bleed. Dot had never bitten me before.

I looked up, about to scold my old cat before I saw that she was trembling.

"You okay, girl?" I scooted forward to hold her, but she stumbled away. My vision blurred slightly as Dot looked like a drunken cat from the cartoons, her crossed legs making her trip over herself. I watched in shock as her mouth began to froth. My eyes began to feel as though there were cotton balls clouding the edges, but I tried to focus on Dot.

She stood staring at me, her head cocked and her mouth open. I mirrored her look, trying to figure out what had happened when it hit me—I had poisoned my cat.

Whatever was polluting my bloodstream was now in Dot's, and her little body couldn't handle it. I glanced back at my arm and saw the same froth that was coming from Dot's mouth spouting from the holes.

"Dot," I sobbed, trying to keep myself upright as overwhelming exhaustion took over my body. "Dot, what have you done?"

I pulled her into my arms and felt her body convulsing. My shoulders shook as I held her, and I tried to stand to take her to her water bowl. I couldn't. Her breathing was rapid and I could feel myself slowly starting to blackout.

I couldn't let her suffer. I flashed back to when my father had to convince me my first dog, Rosco, would feel better in heaven than he did in his old age on earth. He said that right then he was just suffering, and we didn't want that for him.

I moaned as I realized what I had to do. My face was sopping with all the tears I had shed and was now shedding, and my vision was slowly growing dark. If I passed out before her, who knows how long Dot would feel this pain. I had to end her suffering just like when my dad had taken Rosco to the vet.

I reached slowly up to her neck, trying to think of the most humane way to do this. I didn't have a fancy shot like they did at the vet. I squeezed tight, feeling her fur bristle under my fingers. I was barely able to see with the tears and unconsciousness threatening to take over, but I had to take her misery away. I sobbed aloud as she let out a strangled meow, and I felt her breathing shudder to a stop. I laid her down on part of the ripped-up pillow, resolving to give her a proper burial in the morning as I noticed my arm swelling and turning purple.

I tried to lift myself up to get a bandage from the kitchen, but slumped unconscious to the floor, beside my deceased cat.

CHAPTER 16

Jace

I set my keys on my desk, putting my elbows on top of it and resting my head in my hands. Delilah had kicked me out early again last night, and still wasn't here at work this morning. I knew she was a late person, but not this late this consecutively. I had stopped by her desk when I arrived, and again only Edith occupied the space, just as confused as I was.

Deciding my new assignment here at work may help with taking my mind off things, at least until Delilah arrived, I logged into my computer and began reading the pertaining emails. I had once again been assigned to the McGregor file; they decided it was necessary for me to be taken off probation now that Jameson was out of commission. I was currently working with a group of handpicked specialists from both Jameson's old team and my own. We were following up on the leads Jameson had presented before backing out of the infiltration. I remembered talking to him after he had backed out in front of everyone; he had done it out of concern for everyone's safety. At this point, we had extra recon in the works to make sure it was a safe mission. So far so good, according to these emails.

As I read through the reports that had been sent to me, I couldn't help but think again whether it *was* McGregor who had done Jameson in. My team had uncovered nothing different from Jameson's presentation, and I wondered if that was a little too close for comfort for McGregor. It would make sense. The day of this big reveal of where McGregor was hiding out, only to have the lead of the case turn up dead that night.

Security. Security was the only thing that tripped me up on the whole situation. How could anyone but an FBI agent get into the building, anytime? We have the highest security in the city, we are one of the most elite groups. It's not like gangsters just walk in whenever they want.

"Avery," Lars' hand patted my shoulder, shaking me out of my reverie. "Jordine and I are going down to Forensics at noon to hear the results of Jameson's autopsy. We were wondering if you would like to come?"

I felt numb. "They have his body in the building?"

"No, but the pathologist works downstairs. They said he'll be in around ten this morning, and we figure that's enough time for him to get everything together."

Relieved that I wouldn't have to see a corpse, especially the corpse of a good friend, I nodded,

"Sure, I'm curious. Did they say what they're thinking it is?"

"Since it's a confidential case, no, not over the phone anyway," Lars shook his head. "That's why we have to go down to his office. If you ask me, those scientists are crazy as it is, they don't need to be so secretive about it all."

I chuckled under my breath. "They solve mysteries, that's for sure."

"I'll see you 'round noon then?"

"Sure, I'll meet you at the elevators."

Lars walked away, leaving me feeling slightly tense. I was about to find out if my buddy was murdered, or if he had made a stupid mistake. I silently hoped it was the latter, but a part of me wanted even more reason to find McGregor and put an end to him.

Turning back to my computer, I spent most of my morning returning emails. I thought about going and visiting Delilah's desk again, but had an odd feeling about it, so I decided to put it off. Maybe I would hit her up on my way to the elevators at noon.

An IM popped on my computer as I was getting up to get my lunch from the breakroom. Sitting back down, I clicked on Edith's company photo.

She's here, and she is not good.

Delilah?

Who else? She looks like she got attacked by a bull dog.

Don't make fun of her hair, Edith, I know she's

still sensitive about it.

There was a minute before another reply came:

Not talking about hair. Here she comes.

I quickly exited out of the IM, locking my computer and standing once more. As I looked over the top of my cubicle, I saw Delilah walking toward me, and I realized what Edith had meant. Aside from her already crazy hair and her puffy eyes, Delilah looked sick. She had an ace bandage wrapping her arm from her wrist to her elbow, and her hands were covered in band-aids. She walked slowly, as if she was asleep, and flinched when other people walked by. The exotic confidence she normally exuded was replaced by a shriveling paranoia, and as I watched the woman I loved move forward, extreme anxiety filled my body.

"Liles," I walked forward, grabbing her hands gingerly.

She looked at me with tears in her eyes, and I knew we couldn't talk there. Holding her shoulders, I guided her back through the office to the printing room across from her desk corner. Closing the door behind us, I turned to her slowly.

"What happened?" I leaned forward and kissed her cheek. It was wet.

"I can't," she sobbed, breathing deeply and quickly as if she had been holding it in. "She's gone."

My mind immediately went to Delilah's mother. *Hasn't she gone through enough*, I thought impatiently as I continued to watch her struggle.

"Take your time," I held her waist and helped her sit on top of the cleared counter.

She shook her head, sniffing rapidly and using the unbandaged part of her hands to wipe tears from her face. I watched, holding her knees and feeling lost. What had happened to make her like this?

"I. . . I," Delilah took deep gulping breaths, clearly trying to control her tears. "I had to put her down."

My eyes widened. "You did what?"

"Dot," she moaned, and I felt slightly relieved that we weren't talking about her mother. Still worried, though.

"You put Dot down?" A weight sank into my chest. I'm more of a dog person, but that little cat was growing on me.

Delilah nodded slowly, finally starting to calm down.

"When?" It couldn't have been more than 10 hours since I had last seen Delilah *and* Dot, and most of those were at night. How had she found a vet to put her down? "Why?"

"Last night," Delilah sniffed again, finally looking up at me. Her eyes were dilated and red, making the sliver of blue iris sparkle. "Jace, she bit me."

I raised my eyebrows. "She. . . bit you?" I knew Dot didn't bite. But wasn't it a little extreme to put your pet down for that?

Delilah's face hardened, and she backed away slightly. "You don't understand."

I put a hand on her leg, "Help me to, Liles."

Softening again, she put her bandaged hands on mine. "She bit me, while I was having a tremor episode."

I could tell she was hesitant, but she was also becoming more herself the more she talked, so I nodded encouragingly. In the back of my mind, I wondered what had brought on the tremors this time.

"Dot bit me, and then she started acting weird. She stumbled, and looked like a drunk cat, like the ones from *Tom and Jerry*. When I looked back down at where she had bit me," she started unraveling her arm. "My wrist had started swelling, it had turned purple and froth was coming out of the puncture marks."

Unsure if I really wanted to see this gruesome wound, I hesitantly looked down at Delilah's bare wrist. There was nothing; not even a scratch.

She winced as she looked down at it as well. "Not very pretty, I know," she exhaled softly, then went on, "When I looked back up at Dot, the same froth was coming from her mouth, like she had rabies or something."

Delilah began to sniffle again as slow tears began to crawl down her cheeks. I knew she wasn't joking, so I tried not to look as confused as I felt.

"She was in pain, Jace," she started to wrap her completely healthy arm back up. "She was suffering from the same poison that is in me. Her little body...it couldn't handle it."

Delilah hung her head. I had no idea what to say. Had she dreamt this? As far as I could see there wasn't even a little dent in her skin, let alone foaming holes.

"I killed my own cat Jace," she said softly, "I didn't want her to suffer. And I didn't know if I could find a vet in time." She looked up at me again, and if possible, her eyes had grown even more red.

"How?" I couldn't say anything else. I felt slightly disgusted that she had murdered her own pet, but I could see Delilah's thought process and knew that was the only reason she did it.

"Suffocation," Delilah choked out. "It seemed to be the only humane way."

Not able to think of what to say, I let her fall into me and wrapped her in a hug. There was nothing wrong with her arm. Did she hallucinate last night, imagine all of this?

"Liles," I said softly, holding her head in my hand, "Were you feeling okay last night? When this all happened?"

She pulled back, staring at the floor. She spoke slowly, "Like I said, my body was doing that weird twitch thing again. I felt sick, and like I was about to black out when she bit me." She fingered the band-aids on her hands.

"What happened to the rest of your hands?"

"Splinters," Delilah peeled back one of the ones she was playing with like a little girl caught doing something wrong, revealing very real, angry little welts covering her fingers.

"How did you get so many?"

"I accidently broke my coffee table."

I raised my eyebrows. "How do you accidently break a coffee table?"

She looked up at me, her eyes hard. "I don't know Jace," her voice was harsh. "I don't know what happened last night. It's all fuzzy. I think I fell on it when I felt like I was going to pass out or something. Tried to catch myself or something."

"Okay," I raised my hands defensively, "I was just wondering. You said everything's fuzzy?"

"Nothing seems clear. I can picture in my head what Dot looked like though. But I was on the verge of passing out, so the edges of my vision were blurry."

I took a deep breath, trying to keep my cool. "What do you think brought on the tremors?"

"Bad dream."

She didn't make eye contact, looking into the corner of the room behind me. She was done talking. I pulled her into a hug and felt her relax in my arms. I had never seen Delilah so defensive, but I also knew that physical contact was one of her weaknesses.

"I'm sorry you had a bad dream," I whispered in her ear. "And I'm sorry you had to put Dot down. All cats go to heaven though, just like dogs." I kissed her cheek, resolving to not judge her for killing an innocent cat. There must be something else that happened to explain all this.

"Yeah," she sniffed, "Thanks for understanding, Jace. It means more than you know."

I walked her out of the printing room and back to her desk. Edith was thankfully away from hers. "Do you just want to take a sick day?" I asked, "I could come over right after work tonight, if you'd like?"

"No, I came in because I need to finish up some work here before the weekend." Delilah looked up at me gratefully after sitting down. "But we can meet up after work, for sure."

"Sounds like a plan," I started to head out. "Text me if you need anything, okay?"

"Okay."

* * *

I leaned back in my chair, my hands in my hair. My google search of Delilah's symptoms had seemed iffy at best, but the results on my screen made tingles run up my spine. If my assumption was correct, and if Web M.D. had any credit to it, Delilah had hallucinated most of last night. I bit my lip, wondering if Dot was still alive, or if Delilah had killed her under the pretense that she was poisoned. I knew for sure she had hallucinated her injury, at the least.

Glancing at my watch, I promptly locked my computer and headed to the elevators, my mind racing. As I navigated through cubicles, I shot a quick text to Delilah.

Where is Dot now?

As I stepped up to the door leading to the elevators, seeing Jordine and Lars on the other side, I received a quick response.

I buried her this morning in a box.

I caught up to the two as the elevator doors rang open, pocketing my phone.

"Let's hope it wasn't murder," Jordine said shortly as we piled in and she punched the button to floor 4.

We rode in silence, which let my thoughts run freely. Delilah was no longer hallucinating this morning, or she wouldn't have made it in one piece to the building. She clearly still thought she had a disgusting wound, but I've witnessed one too many instances of people convincing themselves of something if they believe in it enough. Was it possible she had imagined the wound, and Dot being poisoned, but had killed her cat in real life? It seemed plausible, especially if Dot was within reaching distance.

The elevator doors slid open, and the three of us walked out into a completely different floor than the one we had left. It looked like a laboratory behind the glass window panes, rows of tables littered with vials and computers. Jordine scanned her all-access badge, and we opened the door to a smell that no living being would enjoy.

I coughed slightly as Lars made a choking noise. Jordine turned to us, and without saying a word told us to both grow up and take it like men.

She led us through the benches, passing men in goggles and women wearing gloves. Finally, we reached a back door leading to what looked like a regular office, with a noodly sort of man sitting behind the desk in the corner, a replica of a skeleton his only company.

"Babineaux," Jordine said with a flare of an accent. "Thank you for being willing to meet with us, I know you've been working hard."

"I have, yes," the man said bluntly, his bulbous nose turned down. He had a faint French accent, but I could tell he must have been here long enough to have Americanized it somewhat.

"Let me introduce my colleagues," Jordine gestured to us in turn, "Jace Avery and William Lars. Boys, this is Andre Babineaux, our Forensics' lab coordinator and one of our top inspectors."

"Pleasure," Lars said stiffly. I merely nodded.

"These two were some of Jameson's colleagues, and have clearance, along with myself, to know his diagnosis."

Babineaux nodded slowly, taking off his glasses and rubbing the bridge of his nose. "I'm afraid I don't have much," he replaced his glasses and motioned to the two chairs on either side of the skeleton.

I remained standing while the others took their seats, feeling too anxious to relax. Babineaux pulled out a stack of papers.

"Time of death, approximately 5:15 Tuesday evening," I felt irked by the way he read it so detachedly. I tried to remember that it was his job to be detached, though. "Cause of death," he hesitated.

"What?" I had never known Jordine as a patient woman, and no department was exempt. She looked at Babineaux shrewdly.

"Cause of death," he continued without looking up from his paper. "Construction accident; victim was crushed beneath an unstable pillar in a construction zone."

All three of us let out the breaths we were holding. I watched as Lars' shoulders sagged slightly, while Jordine's straightened. But something was wrong. It was my job to read people, and Babineaux was once again removing his glasses to rub his nose.

"Why the hesitation?" I asked quietly, making Jordine look back at me in a disapproving way. I shrugged before returning my gaze to Babineaux.

He stood, standing at least 3 inches taller than me, his gangly arms swinging as he walked around his desk.

"I ran all the tests I could," he leaned the backs of his knees on the desk, making me wonder how in the world he fit behind such a tiny thing. "We found DNA from a couple of people in your office on the victim's clothes, but all checked out according to video surveillance."

"Then why the hesitation?" I repeated.

Babineaux looked down at me, his beady eyes glinting slightly. "In the 23 years I have worked here, I have never run across something that confused me. But this man's sternum was broken."

"He was crushed by a pillar," Lars pointed out

stupidly.

"Yes, yes, but all other injuries prove the pillar came from above, a head shot if you will," Babineaux glanced around, as if searching for the answer. "The crack in that man's sternum was in the front, as if he had been hit straight on," he motioned with his hand, pointing it with the palm facing in and pulling it straight into his chest, "As if he were hit with a baseball bat in the chest."

"Couldn't the pillar have put so much pressure on his head that it just cracked the bone down?" Jordine asked. I tried to desensitize myself from the conversation. We weren't talking about Jameson, we were talking about some other poor guy.

"That is the conclusion we came up with," Babineaux looked annoyed. "But in my professional opinion, I don't know if that is quite right."

"Who pulled up as having contact with him?" I asked abruptly. An idea was forming in my head; a terrible conclusion, and one I wanted to be proved wrong immediately.

"Birdelle Caroway on the back, Jace Avery on the arm, Delilah Hadley on the chest, and Maylene Torris on his shoe." He read matter-of-factly from the paper, folding his arms and looking over his glasses at us.

"Birdy patted him on the back before his presentation," Jordine remembered aloud, "And I saw you go up and grab his arm afterwards, Avery."

"Maylene is clumsy, she probably stepped on his foot sometime during the day," Lars said slowly,

"But why would Delilah have touched his chest?"

Babineaux shuffled through more papers. "'Video surveillance shows her stumbling onto an elevator and tripping into him, before pushing a button to the 20th,'" he read again. I was starting to wonder if this guy was anything but a robot, but I was relieved to hear her DNA sample was just from Delilah falling into Jameson.

Something nagged at the back of my mind, but I pushed it down. I struggled to feel satisfied with an accident as the answer like everyone else. Except Babineaux, who, as we left his office, advised he would soon be alerting Jameson's family and friends of the verdict.

* * *

Stay after you clock out for a minute, ok? I typed the message slowly, but Edith's reply came fast:

You got it, we need to discuss some things.

Thankful that I didn't need to explain myself further, I tried to drag my work out for the last hour of the day. After I had returned to my desk, I let what had felt off down in Forensics come forward, and it worried me more than anything had this week; which was saying a lot.

Why had Delilah been going to the 20th floor the day Jameson had died? I guess that was the same day I had gone to talk to Rodolpho, so I had been distracted enough not to notice what she was doing.

But what was even on the 20th floor that she would need? I didn't even know what division operated on that floor.

I received a text from Delilah inviting me to meet her at her apartment, and I replied quickly that I had some work to finish but I would be there soon. A few minutes after the text, I received an IM from Edith giving me the all clear.

"Did she tell you what she did last night?" Edith asked in hushed tones as I walked into her little cubby. People were passing by to get things from the breakroom before the weekend, and there was no door to close off the little office area.

"About Dot?" I sat in Delilah's chair, looking around her desk. Everything seemed in order there.

"Yeah, I can't believe she put her down."

"Did you hear how she put her down?"

"Well, I assumed the vet," Edith watched me closely, "But she also showed me the so-called nasty bite, and I couldn't see a thing."

"She hallucinated," I kept eye contact, pointing to my head. "All of it, she imagined it. Except she did kill her cat. Edith, Delilah killed her cat, she didn't take it to a vet."

Edith's hand clapped to her mouth, her eyes horrified. "Are you sure?"

"Almost positive, and there's something else," I tried to keep my voice level. "Something that could be a lot worse if my suspicions are right."

"Wait, back up. What made her hallucinate?

I have noticed her acting squirmish lately. Do you think she's lost it?"

"I don't know. But it has something to do with the drug, and yes, I think she is feeling some sort of effect from it in her brain."

"Well what's the other thing?"

"Can you pull any images from surveillance cameras?"

"In this building? Not without proper clearance," Edith smirked slightly, holding up her badge. "Good thing I know the security team well."

I paused. "So, um, I'm grateful you have it now," Edith started typing rapidly on her computer. "But why do you have that, exactly?"

"I was trying to find any evidence of Jameson's accident," Edith said, not looking up from her monitor, her fingers flying. "I volunteered to help. But apparently the construction guys on the 17th broke the cameras too, 'cause we found nothing."

"Interesting. Construction zones shouldn't be surveillance free."

"Exactly. Okay, where do you need me to look? And what day?"

"Tuesday, and," I hesitated. "The stairwells."

"All of them?"

"Just to be safe, yeah."

I wheeled Delilah's chair next to Edith's, watching the screens as she pulled up multiple images of empty stairwells. Occasionally two or three people would show up on the flights close to the bottom floor, but they remained empty near higher floors.

And then we saw it. A tall, dark-haired woman running down two flights of steps between the 18th and 17th floors.

"Replay that," I said, pointing at the screen where she was. We watched on replay as Delilah ran from the floor she hadn't even meant to go to, to the floor where Jameson died. The time on the screen read 5:00 exactly. My body froze as realization came from all sides. Delilah's sudden haircut, her broken appliances, her dead cat.

Her wall chart with the word *GUILT* written in the middle of it.

"Delilah is going to the floor Jameson died on," Edith said, her mouth wide open as she stared from the screen to me and back again. "I know it's ridiculous but, are you thinking what I'm thinking?"

"If you're thinking that Delilah may have somehow been a part of Jameson's 'accident'," I said, gagging on my own tongue. "Then I'm afraid we're thinking the same thing."

CHAPTER 17

Delilah

Jameson's autopsy results were in, and no swat teams had broken down my door. Lying down on the couch, I watched the clock above my piano, the minute hand slowly moving forward. Was it too early to tell, or was McGregor right about me being off the hook?

I felt disgusted with myself. I also felt angry that I had invited Jace over. I wanted so badly to just give in to him, tell him everything that had happened, everything I had done. Especially after telling him about Dot. He had been so understanding. My eyes welled up with tears, but I pushed them down; I was done crying over this.

I couldn't tell him though, and I couldn't tell anyone, or they would just become McGregor's next targets. Or I could just turn myself in straight to Jordine. Then the most McGregor could do was watch as I was put behind bars, never to be touched by him again. But did I want that? Did I want to be locked up? No, of course not. And what would happen once I was captive? Would I have another episode of grief and just bust myself out again? Possibly hurting even more people? I hated my options, and the more I thought about them, the more I felt my stomach churn and my arms tremble.

Jace was right about how going to the office had been a bad idea. All day I overheard people talking about me, probably because Edith had run her big mouth off after I had told her about Dot. And I'm sure my drastic haircut didn't help. I sat up, remembering that I had meant to make an appointment with a salon to fix the mess on top of my head after lying to Edith about it.

Standing, I glanced out the window, recalling the inappropriately sunny morning it was as I had buried Dot hours before. Now she lay wrapped in her favorite blanket, in a shoe box in the field behind some park on the outskirts of town. Again, I reminded myself I was no longer going to cry. I walked to the kitchen, pulling out my phone and googling nearby salons as I filled a glass of water. I watched out the window as some couple yelled at each other in the parking lot out front. Even though mine and Jace's relationship may not be the most honest at this point, at least it wasn't like that.

After I had made the appointment, I glanced at the clock again. Jace should have been off work by now, but maybe he had to take care of things at his place before coming here. I willed myself not to get angry with him. He'd told me he had extra things at work he had to take care of. How long could they take though, really?

It's amazing how much presence a single cat could have. My apartment felt strangely empty without the pitter-patter of Dot's little paws. And her panting. I felt more alone than I ever had as I paced about my apartment. Now would be a great time for Jace to come over, or I might start crying again.

And then I realized there were still fragments of my coffee table littering my front room. My mind was so clouded that I had forgotten about the mess till I looked down at my feet, expecting Dot to be slinking around down there. Not knowing when Jace would arrive, and knowing how ridiculous it would look to have the torn up legs and pillow on the floor, I dropped to my knees and started scooping the wood off the carpet.

There wasn't room in my garbage can for the bigger pieces, so I swept them under the couch, hoping that would be good enough for now. I pulled out my vacuum, trying to suck up the little splinters in the carpet. As I turned it off, a knock came to my door. I pushed the vacuum against the wall.

Smoothing my shirt, I pulled open the door. Edith stared up at me.

"Edith?" I asked blankly.

"Hey Delilah, mind if I come in?" she asked delicately. I had never heard Edith speak in such a careful tone, and I automatically knew something was up.

I stepped aside, trying not to sound suspicious as I asked, "What are you doing here?"

"Just thought I'd stop by." She walked into my apartment, looking around curiously as she went. "Plus, my apartment building is under lock down for a drug bust."

"That's unfortunate," I closed the door and followed her back to the living room.

"On a Friday, too," she mumbled, continuing to look around. "They couldn't have picked a worse time to do it. Hey, did you change something since I was last here? Like furniture or decoration wise?"

"No, it's completely the same," I motioned for her to sit before plopping down on the couch as well. "How long before you can go back to your apartment?"

"Don't know. They said they'd call when the investigation was finished, but it hadn't started till just an hour or so ago. If this is a bad time—"

There was another knock on the door. "Well actually," I said as I made my way back to the front of my apartment, "Jace is coming over tonight. If you don't mind third wheeling, I'm sure he won't mind it either."

In truth I *did* mind, and I felt annoyed that Edith would choose my place for a hangout till she could go back home. According to all the stories she had after every weekend, she had much closer friends than me.

"I don't mind," she called after me.

I opened the door, happy to see that it was Jace this time and not another random coworker. Fingers twitching slightly on the doorknob, I forced a smile and pushed down the irritation. I was being a good friend, performing a service. That's how Mom and Dad taught me, right? See a need, fill a need.

He walked in, pulling me into his arms and kissing my cheek. I winced slightly as his arm brushed my bandaged wrist, trying not to touch him with the disgusting wound.

"Hey Liles," he said, continuing to hold on to me as I closed the door.

"Hi Jace," he still didn't let go. "Want to come into the living room with me? We have company tonight."

"I heard," finally pulling back, Jace motioned to the door. "That thing doesn't keep all the sound in, remember?"

"So, you were eavesdropping," we walked down the hallway to the living room, stopping in the entryway.

"Only a little." He winked at me, his smile slightly forced. "Mind if I use your bathroom? I came straight from work and didn't have time to go."

"Go for it." I noticed Edith give him an incredulous look before he walked back. She turned slightly pink when I caught her eye and went back to staring around my apartment.

Something felt off. Not just because Edith was there; Jace was acting odd. Or was that *because* Edith was there? I didn't know what it was, but I didn't like it at all.

"Have any fun plans for the weekend?" I asked

awkwardly, sitting on the couch again. I had always enjoyed working with Edith, but her being in my home tonight felt completely different. I could feel the tension in the air, and I wondered if she knew I was slightly annoyed with her.

"Not particularly." She continued to avoid eye contact with me. "Going to visit my parents tomorrow, then church on Sunday."

"You go to church?"

"When I can, yeah." Edith finally looked at me, surprise in her eyes. "Do I not seem the type?"

"That's not what I meant." I laughed, grateful she had stopped glancing around. It hadn't helped my suspicions.

We made small talk for a while longer, till I was getting worried that Jace had been swallowed up in the toilet. I excused myself, walking down the hallway and seeing the bathroom door ajar and the lights off. Jace walked out of my bedroom.

"What are you doing?" I asked, scrunching my eyebrows at him.

"Uh-oh, caught in the act." Jace swaggered toward me, smirking slightly. That seemed hard for him as well, as if he was suddenly nervous around me. "I was leaving a note on your dresser. Since we have a guest tonight."

"Yeah. . ." I said, leading him slowly back down the hall as I whispered, "I feel awkward leaving Edith alone in my living room."

Entering the room, I noticed Edith sitting with her back rigidly straight. She wasn't understanding the fluffiness of my sofa at all; usually people were swallowed right up in it.

"Been a beautiful day," Edith said, once again not making eye contact with me. I followed her gaze and realized she was staring down Jace.

"And a beautiful night," I said, looking back at Edith. I focused on my peripheral vision, however, and saw Jace mouth something.

What was going on?

Without my coffee table to take up room, the space between the couch and the piano felt like a chasm. I pulled out the piano bench and sat down, motioning for Jace to take the other side of the sofa. My mother was a lot of things, but never once was she a bad hostess, and neither was I. She taught me the guests always get the most comfortable seats in the house.

There was an awkward silence, where Edith watched Jace, he kept his eyes on me, and I glanced back and forth between the two of them.

"Okay," I said, feeling sorely left out. "What in the world is going on? Edith stop staring at my boyfriend like that."

It came out snappier than I had meant it, and it was the first time I had called Jace my boyfriend, but it did the job just the same. Edith's face turned beet-red and she turned to me, pursing her lips. Jace clasped his hands and looked at the ground.

"Sorry," she said, then added in an attempt at humor: "I guess I didn't believe you two were actually dating. Had to see it for myself." She gave a weak grin.

My leg pulsed slightly. I prayed neither of them had seen it as I tried to remember this was just her type of personality.

Jace cleared his throat. "Liles, Jameson's autopsy came back today. I thought you'd like to know what they found."

"Sure." I dragged my sweaty palms across my jeans.

"Well, they found mine and your DNA on him, plus some other people." Jace gave a harsh chuckle. I looked at him and saw him tugging at his collar. That was not a normal habit. "But I mean how could you not, bumping into people in that crowded office all day, right?"

"Right." I smiled. Or at least I tried to; I'm not quite sure how it looked.

"Well, they ruled it as an accident, so that's good, right?"

"Right," I repeated. He didn't seem so convinced.

"They, uh, found something funny, though, in some surveillance footage."

"I stumbled," I said before I could stop myself. Edith's head snapped up, looking between me and Jace. "I mean, that's where my DNA came from, right? When I fell in the elevator?"

"Oh yeah, they saw that bit," Jace said slowly, looking me in the eye. "But we found something else, too, we thought you might be interested in."

My heartbeat thundered. I was surprised they

couldn't hear it as it pounded in my ears. Had McGregor been wrong? Was there still evidence of me killing Jameson?

"Oh?" I tried to sound nonchalant. "What's that?"

"Well, we found footage of you running down the stairwells just minutes before Jameson's estimated time of death," Jace's voice had grown solemn, and less forced. This was no act. "Exiting the 18th floor to enter the 17th, which we know is where they found his body the next morning."

My arm twitched out, leaving Edith staring at me with wide eyes. A lump had formed in my throat, making it hard to swallow, or even breathe. I opened my mouth, but no sound came out. I counted to ten in my head, feeling a slight tremor building in my core.

"Liles..." Jace had scooted to the edge of the sofa. He hadn't let himself be swallowed up either. "Why did you take the elevator to the 18th if you had meant to get off at the 17th? And why had you punched the 20th first?"

"And what business did you have on the 17th in the first place?" Edith added. Jace shot her a warning look.

My eyes widened as I looked between the two of them, realizing what was going on.

"This is why you're here, Edith? Jace, you brought her for an interrogation?" I stood up.

Jace shot up as well. Edith cowered on the couch. "It's not an interrogation, Liles. With that evidence, it doesn't look very good, but if you have a plausible explanation, we can just forget about it and Edith can go home. And we can have a date night."

Something in his eyes was sad, almost pleading. But I felt violated, furious that they had gone behind my back. "Where did you get the footage from? How do you know it wasn't a different day entirely?"

"Because we know, Delilah." Edith finally stood up, looking considerably smaller than usual next to Jace. I hated that they were standing together... against me.

"How long have you guys been going behind my back?" I accused. I had wanted to tell Jace, but now I just felt angry that he had done his stupid investigative work on me.

"We are just worried about you." Jace reached out, but I dodged his touch, feeling the tremors magnify within me.

"Why? Because I killed my cat?" I yelled. I didn't care who heard at this point.

"Take off the bandage Delilah," Edith said quietly, tears in her eyes. "When you showed me earlier, and explained your wound. . . Liles, there isn't anything there."

I scoffed. I had seen it with my own eyes; the inflammation, the discoloration, the froth.

"No," I said, moving toward her. "Edith, I

think you chose not to look because of how horrible it is. Well, you don't have poison running through your veins! I do Edith! I'm poisoned, and I poisoned my cat! It's as simple as that, okay?"

Edith flinched but held her ground. I glared down at her as Jace said from the side. "Delilah, I didn't see anything either."

It had been months since he had called me Delilah. Ever since we started. . .whatever we were, I was Liles. Our relationship had just begun and was already falling apart, and it was because of Edith and whatever lies she was feeding him.

"Don't listen to her, Jace." I continued to watch Edith as she stared up at me with a tear-streaked face. "She's jealous of us. She's jealous that my accident was worse than hers, and that I got more attention for it. Well, guess what Edith? It isn't that great! Do you know what it's done to me?"

Finally, she stepped back, whimpering slightly as she shook her head. Of course, she had been jealous of the attention I had. I guess being shot in the leg hadn't been enough for her.

"Delilah, that's not what's going on," Jace said, stepping closer to us. "We think you hallucinated Dot getting poisoned—"

"Oh, did I 'hallucinate' killing her, too, or did she just conveniently run away the same night I had this 'hallucination'?" I asked hysterically, feeling tears fill my own eyes.

Jace hung his head. "No, we think you really did kill her, but under false pretenses."

"You think I wanted to kill her?" I rounded on him, but he stood his ground, looking firmly into my eyes. "You think I made all this up so that I could get rid of one of my best friends?" Congestion was building in my nose as my fingers twitched angrily. I balled them into fists.

"Delilah, no." He glanced at my mirror. I looked over as well. My reflection was terrifying, so I quickly glanced away, trying to soften my expression as I remembered I was yelling at my first and only boyfriend. But he was also going behind my back with Edith for who knows how long. My arms began to shake.

"Delilah, I've been worried about you for a while." He moved forward, trying to grab my hands. I struggled to hold them steady. "I'm sorry, but I did go behind your back. Not with Edith, though. I came here one day, while you were at work. I was hoping I could find out what was altering your moods. I found your broken counter, microwave, and piano."

I bit my lip, watching him as shame clouded his face.

"I found the diagram behind your mirror, too," Jace said quietly. I felt the color drain from my face as he looked back up at me and watched as his face began to pale as well. "Delilah, why did you go to the 17th floor that day? Did you see Jameson up there?"

He was still holding my hands as my whole body shook. Tears slid down my face as I nodded slowly. I heard Edith gasp behind me.

"Did you see who killed him?"

I held my body rigid but felt the boiling inside me grow. I had to do something before I blacked out, but I was surrounded by people who didn't know what I could do yet. And right now, out of anger and despair, this was not the time to show them.

"She *is* crazy," I heard Edith whisper behind me.

That was it. I felt like a camel that just broke its back. I tore out of Jace's grasp, sending him flailing into the wall behind him as I rounded on Edith, a yell escaping my lips. She looked horrified and surprised.

"What?" she squeaked, backing away from me but running into the side table of my sofa.

"What did you say?" I growled, advancing slowly, my hands balled into fists once more.

"I didn't say anything," she cried, bracing herself against the table as I drew near.

"Delilah," Jace was coming up behind me. I turned and pushed out, not knowing how close he was or how hard I was trying. My vision grew slightly fuzzy as I watched him fly backward, breaking the top half of my window.

"Say it again, Edith," I turned back to her. "What, you think I'm crazy? Think I've lost it?"

"I didn't say anything," Edith repeated, sobbing uncontrollably.

"You all think I killed him," I said, looking around at Jace, who was slowly getting up from the glass covered floor. His arm was bleeding heavily.

There was a silence. And then Edith spoke.

"Did you?"

I reached out with a straight arm, grabbing her neck and lifting her off her feet in a split second. She choked and spluttered, her legs kicking out feebly, but I was too far away. I could feel her windpipe in my fingers, and relished the thought of crushing it, so no one could hear her call me crazy again. I saw out of the corner of my eye Jace's astonished face.

"In conclusion..."

The voice sounded familiar but not like anyone in the room. I glanced around, wondering if it had come from outside.

"Delilah, no!" I heard Jace yell.

I turned my attention back to the struggling Edith. It would be so quick, so easy. Blurriness edged into my vision as I tightened my grip slightly, watching as her face began to turn purple.

"The subject is insane..."

There it was again. I stopped, pulling my full attention away from Edith. And that's when I noticed Jace's gun trained on my head.

"Delilah, put her down." He had tears running down his face. I had never wanted to see him cry again, but here we were.

I seemed to turn in slow motion, and on my way to look back at Edith I glanced in the mirror and saw my reflection staring back at me, a wild grin on its face.

I wasn't smiling. And then it spoke, but my mouth wasn't moving.

"You. Are. Insane."

EPILOGUE

Jace

I tried to smooth my messy hair with my hand as I waited in the white chair, careful to keep the bouquet of flowers in my hand upright. I felt out of place as nurses and secretaries bustled past, keeping their eyes on their clipboards and using their badges to access doors on all ends of the entry hall.

"Jace Avery?" A voice called. I looked up to see Nurse Garn hobbling toward me, her overweight body rocking back and forth with each step.

"Nurse," I stood, shaking her stubby hand.

"The dedication you have," she mumbled as she walked me out of the entry hall, beeping us into an adjourning hallway. "A handsome man like you can't wait around forever."

"It won't be forever," I assured her.

It had been a month since Delilah's attempt on Edith's life. Right before she could do lasting damage on Edith, though, she had passed out. Edith hadn't pressed any charges, though she now spoke with a slight rasp and coughed constantly.

Delilah had confessed about everything that had happened. It was a shock to hear that my girlfriend had killed my best friend and her cat and had superhuman strength. But the fact that it was all because of the drug, and the thoughts it had put into her mind, (not to mention the voices in her head and her hallucinations), had helped her in pleading insane to the case Jameson's family held against her. It was a rough couple of weeks in court, but she finally agreed to be held in an institution for the criminally insane.

She wasn't criminal, though. She knew it, and I knew it. And that's why I kept coming back. I was her boyfriend, after all, even if it had only been official for two days, and in the midst of her mental breakdown.

Nurse Garn huffed as she led me down endless white hallways. "Keep those flowers low, young man," she nagged. "Some of these patients don't appreciate so much color."

"You got it, Garnie." It was Delilah's nickname for her, and it had grown on me.

Eventually, we reached the only door in the hallway with a window in it. Nurse Garn reached down, swiping her badge and pushing it open.

"You have a handsome visitor sweetheart," she said slowly, as if talking to someone who couldn't understand her. "He's come a few times, if you can remember."

I walked in, holding up the blue calla lilies for Delilah to see. Even though she was required to where the white robe, it made her look angelic as she sat in her chair, looking out the window. Her skin had lost some of its rich caramel color, but her eyes remained a shiny blue and her hair had been fixed to a stylish and even pixie, making the definition of her cheekbones and jawline that much more impressive.

Her smile made the whole room even brighter than the white walls ever could.

"I remember." She stood, holding out her arms. "And Garnie, I'm not like the other people in here. Just talk to me normally, please."

This was the third time I had heard her request it, and each time Nurse Garn had answered in the same way, which she rehearsed now:

"Whatever you want, sweetheart." Then she added, "You've got only a couple minutes before your next session though, so you may want to keep it quick."

I frowned as she closed the door. "I'm sorry, Liles, I didn't know you had therapy today, or I would have come at a better time."

She pulled me into her arms, and the contact felt almost back to normal, or at least the normal one date we had before her accident.

"Seeing you anytime is worth it," Delilah motioned to the white bed, setting the lilies in the vase on the desk, replacing the withered yellow ones I had brought last time. "I wish I could take better care of your beautiful flowers, but they don't get much sunlight over here. Plus, the staff doesn't have the greenest of thumbs, if you know what I mean."

She rolled her eyes. This was the best I had seen her in months.

"That's okay, at least you can count on me bringing them every time," I smiled, but she looked saddened by my statement. "What's wrong?"

"Are you going to keep coming back?" she avoided my eyes. "Everyone keeps saying you won't wait around for me because I'm nuts."

I pulled her chin up, making her eyes meet mine. "We've come this far, haven't we? Plus, we have a new lead."

Her eyes grew wide. "You found him?"

"We think we may have. We've actually been following a trail of others like you, who have had these 'accidents' with McGregor's men. Remember when I told you about what Rodolpho had said?"

Delilah's face grew shrewd. "I'm not the only one."

"No," I said sourly. "But they all are affected differently, remember? Maybe it didn't affect their brains like it did yours, you know? And the more we find of them, the closer we get to McGregor—"

"And an antidote," Delilah smiled. We had talked about this in almost every one of my visits.

"Exactly. That's why I keep coming back." I leaned forward and kissed her cheek. "I'm not giving up on you. I'm more worried you'll be cured and realize you really don't want me," she gave me an incredulous look. "What? You can't blame me—you decided we should be together around the same time you started hallucinating." This was also a common subject of our visits.

Her shoulders sagged slightly. "You know I meant it. I told you, it's times like these I feel completely normal again. I would think I was if it wasn't for the five doctors that diagnosed me with insanity."

She looked out the window longingly, and I held her hand.

"You know, I could break out of here if I wanted," Delilah said quietly, squeezing my hand. "These walls wouldn't be able to hold me. But, I know if I do, McGregor will find me."

I squeezed her hand back. "Not if I can help it," and then I backtracked. "But don't break out okay?"

She laughed. "I won't. I don't know if I'd be able to handle all the voices in my head if I did. The doc says it's brought on if I interact with more than one person for over an hour. It sucks, especially in group therapy." She sighed.

"I know," my phone buzzed, and I pulled it out for both of us to see. "But at least I get you to myself when I come because of it."

Delilah laughed before we both looked down at the message on my phone that read:

First contact with another victim, seems to know what we're talking about. Willing to help. Bringing them in.

It was from Lars. Delilah's smile faded. "I wonder if they were brutally thrown against a wall."

"I guess we'll find out," I replied, looking up into her sad eyes, "But this means I have to go, plus —"

Nurse Garn came in at that very moment without so much as a knock.

"Time for therapy dearie," she said, tottering in and pushing me off the bed and into the hall. "Bring something a little less colorful next time, alright?"